The World of Thrush Green

Also published in Large Print
from G.K. Hall by Miss Read:

Village Christmas
News from Thrush Green
Tyler's Row

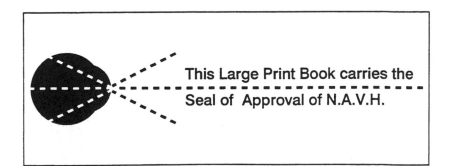

This Large Print Book carries the
Seal of Approval of N.A.V.H.

The World of Thrush Green

Miss Read

Illustrations by John S. Goodall

G.K. Hall & Co.
Thorndike, Maine

Published in Large Print by arrangement with Houghton Mifflin Company.

G.K. Hall Large Print Book Series.

Printed on acid-free paper in the United States of America.

Typeset in 16 pt. News Plantin by Heidi E. Saucier.

Library of Congress Cataloging-in-Publication Data

Read, Miss.
   The world of Thrush Green / Miss Read ;
illustrations by John S. Goodall.
      p.   cm.—(G.K. Hall large print book series)
   ISBN 0-8161-5507-0 (acid-free paper).
   ISBN 0-8161-5508-9 (pbk. : acid-free paper)
   1. Thrush Green (Imaginary place)—Fiction.
2. Country life—England—Fiction. 3. Large type books.
I. Title.
[PR6069.A42A6   1993]
823'.914—dc20   93-16776
                                                            CIP

Contents

Author's Note

I should like to pay tribute to the artist, John S. Goodall who, for over thirty years, has illustrated all my books about Thrush Green and Fairacre.

He has portrayed the English countryside and the people who live there with an incomparable combination of skill, affection and humour which has always delighted me and, I know, countless readers.

I deeply appreciate my long and happy association under the distinguished imprint of Michael Joseph and it is therefore to that company and to John that I dedicate this book.

I should also like to thank Mr T. E. Worley of Witney who has searched out and provided the excellent photographs of Witney which are reproduced in the book.

Introduction

I HAVE NEVER made any secret of the fact that the village of Thrush Green was based, outrageously loosely, on Wood Green at the northern end of the Oxfordshire town of Witney (or Lulling in the books), where I spent most of the war years from the winter of 1940 to that of 1945. I use the expression 'outrageously loosely' because I have taken great liberties with the place, erecting a monument to a fictitious Victorian missionary called

This is the view Ella Bembridge would
see from the front of her cottage

Nathaniel Patten, depositing a village school where there is none, and adding a rectory at the southern end of the green which I greatly enjoyed burning down in a later book. There is a touch of the arsonist in us all, I suspect, and anyway it was a hideous building to find in such a delectable Cotswold setting.

How I came to light upon Wood Green as a background for the Thrush Green books might be of interest to those who like to know how a writer's mind works. By 1958 I had written three novels in quick succession about the quite imaginary village of Fairacre. These all used the village schoolmistress, Miss Read, as their narrator, but I found writing in the first person was irksome. Also I was getting rather tired of those characters, and if anyone had told me that I should write a good many more stories about Fairacre, its school and its inhabitants, I should have been profoundly surprised.

I think it was J. B. Priestley who said that there was no need to pity the novelists, as 'they are only playing with their dolls'. The time had come to find a new set of dolls for me to play with, and this time I was determined to write in the third person. It is advice I give to all budding authors of fiction. Trying to observe the verities of time and place, when acting as narrator, can be a traumatic experience, take my word for it.

So where should I sport this time, in 1958? I wanted a village. I wanted a few well-defined characters. What did Jane Austen advise her niece Anna when the girl was embarking on her first novel?

'You are now collecting your People delightfully, getting them exactly into such a spot as is the delight of my life; three or four Families in a Country Village is the very thing to work on.'

No one could give better guidance. Although I was lucky enough to have been brought up in a Kentish village, Wood Green was closer to me in time and place, and I had spent five amazingly happy years there considering that it was war-time and that my husband was busy in the RAF with flying duties. Our daughter had been born during that time, and almost every day I pushed the pram up the steep hill that led to Wood Green from Witney. I saw those lovely Cotswold houses in sunshine and shower, while bombers lurched back to air bases nearby and army convoys thundered south from the Midlands.

It was a strange world, and one's senses were made more acute by the times. There were several of us young mothers, far from home, wheeling our babies in Witney and Wood Green, and friendships were forged then that have lasted a lifetime. And the people of Witney were outstandingly kind and welcoming to the strangers in their midst. Scarcity of housing, of food, of clothing, and of all the other necessities of living did not quench their generosity and I hope we showed that we were grateful.

And so, in 1958, it was to Wood Green that I returned in spirit. I had long wanted to write a book wherein all the happenings take place in one day. It is a great challenge, and now that I was freed from that wretched first person as narrator, I felt that I could try my luck on this new project.

Thus 'Thrush Green' was born. It seemed a good idea to make that one day a particularly interesting one, and so I decided to have Mrs Curdle's fair on May 1st.

Witney has a splendid annual Mop Fair in September, but that is held on a larger green, the Leys, at the other end of Witney. For my purposes, the smaller affair at Thrush Green fitted very well, and I began my book: 'Thrush Green Chapter One. The Day Begins.'

When I write a novel, the place comes first, the people second. In this case, Wood Green was there, already laid out, and it only remained for me to people the houses. I can truthfully say that every one of the Thrush Green characters is of my creation. The nearest I came to reality was to have Doctor Bailey and his wife living in a house very close to that of the doctor whom I knew during the war. But the latter's surgery was in the High Street of Witney, and I was obliged to build a surgery for Doctor Bailey beside the house.

Much has happened to Witney and its neighbourhood over the last forty-odd years. The path down which I used to push my daughter in her pram and I made into the path beside Albert Piggott's cottage led to open fields and the imaginary Lulling Woods, but now leads to a housing estate. More houses have been built along the New

10

Yatt Road, and between that road and the larger Woodstock Road. Witney itself is greatly altered with at least two important roads leading from the High Street, where once were large gardens or paddocks.

But Wood Green itself is little changed, and when it was filmed for a short television programme about Thrush Green, it warmed my heart to see it so close to my memories of it.

Long may it remain so!

The Setting

WHEN I BEGAN to write about Thrush Green in 1958, I described it in the first few pages of the book I called *Thrush Green*, and a little later as seen by Ruth Bassett from the bedroom window of her late grandfather's beautiful house overlooking the green.

Thrush Green stood on high ground at the northerly end of Lulling, a small sleepy prosperous town, which had been famous in the days of the wool trade.

The town itself lay some half a mile distant, its gentle grey houses clustered, in a hollow, on each side of the twining silver river, like a flock of drowsy sheep. The streets curved and twisted as pleasantly as the river, but were shaded by fine lime trees, now breaking into delicate leaf, instead of the willows, soon to shimmer summer through, above the trout-ringed reaches of the River Pleshey.

The High Street tilted abruptly to rise to Thrush Green. It was a short sharp hill, 'a real head-thumper of a hill' in hot weather, as old Mr Piggott, sexton of St Andrew's, often said. In the grip of winter's ice, the same hill was feared by riders, drivers and those on foot. Years before, a wooden handrail, polished by generations of hands, had lined the high pavement, but the town council had decided that it served no useful purpose and detracted from the charm of the stone-walled cottages perched high on the bank above, and when the handrail had become shaky with age it had been dismantled, much to the annoyance of the Thrush Green residents. The green itself was triangular, with the church of St Andrew standing at the southerly point. The main road from Lulling to its nearest neighbouring Cotswold town ran along one side of Thrush Green, and a less important lane threading its way to half a dozen or so sleepy little hamlets, skirted the other side. Across the base of the triangle at the northern end ran a fine avenue of horsechestnut trees, linking the two roads and, behind them, facing towards St Andrew's, across the green, stood five sturdy old houses, built of that pleasantly sunny Cotswold stone which reminds one of honeycombs, golden afternoons and warm and mellow bliss.

[THRUSH GREEN]

The view from its window across Thrush Green never ceased to enchant Ruth Bassett. If she looked left she saw the wider road to Lulling, with a few comfortable houses standing well back in leafy gardens. The tallest one belonged to old Doctor Bailey, who had attended

16

to Lulling's ills for almost fifty years, and who had known the Bassett girls since they were babies.

To the right, on the narrow dusty lane, lay the village school behind a row of white palings. A stretch of mown grass lay between the palings and the road, and on hot days the children left their stony playground and lay and rolled on the grass just outside. Only if their teacher were with them were they allowed to cross the dusty lane to play on the greater green, for Miss Watson was a woman who had no doubt at all that each and every pupil would be run over and either maimed or killed outright if she were not there to keep an eye on their movements.

Beside the school stood the little school house, and beside that a row of small cottages. In the last lived old Mr Piggott, the sexton of St Andrew's. As The Two Pheasants stood next door to his house, he was handy not only for his work at the church on the green, but also for his only pleasure. He had been a source of fear to the two Bassett girls when they were small. Always grumbling, he had threatened them with all kinds of dreadful punishment if he had caught them walking in St Andrew's churchyard or sheltering in the porch. Now, bent and rheumaticky and crosser than ever, Ruth and her sister Joan Young found him a figure to be pitied rather than feared, but both agreed that he was an evil-tempered old man and they felt very

17

sorry for his only daughter Molly who kept house for him.

[THRUSH GREEN]

It was Molly Piggott, later to be Molly Curdle, who took out Ruth Bassett's little nephew Paul Young each afternoon.

In the winter they kept to the roads or, if the earth were hard with frost, they might play on Thrush Green with a bat and ball in view of Paul's home. Occasionally they walked down the steep hill to Lulling to shop for something which Joan had forgotten. But more often they took the little leafy lane which led from Thrush Green to Upper Pleshy, Nod and Nidden, the lane that threaded half a dozen or more sleepy thatched villages, like hoary old beads upon its winding string, before it emerged upon the broad highway which led to Stratford-upon-Avon.

Sometimes their expeditions were more adventurous. Molly and Paul knew all the true joys that were within an hour's walking time of Thrush Green. There was the pond that lay, dark and mysterious, along the lower road to Lulling Woods, mirroring the trees that stood around it. Sometimes in the summer Paul had taken a bright wooden boat on a string and floated it there, beating at the water's edge with a fan of leaves to make waves. In the spring, vast masses of frogs' spawn floated just beneath the surface, like submerged chain-mail cast there by some passing knight. And on one day of hard frost, Paul and Molly had slid back and forth across the shining ice, screaming with delight, watched by a bold robin who sat fearlessly nearby on a low bare branch preening the pale grey feathers that edged the bronze of his breast.

There were other places that they loved which were accessible only in the summer. There was the steep path through Lulling Woods, cool as a cathedral, even on the sultriest day. There was the field path to Nod, where the grass brushed Paul's shoulder in high summer and he looked at marguerites and red sorrel at eye-level. A bower of briar roses guarded the final stile that led into Nod and, in later life, Paul never smelt that sharp breathtaking sweetness of the wild rose without remembering the languor and warm happiness of those golden afternoons with Molly Piggott.

[THRUSH GREEN]

In the course of *Thrush Green*, Molly received a proposal of marriage from Ben Curdle. While the preparations for the fair were in progress, the young man made his way from the green to The Drover's Arms by way of Lulling Woods.

Ben's heart was light as he swung along through the meadows that lay before the heights of Lulling Woods. In the sunshine, the buttercups were opening fast, interlacing their gold with the earlier silver of the daisies. For the sheer joy of it, young Ben left the white path and trod a parallel one through the gilded grass, watching his black shoes turn yellow with the fallen pollen.

The field fell gently downhill to his left, tipping its little, secret, underground streams towards the River Pleshey, a mile distant. Dotty Harmer's cottage was the only house to be seen here, basking among the buttercups like a warmly golden cat.

Dotty herself was in the garden, a straw hat of gigantic proportions crowning her untidy thatch of hair. She waved to the young man and called out something which he could not catch.

He waved back civilly.

'Nice day, ma'am,' he shouted, for good measure.

'Rum ol' trout,' he added to himself, noting her eccentric appearance. 'Not quite the ticket, I should think. Or else gentry.'

He forgot her as soon as the cottage was behind him. A bend in the path brought him to a stile at the entrance to Lulling Woods. It was nearly a mile of steep climbing, he knew, before he would emerge on to the open heathland where The Drover's Arms stood.

His spirits were buoyant. So she'd missed him! She hadn't forgotten him! Everything pointed to happiness. He forged up the narrow path, slippery with a myriad pine needles, as though his feet were winged.

It was very cool and quiet in the woods after the bland sunshine of the meadows. Above him, the topmost twigs of the trees whispered interminably. An occasional shaft of sunlight penetrated the foliage and lit up the bronze trunks of the pines, touching them with fire. A grey squirrel, spry after its winter sleep, startled Ben by scampering across his path. It darted up a tree with breathtaking ease, and the young man watched it leaping from bough to bough, as light and airy as a puff of grey smoke.

The primroses were out, starring the carpet of tawny dead leaves, and the bluebells, soon to spread their misty veil, now crouched in bud among their glossy leaves in tight pale knots. The faint but heady perfume of a spring woodland was to stay with Ben for the rest of his life, and was connected, for ever, with a lover's happiness.

[THRUSH GREEN]

Some hours later, Ben returned to his duties at the fair. There was much to do before the festivities began.

Although twilight had not yet come, the lights of the fair were switched on at a quarter past six, and the first strains of music from the roundabout spread the news that Mrs Curdle's annual fair was now open.

The news was received, by those who heard it on Thrush Green, in a variety of ways. Sour old Mr Piggott, who had looked in at St Andrew's, let fall an ejaculation quite unsuitable to its surroundings, and emerging from the vestry door, crunched purposefully and maliciously upon a piece of coke to relieve his feelings.

Paul Young, beside himself with excitement, was leaping up and down the hall, singing at the top of his voice. Occasionally, he broke off to bound up to Ruth Bassett's bedroom where she was getting ready. The appalling slowness with which she arranged her hair and powdered her face drove her small nephew almost frantic. Would she *never* be ready?

To young newly-appointed Doctor Lovell, returning from a visit to Upper Pleshey in his shabby two-seater, the colour and glitter of the fair offered a spectacle of charming innocence. Here was yet another aspect of Thrush Green to increase his growing affection for the place. He could settle here so easily, he told himself, slipping into place among the friendly people of Lulling and Thrush Green, enjoying their companionship and sharing their enchanting countryside.

[THRUSH GREEN]

Where They Live

IT MAY SEEM paradoxical to describe Mrs Curdle's gipsy caravan first, for it only stood on the green for a day or two at the end of April and beginning of May each year.

But then it was the focal point of Thrush Green's interest, and the fair, the fun, and the great Mrs Curdle herself dominated the scene. For the rest of the year, the Thrush Green inhabitants remembered it, and looked forward to her next visit.

As it happened, in the first book, Mrs Curdle paid her final visit to the place, but her grandson Ben took over the fair and continued in the old lady's footsteps for several years. Her spirit still dominated Thrush Green, and her remains lay at rest in St Andrew's churchyard.

Here is a description of her home.

Mrs Curdle heard St Andrew's clock strike seven as she lifted the boiling kettle from her diminutive stove. She had been up and about for over an hour, moving slowly about her caravan, straightening the covers on the bunk, shaking the rag rug and even giving the brass on her beloved stove an early rub with metal polish.

The stove was the delight of her heart and had been built especially by a friend of her late husband's to fit neatly into the end of her tiny home. The top was of gleaming steel which Mrs Curdle rubbed up daily with emery paper, hissing gently to herself like a groom to a horse, as her busy hand slid back and forth across the satin of the surface.

A circular lid could be lifted off and the fire then sent up its released heat to Mrs Curdle's kettle, stew-pot or frying-pan. When the food was cooked, or the teapot filled, it could be kept hot by standing it further along the hob, and frequently the top of the little stove was filled with a variety of utensils each giving off a rich aroma, for Mrs Curdle was a great cook.

The front of the stove was black but decorated with a great deal of brass. The knobs and hinges of the tiny oven door gleamed like gold against the jetty blacklead. Another door, covering the bars of the fire, could be let down and formed a useful ledge. It was here that Mrs Curdle heated her great flat-iron, propping it up on its back with the ironing surface pressed to the glowing red bars.

[THRUSH GREEN]

Paul Young, like all the local children, was fascinated by Mrs Curdle.

Molly had told him all about Mrs Curdle and gipsies' ways. She would be standing by her glittering stove, cooking hedgehogs, Paul had no doubt. He had once, fearfully, climbed the three steps to Mrs Curdle's caravan and had gazed, fascinated, at the glory within, the half-door had been shut, but by standing on tiptoe he had seen the shelves, the tiny drawers, the cupboards, the gleaming brass and copper and the rows of vividly painted plates as breathtakingly lovely to the child as the bright birds which he had seen the week before at the Zoo, sitting motionless upon their perches, in a splendour of tropical plumage.

No one had been in the caravan. Only a clock ticked and a saucepan sizzled, now and then, upon the diminutive stove. Molly had stood beside him and had pointed out one particularly small drawer close by the door. It had a curious brass handle, embossed with leaves and fruit.

'She puts the money in there,' had whispered Molly, in the child's ear.

'What money?' Paul had asked.

'The fortune-telling money. See, she leans over this door and reads your palm and you pays her a bit of silver, sixpence say, or a shilling, and she pops it in this little drawer just beside her. Real handy, isn't it, Paul?'

He had nodded, open-mouthed, and would have liked to have stayed longer, just gazing at the beauties, but Molly had hurried him away.

[THRUSH GREEN]

If Mrs Curdle's abode was the smallest on Thrush Green, then the Youngs' house was certainly the largest and one of the oldest.

Travelling clockwise round the green, Joan and Edward Young's house stood at twelve o'clock, a dominant position well suited to its size and dignity.

The finest house at Thrush Green, everyone agreed, was that occupied by Joan and Edward Young. Built of honey-coloured Cotswold stone, some hundred or so years ago, it had a beautiful matching tiled roof, mottled with a patina of lichen and moss. It looked southward, across the length of the green, to the little market town of Lulling hidden in the valley half a mile away.

The house had been built by a mill owner who had made a comfortable fortune at the woollen mill which straddled the river Pleshey a mile or two west of Lulling. It was large enough to house his family of six, and three resident maids. A range of stone-built stables, a coach house and tack room, stood a little way from the house, and at right angles to it. Above the stable was the bothy where the groom-cum-coachman slept, and immediately above that was the stable clock.

The Youngs often wondered how on earth people managed without such storage space. Nowadays the buildings were filled with furniture awaiting repair, lawn-mowers, deck chairs, tea chests full of bottling equipment or archaic kitchen utensils which 'might come in useful one day', two deep freezers and a decrepit tricycle and a rocking horse, the property of Paul Young, their only child. Everything needing a temporary home found its way into the stable and then became a permanency. Sagging wicker garden chairs, shabby trunks, cat baskets, camping stoves, old tennis racquets, fishing waders, and Paul's pram, unused for nine years, were housed here, jostling each other, and coated with dust, bird droppings and the debris from ancient nests in the beams above.

'If ever we had to move,' said Edward to Joan one sunny afternoon, 'I can't think how we'd begin to sort out this lot.'

He was looking for space in which to dump two sacks of garden fertiliser.

'Those new flats in Lulling,' he went on, 'have exactly three cupboards in each. People seem to cope all right. How do we get so much clobber?'

'It's a law of nature,' Joan replied. 'Abhorring

a vacuum and all that. However much space you have, you fill it.'

[RETURN TO THRUSH GREEN]

Here we are, thought Joan, surveying the garden through half-closed eyes, in mid-April and the daffodils and narcissi are only just in their prime. Would the primroses be starring the banks along the lane to Nidden, she wondered? As children, she and her sister Ruth had reckoned the first outing to pick primroses as the true herald of spring.

How lucky they had been to have grandparents living at Thrush Green, thought Joan, looking back to those happy days with affection. She and Ruth lived most of the year in Ealing, where their father owned a furniture shop. They lived comfortably in a house built in King Edward's reign. The garden was large for a town house. The common was nearby, and Kew Gardens a bus ride away. But to the little girls, such amenities were definitely second-best.

'It's not *the country!*' they protested. 'Why can't we live in *the country?* Why don't we go to Thrush Green for good?'

'Because my living's here,' said Mr Bassett, smiling. 'There are four of us to keep, and the house and garden to care for, and your schooling to be paid. If I don't work, then we have nothing. You must think yourselves lucky to be able to go to Thrush Green as often as you do.'

He too adored Thrush Green, and when his

parents died, the house became his. Barely fifty, he intended to continue to live and work in Ealing. By this time, Joan had married Edward Young, an architect in Lulling known to the Bassetts since childhood, and the young couple had lived in the house ever since.

'But the day I retire,' Mr Bassett had said, 'I'll be down to take over, you know!'

'I'll build a house in readiness,' promised Edward. That was over ten years ago, thought Joan, stretching out her legs into the sunshine, and we still have not built it. Perhaps we should think about it, instead of drifting on from day to day. Father must be in his sixties now, and had not been well this winter. The time must come when he decides to retire, and it's only right that he should come to Thrush Green to enjoy his heritage. They had been wonderfully blessed to have had so long in this lovely place.

The telephone bell broke in upon her musing, and she left the sunshine to answer it.

[RETURN TO THRUSH GREEN]

Within fifty yards of the Youngs' home, across the road which led northward to the Midlands, stood the house called Tullivers at one on our imaginary clock.

Tullivers, as it was called, had been the home of old Admiral Josiah Trigg and his sister Lucy for almost thirty years, and when he died, suddenly one hot afternoon, after taking the sharp

31

hill from the town at a spanking pace, his sister continued to muddle along in a vague, amiable daze for another eighteen months before succumbing to bronchitis.

'If it's not the dratted hill,' pronounced old Piggott the sexton gloomily, 'that carries off us Thrush Green folks, it's the dratted east wind. You gotter be tough to live 'ere.'

You certainly had to be tough to live at Tullivers after the Admiral had gone, for Lucy Trigg, in her eighties, could not be bothered to have any domestic help, nor could she be bothered to light fires, to cook meals for herself, nor to clean the house and tend the garden.

Winnie Bailey, the soul of tact, frequently visited, did what she could in an unobtrusive way, but knew she was fighting a losing battle. The curtains grew greyer, the window panes misty with grime, the doorstep and path were spattered with bird droppings, and the docks and nettles rioted in the borders once tended by Lucy's brother and kept trim and shipshape with pinks, pansies and geums neatly confined within immaculate box hedges.

It wasn't as if Lucy Trigg were senile. Her mind, in some ways, was as clear as ever. She played a good game of bridge with her neighbours. She attacked, and overcame, the challenge of the *Daily Telegraph* crossword puzzle each morning, and played her dusty piano with fingers still nimble despite arthritis. It was simply that the squalor of her house did not affect her. Her world had shrunk to the few things which still had interest for her. The rest was ignored.

It was fortunate that Tullivers was a small house with a small garden. Doctor Bailey, as a young man, had been offered the major part of the next door garden by the Admiral's predecessor. He had bought it for thirty pounds, enclosed it with a honey-coloured Cotswold stone wall, and planted a small but fine orchard, now at the height of its production. Thus the Baileys' garden was L-shaped, and the remaining portion of Tullivers' land, a mere quarter of an acre, allowed room for only a lawn, a few mature lilac and may trees and the flower border which had been the Admiral's particular pride.

An Albertine rose grew splendidly over one end of the house, and winter jasmine starred the front porch in the cold of the year. Inside were two fairly small square rooms, one each side of the front door, with a roomy kitchen built on at the back.

Above stairs were two modest bedrooms and a bathroom with Victorian fittings and a geyser which made threatening rumbles, wheezes and minor explosions when in use.

Tullivers, in its heyday, was always known as 'a snug house' by Thrush Green people. It stood at right angles to the road, and rather nearer it than most of the larger houses which stood back in their well-kept gardens.

It faced south, across the Baileys' front garden, towards the roofs of Lulling in the valley below, a mile distant. It crouched there, as snug as a contented cat, catching the sunshine full on its face.

To see Tullivers so neglected had grieved Thrush Green. Its dereliction over the past two years had been a constant topic of conversation. It had been left to a nephew of Lucy Trigg's, also a naval man, who put it in the hands of a London estate agent to sell for him whilst he was abroad.

'Pity he didn't let the local chaps have it,' was the general opinion. 'Keep a sharper eye on it. Should have gone within the month.'

There had been one or two prospective buyers, pushing their way through the tall weeds, with papers describing the property's charms in their hands, but the general neglect seemed to dishearten them. Heavy snow in January and February kept other possible buyers away, and by the time the crocuses and daffodils were decking the rest of the Thrush Green gardens, Tullivers was looking at its worst.

Birds nested in the porch and in the guttering, and a bold jackdaw started to build in the cold unused chimney. Mice had found shelter in the kitchen, and spiders spun their webs unmolested. The children at the village school eyed the blank windows speculatively, and the bigger boys fingered the catapults hidden in their pockets, longing to pick up pebbles and let fly at this beautiful sitting target. What could be more exhilarating than the crack of a glass pane, the dramatic starring, the satisfying hole?

Two of the most daring had been observed in the garden by Miss Watson, the headmistress, who lived across the green at the school-house, and she had delivered dire warnings during assembly the next morning. The two malefactors had been displayed to the assembled school as 'Trespassers Loitering with Criminal Intent', and were suitably abashed. Thrush Green parents, fortunately, were still unspoilt by modern educational theories, and heartily approved of Miss Watson's strong line. Miss Fogerty, who was in charge of the infants' class, added her own warnings when she regained the classroom, and the infants approached their morning's labours in a suitably sober mood. It says much for the two ladies, and the parents of Thrush Green, that the little house remained safe from children's assaults, despite temptation.

[NEWS FROM THRUSH GREEN]

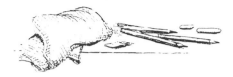

Luckily, succour was at hand. The months of winter which had added to Tullivers' dereliction and had kept buyers away, now gave way to spring.

One bright April day, a red Mini stopped outside Tullivers and a tall woman, paper fluttering from a gloved hand, made her way into the house.

Miss Fogerty was on playground duty that morning. Standing on the sheltered side of the school, teacup in hand, she watched with mounting excitement. Around her squealed and shouted the sixty or so pupils of Thrush Green Church of England Primary School. During those delirious fifteen minutes of morning play-time, they were variously spacemen, horses, footballers, boxers, cowboys or — among the youthful minority — simply mothers and fathers. The noise was ear-splitting. The bracing Cotswold air produces fine healthy lungs, and the rumpus made at play-time could be clearly heard by fond parents who were safely half a mile away.

Agnes Fogerty, quiet and still as a mouse, and not unlike that timid animal in her much-pressed grey flannel skirt and twin-set to match, stood oblivious of the chaos around her. Somehow, she sensed that the stranger would take on Tullivers one day. There was something purposeful about that stride towards the front door, and the deft slipping of the key into the lock — almost as though the house were hers already, thought little Miss Fogerty.

Needless to say, many other people observed the stranger's entry to Tullivers. Thrush Green, to the uninitiated, might have seemed remarkably quiet that morning. The school-children apart, not more than two or three people were to be seen. There were, of course, almost a dozen unseen — hidden behind curtains, screened by garden shrubs, or cocking a curious eye from such vantage points as porches and wood sheds.

Albert Piggott, languidly grubbing up the dead winter grass at the foot of the churchyard railings, kept the stranger comfortably in view. He approved of the red Mini. Must have a bit of money to drive a car, and that great leather handbag had cost something, he shouldn't wonder. He knew a decent bit of leather when he saw it. Plastic never deceived Albert Piggott yet. A handsome gal too, with a nice pair of long legs.

[NEWS FROM THRUSH GREEN]

The stranger, who did indeed take Tullivers, was a young married woman called Phyllida Prior, who had a small son Jeremy to keep her company. But, to the great interest of all at Thrush Green, no husband was to be seen when she moved in.

Dr Bailey and his wife Winnie lived next door, at two o'clock on the green, and promptly befriended Phyllida Prior when she arrived.

Their house was the tallest on Thrush Green, and when we first meet the good doctor, in the book of that name, he is an elderly man contemplating retirement.

His link with the redoubtable Mrs Curdle is a long one, and strengthened by her annual visit at the time of the fair. Always she brought with her a rather odd bunch of flowers for her old friend.

'Those flowers!' said the old man, shaking his head. 'A bigger and brighter bunch each year it seems.'

Mrs Curdle's annual bunch of flowers constituted something of a problem in the doctor's house, for they were artificial and lasted for ever. They were indeed works of art, great mop-headed beauties made from finely-cut wood shavings which curled into unbelievable shapes. Mrs Curdle had learnt this handicraft as a young girl and was an expert. When the flowers had been made, she dyed them yellow, pink, orange and scarlet and mounted them among evergreen twigs of laurel. They made a dazzling bouquet, not without charm, but the bunch which was presented each May Day by Mrs Curdle in person to the doctor was of such gargantuan proportions that Mrs Bailey was hard put to it to find a suitable place for it.

Each year Mrs Curdle asked to see how the previous year's bouquet had worn, so that the doctor and his wife were in honour bound not to destroy these offerings.

'Do you realise, my dear,' said the doctor, 'that we've had a bunch of Curdle blooms ever since 1915?'

'Forty-odd years with the top shelf of the pantry occupied,' commented Mrs Bailey. 'And then having to remember to unearth them before the day! Really, I shan't know myself.'

Outside, the blackbirds scolded and the sound of children playing on the green, glorying in the first few outdoor games of spring, could be faintly heard. Mrs Bailey stole a glance at her husband. His blue eyes were gazing far away and his wife knew that he was thinking of that distant evening when he and Mrs Curdle had first met, on just such an April evening, many years ago.

Doctor Bailey was then a young man in his twenties, newly qualified and recently married and settled in this his first practice. The tall house on Thrush Green had been but sparsely furnished for the young couple had great aspirations but little money, and most of the furniture was solid Victorian stuff given by their parents. The large room to the left of the graceful hooded front door was young Doctor Bailey's surgery. Later, as his family came into the world, it was to be the dining-room and a new surgery was built at the side of the house, but when Mrs Curdle first knew him, the doctor and his wife dined in the sunny little room at the back of the house, conveniently near to the kitchen.

They had been at supper on that far-distant evening when Mr Curdle, white with panic, had drummed madly on the glass of the hall door. The little maid of-all-work had been disdainful, telling the wild-eyed rough-looking man that Doctor Bailey had finished his evening surgery and was not at home.

At this, the sorely-tried husband had broken into such cries of frustration and wrath that the good doctor had thrust aside his plate and gone out into the hall to discover what all the hullabaloo was about.

'It's me missus, sir,' had said Mr Curdle, clutching the doctor's arm. 'It's on the way — afore time. Ain't never seen her this way afore!'

'I'll come,' had answered the doctor, picking

up his bag from the hall table. The maid had retired, tossing her head at the thought of such low people as them gyppos having the sauce to interrupt the master at his supper.

[THRUSH GREEN]

On the same side of the road, some hundred yards farther south, at four o'clock, stood a small cottage where Dimity Dean and her friend Ella Bembridge lived.

At first sight they seemed an ill-assorted pair.

Ella Bembridge was a formidably hearty spinster of fifty-five who had lived, with a wilting friend of much the same age, in a small cottage on the Lulling corner of Thrush Green for the past ten years. It was generally agreed that Ella ruled the roost and that 'poor Miss Dean' had a pretty thin time of it.

Deborah Dean had been nicknamed Dimity

so long ago that the reason for the diminutive had been lost in the mists of time. Now, at the age of fifty-odd, the name was pathetically incongruous, calling up as it did someone fresh, compact and sparkling, with an air of crisp, but old-world domesticity. Dimity nowadays resembled a washed-out length of grey chiffon, for she was a drooping, attenuated figure, with lank, mouse-grey locks and a habit of dressing in shapeless frocks, incorporating unpressed pleats and draped bodices, in depressingly drab shades. Doctor Lovell, who knew both women slightly, suspected that she was brow-beaten by the dominating Ella and would have liked to try the effects of an iron tonic on Dimity's languid pallor.

It was an odd thing, mused Doctor Lovell, that it was Ella who was the artistic one of the pair. Dimity ran the house, it appeared, and it was her slender arms that bore in the coal scuttles, the heavy shopping baskets and the laden trays, while Ella's powerful hands designed wood blocks, mixed paint and stamped the lengths of materials which draped their little cottage.

Occasionally Ella took the train to town with a portfolio of hand-blocked patterns, and usually she returned, blown but jubilant, with a few orders from firms who appreciated her strong shades of olive green, dull beetroot and dirty yellow madly ensnared in black mesh.

[THRUSH GREEN]

43

But the friendship endured, and when Dimity did get married later, their affection survived the break.

Their snug cottage looked across the road to the ugliest house on the green, the Rectory, which stood at six o'clock, dead opposite the Youngs across Thrush Green, and was consequently a source of continuous irritation to Edward, the architect, who could see it from every south-facing window of his house.

The rectory, some hundred yards from St Andrew's, was a high Victorian monstrosity, facing north, and perched on a small mound the better to catch the chilly winds of the Cotswold country.

It was, thought Harold Shoosmith, the newcomer to Thrush Green, as he waited on the doorstep, the most gloomy house in Thrush Green. Unlike its neighbours which were built of local stone, the vicarage had been encased in grey stucco early in its life. The ravages of time had caused pieces to break away here and there, so that newer patches of different grey made the whole affair appear shabbier than ever.

Large sash windows and a tall narrow front door were all in need of paint, but there was little money to spare, as Harold knew too well. In any case, Charles Henstock cared little for creature comforts, and had lived there for several years, alone, in appalling conditions of cold

and discomfort, until his marriage to Dimity
Dean, a few years before, had brought companionship and a slight mitigation of the hard-
ship of his surroundings.

Dimity opened the door to Harold and greeted
him with cries of welcome.

'What a day you've brought with you! I'm
in the kitchen, and the sun is just streaming in.'

She led the way, still chattering, down the
long dark corridor which acted as a wind tunnel,
and kept the rectory in a state of refrigeration
during the winter months. Harold's feet echoed
on the shabby linoleum, and he thought guiltily
of his own carpeted home across the green.

[BATTLES AT THRUSH GREEN]

Charles and Dimity's bleak surroundings worried Harold continuously but there was little he
could do.

But one winter evening, Charles Henstock
paid a call upon his friend Harold Shoosmith.

It was clear and cold. The stars were already
pricking the sky, and frost was in the air.

Charles was glad to settle by Harold's log fire,
and to accept a small whisky and water.

He looked about the room appreciatively.
There was a fine cyclamen on the side table,
leather-bound books on the shelves, and a well-
filled tantalus on the sideboard. Everywhere the
hand of Betty Bell was apparent in the glossy
furniture, the plump cushions, the shining glass.

45

'You manage to make things so very comfortable,' commented Charles. There was a wondering note in his voice. 'Somehow the rectory never achieves such snugness.'

Harold could hardly point out that good curtains and carpets were one of the basic requirements for soft living, and an ample income another, to supply other amenities including first-rate domestic help.

'I have the advantage of lower ceilings, for one thing,' said Harold, 'and not such an exposed position. Those Victorian Gothic buildings never were designed for cosiness.'

'Dimity does wonders,' went on Charles, nursing his glass. 'When I think how bleak the house was when I lived there alone, I never cease to be thankful for her presence. Do you remember Mrs Butler who kept house for me?'

'I shall never forget her,' said Harold firmly.

'I have never, in all my travels, met a meaner, tighter-fisted old harridan.'

Charles looked shocked. 'Oh, I wouldn't say that,' he protested.

'Of course, you wouldn't. But it's true. I remember the disgraceful way she allowed you to be neglected when you had flu, only bringing up a water biscuit or two when she deigned to climb the stairs! You were sorely put upon, you know that, Charles. Saints often are.'

'She was rather *frugal*,' admitted the rector. 'But why I mentioned her was that I heard by chance that she has married again.'

'Poor devil,' said Harold. 'I hope he belongs to a good club.'

The night air was sharp as the rector crossed the green a little later. Already the grass was becoming crisp with frost. Two miles away, at Lulling Station, a train hooted, and from Lulling Woods, in the valley on his right, an owl quavered and was answered by another.

His tall house loomed over him as he unlocked the front door. It looked gaunt and inhospitable, he realised. His thoughts turned on the conversation he had just had with Harold.

He found Dimity in the sitting-room, close to the fire. It was half the size of the one he had just left, he noticed, unusually observant. One could see the edges of the iron basket which held the fire. The coals were burning only in the centre of the container.

He looked aloft at the distant ceiling, and at

47

the expanse of sparsely-curtained window space. Although the night was still, some wayward draught stirred the light drapings.

The lamp by which Dimity was seated had a plain white shade which threw a cold light upon the knitting in her hands. Harold's lampshades, he remembered, were red, and made a cheerful glow.

'I've just come from Harold's. His fire seems enormous. I'm beginning to think we must give a very chilly welcome to visitors here. But my main concern is for you. You know that you tend to be bronchial. We really must keep a better fire, or see if we can put in some central heating of some sort.'

'Charles dear,' said Dimity, 'it simply can't be done. Do you know how much coal costs?'

'Harold told me. I couldn't help thinking that he must have made a mistake. Why, as a boy, I remember coal carts coming to the house with a large ticket displayed, saying two-and-six a hundredweight.'

'And that,' pointed out Dimity, 'was over half a century ago! Times have changed, and I'm sorry to say that Harold's figure is the correct one.'

'There must be many ways of making this place snugger,' argued Charles, looking about him with fresh eyes. 'What about a red lampshade, like Harold's?'

'We could do that,' said Dimity, nodding.

'And a screen? My mother had a screen. She

said it kept off draughts. And a sausage filled with sand at the bottom of the door. That would help.'

Dimity suddenly burst into laughter. 'Oh Charles! To see you as a domestic adviser is so funny! And such a change! What this house really wants is double-glazing, central heating, thick curtains and carpets, cellars stuffed with coal, and a log shed filled with nice dry logs. But we should need to find a crock of gold, my dear, to provide ourselves with all that.'

'But the shade,' pleaded Charles. 'And the screen?'

'We'll manage that, I think,' smiled Dimity. 'And I'll make the door sausage before the week is out. By the way, its proper name is a draught-excluder.'

'Let's hope it lives up to it,' said Charles, recklessly putting two lumps of coal on the fire.

The subject still occupied Charles's mind later that night. Beside him, Dimity slept peacefully, but the rector could not rest.

There was no doubt about it, he was failing as a husband if he could not provide such basic things as warmth and shelter for his wife. The poor rector tossed unhappily. Something must be done. He had certainly been failing in his duty towards Dimity. Because she was so uncomplaining, he had let things slide.

'Sins of omission!' sighed Charles, thumping his pillow. 'Sins of omission! They must be rectified.'

He fell asleep soon after three o'clock, and dreamt that he was stuffing a red draught-excluder with sausage meat.

[BATTLES AT THRUSH GREEN]

Albert Piggott's cottage stood at seven o'clock. It was even closer to St Andrew's church than the Rectory, which was useful, as Albert was sexton, verger and general caretaker to the building and the churchyard. Not that this Pooh-Bah of a person let his duties worry him, even though they were within his sight at all hours.

His first wife, Molly's mother, had died some time before, and the girl kept the cottage clean and sweet until marriage to Ben Curdle removed her. After that Albert was content to live in squalor, taking most of his refreshment next door at The Two Pheasants to save cooking.

Doctor Bailey, and later Doctor Lovell, remonstrated in vain about a diet of beer, pickled onions, pork pie and cold sausages, occasionally varied by Albert's own cooking in a disgusting frying pan when the spirit moved him. Every now and again, Albert's digestive system revolted, and his hard-pressed medical advisers were called in, prescribed tablets, and read the riot act yet again.

The arrival of Nelly Tilling, an old school friend, soon altered the interior of Albert's abode. Her first sight of it gave her a severe shock.

Wind-blown and panting, Mrs Tilling thank-

50

fully accepted the armchair which Mr Piggott indicated.

'I'll just tidy these up,' said her host, stuffing a dozen or so unwashed socks behind the grubby cushion. Mrs Tilling viewed the proceedings with some misgivings, but sat herself down gingerly on the edge of the seat.

'Make yerself at 'ome,' said Mr Piggott, passing her an out-of-date copy of the parish magazine. 'I'll put on the kettle.'

He moved into the little kitchen which led from the sitting-room and soon Nelly could hear the tap running. Her eyes wandered round the unsavoury room. If ever a house cried out for a woman's hand, thought the lady dramatically, this was it!

She noted the greasy chenille tablecloth which was threadbare where the table edge cut into it — a sure sign, Nelly knew, that the cloth had been undisturbed for many months. Her eyes travelled to the dead fern in its arid pot, the ashes in the rusty grate, the festoons of cobwebs which hung from filthy pelmets and picture rails and the appalling thickness of the dust which covered the drab objects on the dresser.

The only cheerful spot of colour in the room was afforded by St Andrew's church almanack which Mr Piggott had fixed on the wall above the rickety card table which supported an ancient wireless set.

Mrs Tilling, who began to find the room oppressive and smelly, left her sock-laden armchair (from whence, she suspected, most of the aroma emanated), and decided to investigate the kitchen.

Mr Piggott was standing morosely by the kettle waiting for it to boil. It was typical of a man, thought his guest with some impatience, that he had not utilised his time by putting out the cups and saucers, milk, sugar and so on, which would be needed. Just like poor old George, thought Nelly with a pang, remembering her late husband. 'One thing at a time,' he used to say pompously, as though there were some virtue in it. As his wife had pointed out tartly, on many occasions, she herself would never get through a quarter of her work if she indulged herself in such idleness. While a kettle boiled she could set a table, light a fire, and watch over a cooking breakfast. Ah, men were poor tools, thought Mrs Tilling!

The kitchen was even dirtier than its neighbour. A sour fustiness pervaded the dingy room. In a corner of the floor stood a saucer of milk which had long since turned to an unsavoury junket embellished with blue mould. Beside it lay two very dead herrings' heads. A mound of dirty crockery hid the draining board, and the sight of Mr Piggott's frying pan hanging on the wall was enough to turn over Mrs Tilling's stout stomach. The residue of dozens of past meals could here be seen embedded in grey fat. Slivers of black burnt onion, petrified bacon rinds, lacy brown scraps of fried eggs and scores of other morsels from tomatoes, sausages, steaks, chops, liver, potatoes, bread and baked beans here lay cheek by jowl, and would have afforded a rich reward to anyone interested in Mr Piggott's diet over the past year.

'Where d'you keep the cups?' asked Nelly Tilling, when she had regained her breath. Her gaze turned apprehensively towards the pile on the draining-board. Mr Piggott seemed to sense her misgivings.

'Got some in the other room, in the dresser cupboard,' he said. 'My old woman's best,' he explained. 'Molly used 'em sometimes.'

'You get them while I make the tea,' said Mrs Tilling briskly. 'This the pot?' She peered into the murky depths of a battered tin object on the stove.

'Ah! Tea's in,' said Mr Piggott, making his way to the dresser.

The kettle boiled. With a brave shudder Nelly poured the water on the tea leaves, comforting herself with the thought that boiling water killed germs of all sorts.

Five minutes later she put down her empty cup and smiled at her companion.

'Lovely cup of tea,' she said truthfully. 'I feel all the better for that. Now I must go over to Doctor Lovell's for my pills.'

'It's still raining,' said Mr Piggott. 'Have another cup.'

'I'll pour,' said Nelly. 'Pass your own.'

'It's nice to have someone to pour out,' confessed Mr Piggott. He was beginning to feel unaccountably cheerful despite the disappointment of missing his customary pint of beer. 'This place needs a woman.'

'I'll say it does!' agreed Nelly, warmly. 'It needs a few gallons of hot soapy water too! When did your Molly see this last?'

'About a year ago, I suppose. She's coming again Christmas-time — she and Ben and the baby. Maybe she'll give it a bit of a clean-up then.'

'It wouldn't hurt you to do a bit,' said Nelly roundly. 'Chuck out that milk and fish for one thing.'

'The cat ain't had nothing to eat for days,' objected her host, stung by her criticism.

'That don't surprise me,' retorted Nelly. 'No cat would stay in this hole.'

'I got me church to see to,' began Mr Piggott, truculently. 'I ain't got time to —'

'If Molly comes home to this mess at Christmas, then I'm sorry for her,' asserted Mrs Tilling. 'And the baby too. Like as not it'll catch something and die on your very hearth-stone!'

She paused to let the words sink in. Mr Piggott mumbled gloomily to himself. The gist of his mutterings was the unpleasantness of women, their officiousness, their fussiness and their inability to let well alone, but he took care to keep his remarks inaudible.

'Tell you what,' said Mrs Tilling in a warmer tone, 'I'll come up here and give you a hand turning out before Christmas. What about it?'

Mr Piggott's forebodings returned. What would the neighbours say? What was Nelly Tilling up to? What would happen to his own peaceful, slummocky bachelor existence if he allowed this woman to have her way?

Nelly watched the thoughts chasing each other across his dour countenance. After a few minutes she noticed a certain cunning softness replacing the apprehension of his expression, and her heart began to beat a little faster.

'No harm, I suppose,' said the old curmudgeon, grudgingly. 'Make things a bit more welcoming for Molly, wouldn't it?'

'That's right,' agreed Mrs Tilling, rising from her chair and brushing a fine collection of sticky crumbs from her coat. 'One good turn deserves another, you know, and we've been friends long enough to act neighbourly, haven't we, Albert?'

Mr Piggott found himself quite dazzled by the warmth of her smile as she made for the door, and was unable to speak.

The wind roared in as she opened the front door, lifting the filthy curtains and blowing the parish magazine into a corner. Might freshen the place up a bit, thought Nelly, stepping out into the storm.

'Thanks for the tea, Albert. I'll drop in again when I'm passing,' shouted the lady, as she retreated into the uproar.

Mr Piggott nodded dumbly, shut the door with a crash, and breathed deeply. Mingled pleasure and fury shook his aged frame, but overriding all these agitations was the urgent need for a drink.

'Women!' spat out Mr Piggott, resuming his damp raincoat. 'Never let a chap alone!'

His mind turned the phrase over. There was something about it that made Mr Piggott feel younger — a beau, a masher, a man who was still pursued.

'Never let a chap alone!' repeated Mr Piggott aloud. He pulled on his wet cap, adjusting it at an unusually rakish and dashing angle, and made his way, swaggering very slightly, to his comforts next door.

[WINTER IN THRUSH GREEN]

True to her word, Nelly Tilling called frequently at Albert Piggott's house, and enjoyed cleaning up the place and cooking her old friend a meal.

Two hours later Nelly sat, blown but triumphant, on the kitchen chair and surveyed her handiwork.

She had cause for pride. A bright fire glowed behind gleaming bars, and the bacon pie was already in the oven beside it and beginning to smell most savoury. The thin little cat, her repast spread on a newspaper in the corner, dug her sharp white teeth into the cod's head, closing her eyes in bliss the while.

The floor, the walls and the wooden table had all been lustily scrubbed. Albert's dingy sink had been scoured to its original yellow colour, and the window above it gleamed and winked with unaccustomed cleanliness.

Taking a steady look at it, thought Nelly to herself, easing off her shoes for greater comfort, it wasn't such a bad little house, and certainly very much more conveniently placed for shopping than her own cottage at Lulling Woods.

Two rooms up and two rooms down would be just a nice size for Albert and herself, and her own furniture would look very handsome in these surroundings. The few poor sticks that Albert had collected over the years were fit for nothing but firewood.

She allowed her mind to dwell for a minute on her old schoolfellow in the role of husband. True, he was no oil painting, but she had long passed the age of needing good looks about her, and anyway, she admitted to herself with disarming frankness, her own beauty had long since gone.

And, of course, he was a miserable worm. But, Nelly pointed out to herself, he had some justification for it. The drink had something to do with it, no doubt, but lack of a decent woman in his house was the real cause of the trouble. She cast an appraising eye over the clean kitchen and listened to the music of the sizzling pie. With a cheerful place like this to come home to, thought Nelly, The Two Pheasants would lose its appeal. And if by any chance it didn't, then Nelly Tilling would put her foot down — for hadn't she seen, with her own eyes, young Albert Piggott in a Norfolk jacket much too small for him, signing the pledge all those years ago?

The advantages of the marriage were solid ones. Albert earned a steady wage, was a good gardener and could afford to keep a wife in reasonable comfort. There would be no need for her to go out to work. The Drover's Arms was a pleasant enough place to scrub out, but Nelly disliked seeing people drinking. She would not be sorry to give up the job there.

At Thrush Green she would be able to pick and choose her employers. Miss Ruth or Miss Joan, as she still thought of Mrs Lovell and Mrs Young, could probably do with a hand. She remembered the great flagged kitchen floor at the Bassetts' house and her heart warmed.

Or better still, there was the village school

practically next door! The thought of those yards of bare floorboards, pounded day in and day out by scores of muddy boots, fairly crying out for a bucket of hot suds and a good brush, filled Nelly's heart with joy. There was a cloak-room too, if she remembered rightly, with a nice rosy brick floor that really paid for doing. And there was something about a large tortoise stove, freshly done with first-class blacklead and plenty of elbow-grease, that gladdened your eyes. She had heard that Miss Watson wasn't best pleased with the present cleaner. A word dropped in the right ear, Nelly told herself, might bring her the job if she decided to earn an honest penny at Thrush Green.

She heard the sound of Albert's footsteps approaching, heaved her bulk from the chair, and opened the oven door. A glorious fragrance filled the room. On top of the hob, the winter greens bubbled deliciously. The mingled scents greeted Albert as he opened the back door.

'Cor!' breathed Mr Piggott with awe. 'That smells wholly good, Nell.'

His face bore an expression of holiness and rapture which his habitual place of worship never saw. Albert was touched to his very marrow.

Nelly was not slow to follow up this advantage.

'Sit you down, Albert,' she said warmly, 'in a real clean kitchen at last, with a real hot meal to eat.'

She withdrew the fragrant dish from the oven, and put it, still sizzling, before the bedazzled sexton.

'There!' breathed the widow proudly, setting about her wooing with a bacon pie.

[WINTER IN THRUSH GREEN]

Nelly's Bacon Pie

175 g (6 oz) cooked boiled bacon
175 g (6 oz) potato
1 teaspoon chopped parsley
1 onion, finely chopped
pepper
stock, preferably from boiling the bacon
250 g (½ lb) puff pastry
egg yolk for glazing

Dice the bacon and potato and put it into a pie dish, with the parsley and onion; add pepper to taste. Add stock so that it comes halfway up the pie dish.

Cover with puff pastry and decorate with cut-out pastry leaves. Glaze with egg yolk, and then cook in a moderate oven (Gas mark 5/190°C/375°F) for an hour, or a little more.

(Serves 4)

Nelly Tilling's plans went ahead steadily, despite little or no encouragement from the man of her choice. At last she decided upon action, and set out one afternoon to clinch the matter.

She found him in his kitchen, immersed in the newspaper spread out before him on the table. The odour of fried bacon surrounded him, and a dirty plate and cutlery, pushed to the corner of the table, showed that Albert had just finished his evening meal.

He grunted by way of greeting as the fat widow dumped herself down on the other chair, but did not raise his eyes from his reading.

'It says 'ere,' said Albert, 'that that fellow as robbed the bank yesterday got away with twenty thousand.' His voice held grudging admiration.

'I just been up the school,' answered Nelly, undoing her coat.

'Oh, ah?' said Albert, without interest. 'This chap knocked three o' the bank fellows clean to the floor, it says. Alone! Knocked three down, alone!'

'I can 'ave that job if I want it,' said Nelly. 'I've said I'll start Monday. It's a good wage, too.'

' "He told our reporter," ' read Albert laboriously, ' "that he was lying in a wolter of blood." Think of that!' said Albert ghoulishly. ' "A wolter of blood." ' He began to pick a back tooth with a black finger-nail, his eyes still

61

fixed upon the print.

'It'll be quite a step every day from Lulling Woods,' went on Nelly, delicately approaching her objective. 'I'm supposed to go in first thing in the mornings too, to light the stoves and dust round.'

'Oh, ah?' repeated Albert absently. He withdrew a wet forefinger from his mouth and replaced it damply on a line of print. ' "He was detained in hospital with a suspected skull fracture and rather serious injuries to the right eye." '

'I wish you'd listen,' said Nelly, exasperation giving an edge to her tones. 'I got something to tell you.'

Albert stopped reading aloud, but his eyes continued to follow his moving forefinger.

'Don't you think the time's come, Albert,' wheedled Nelly, 'when we thought of setting up here together? I mean, we've known each other since we was girl and boy, and we seem to hit it all right, don't we?'

A close observer might have noticed a slight stiffening of Albert's back, but otherwise he gave no sign of hearing. Only his finger moved a little more slowly along the line.

'You've said yourself,' continued Nelly, in cooing tones, 'how nice I cook, and keep the house to rights. You've been alone too long, Albert. What you wants is a bit of home comfort. What about it?'

A slight flush had crept over Albert's unlovely

countenance, but still his eyes remained lowered.

' "It is feared," ' Albert read, in an embarrassed mutter, ' "that 'is brain 'as suffered damage." '

'And so will yours, my boy!' Nelly burst out, rising swiftly. She lifted Albert's arms from the table, sat herself promptly down on the newspaper in front of Albert and let his arms fall on each side of her. She put one plump hand under his bristly chin and turned his face up to confront her.

'Now then,' said Nelly, giving him a dark melting glance. 'What about it?'

'What about what?' asked Albert weakly. It was quite apparent that he knew he was a doomed man. At last he was cornered, at last he was caught, but still he struggled feebly.

'You heard what I said,' murmured Nelly seductively, patting his cheek. 'Now I've got the job here, it'd all fit in so nice.'

Albert gazed at her mutely. His eyes were slightly glazed, but there was a certain softening around his drooping mouth.

'You'd have a clean warm house to live in,' went on his temptress, 'and a good hot meal midday, and all your washin' done.'

Albert's eyes brightened a little, but he still said nothing.

Nelly put her head provocatively on one side. 'And me here for company, Albert,' she continued, a little breathlessly. Could it be that

Albert's eyes dulled a little? She put her plump arms round his shoulders and gazed at him closely.

'Wouldn't you like a good wife?' asked Nelly beseechingly.

Albert gave a great gusty sigh — a farewell, half-sad and half-glad, to all his lonely years — and capitulated.

'All right,' said he. 'But get orf the paper, gal!'

[WINTER IN THRUSH GREEN]

Almost next door stood Albert's second home, The Two Pheasants, at eight o'clock on our time-piece.

It was a snug little inn, well furnished with beams and cushioned settles. Mr Jones the landlord and his wife lived in comfort above the two bars, and were as cheerful and welcoming as the best hosts should be.

He was also well skilled in diplomacy, hearing a great deal of gossip and complaint but discreet enough to keep it to himself. Here he listens to Albert's diatribe about the churchyard.

It was generally agreed that the churchyard of St Andrew's was an exceptionally pleasant place.

Albert did not agree, as he told his long-suffering neighbour, Mr Jones of The Two Pheasants, one bright morning as soon as the pub was open.

'Them dratted tombstones was put too close to the outside wall when they done the job.'

64

He took a noisy slurp of his beer.

'Young Cooke,' he went on, replacing the dripping glass on Mr Jones's carefully polished bar counter, 'can't get the mower between them and the wall.'

'Oh, ah!' replied Mr Jones without much interest. Albert and his young assistant had been at loggerheads for years now. The publican had heard both sides of the many arguments between the two, and for far too long.

'Means I had to get down on me hands and knees with the bill-hook, round the back, like. Not that easy at my age. Not after me Operation.'

A shadow fell across the sunlit floor. Percy Hodge, a farmer from the Nidden road hard by, was seeking refreshment.

'You ain't still on about your innards, are

you?' he queried. 'I reckon all Thrush Green knows about them tubes of yours. And fair sick of 'em too. Half a pint, please.'

Albert's face grew even more morose. 'All right for you. Never had a day's illness in your life!'

'Ah! But I got my troubles.'

He pushed some coins across the counter and settled on the next stool to Albert.

'Oh? Your Doris come back?'

Percy drew in his breath noisily.

'Now, Albert,' began Mr Jones. 'We don't want no trouble between old friends.'

'Who's talking about old friends?' enquired Albert nastily. Percy's breathing became heavier.

'You keep Doris's name out of this,' he said. 'I don't keep on about your Nelly, though we all know what she is!'

'*Gentlemen!*' cried Mr Jones in alarm.

Percy and Albert fell silent and turned their attention to their glasses. A distant clanking sound, followed by a steady chugging, proclaimed that the cement mixer was at work on the new retirement homes.

'By the time them places is finished,' said Albert, 'our lot'll all be in the graveyard. Be about ready for young Cooke, I reckon.'

'Wonder who they'll choose?' asked Percy, secretly glad to pick up this olive branch. 'You put your name down?'

'What, with my Nelly to look after me? And

my girl Molly across the green at the Youngs? No point in me havin' a try. They'll be looking for old folk on their own.'

'Well, I've put my name forward,' said Percy. 'I'm old, and on my own.'

His listeners seemed taken aback. Albert was trying to work out how much younger Percy was than he himself. Mr Jones was shocked at the cheek of a man who was only middle-aged, and had a house and a living, in applying for one of the new homes. But he forebore to comment. He did not want any trouble in his respectable hostelry, and both customers were touchy.

'You'll be lucky!' commented Albert at last, putting his empty glass down. 'Must get back to my bill-hook. I'd like to meet the chap as set them tombstones round the wall. I'd give him a piece of me mind.'

'He got hurt in a car crash, other side of Oxford,' volunteered Percy. 'My cousin told me. Broke his arm, he said.'

'No more'n he deserved,' said Albert heartlessly, and hobbled back to his duties.

[AT HOME IN THRUSH GREEN]

At nine o'clock, looking across the green to the Baileys' house, stood the village school, a sturdy one-storey building of Cotswold stone in a playground of generous proportions. There were two classrooms, one occupied by Miss Dorothy Watson, the headmistress, and the other by the young

67

teacher in charge of the lower juniors. Miss Agnes Fogerty is the infants' teacher in a temporary building across the playground.

The school-house, standing at ten o'clock, is a small Victorian building, erected at the same time as Thrush Green school. It was a pleasant two-bedroomed house with a long garden running between the school playground and the Shoosmiths' garden next door.

Some of the most exciting events have occurred in this imaginary place, and I am always disappointed when I visit Wood Green to find that no school, no school-house, no children and, above all, no Miss Watson or Miss Fogerty are to be seen. It gives me quite a shock.

I grew increasingly fond of Dorothy Watson, the headmistress, and her assistant Agnes Fogerty. When we first meet them, Dorothy is living alone in the school-house and Agnes is in lodgings along the main road which leads eventually to the Midlands.

Little Miss Fogerty was in considerable awe of Miss Watson, but a burglary was to alter their relationship.

The school was empty when Miss Fogerty clattered her way over the door scraper to her classroom. That did not surprise her, for Miss Watson lived at the school-house next door, and might be busy with her last minute chores. She usually arrived about a quarter to nine, greeted her colleague, read her correspondence, and was then prepared to face the assembled school.

Miss Fogerty hung up her tweed coat and her brown felt hat behind the classroom door, and set about unlocking the cupboards. There were little tatters of paper at the bottom of the one by the fireplace, where the raffia and other handwork materials were kept, and Miss Fogerty looked at them with alarm and suspicion. She had thought for some time that a mouse lived there. She must remember to tell Mrs Cooke to set a trap. Mice were one of the few things that Miss Fogerty could not endure. It would be dreadful if one ran out while the children were present and she made an exhibition of herself by screaming! After surveying the jungle of cane, raffia and cardboard which rioted gloriously together, and which could well offer a dozen comfortable homes to abundant mice families, Miss Fogerty firmly shut the door and relocked it. The children should have crayons and drawing paper this afternoon from the cupboard on the far side of the room, she decided. Mrs Cooke must deal with this crisis before she approached the handwork cupboard again.

The clock stood at five to nine, and now the cries and shouts of two or three dozen children could be heard. Miss Fogerty made her way to the only other classroom, and stopped short on the threshold with surprise. It was empty.

Miss Fogerty noted the clean duster folded neatly in the very centre of Miss Watson's desk, the tidy rows of tables and chairs awaiting their occupants, and the large reproduction of Holman Hunt's 'The Light of the World', in whose dusky glass Miss Fogerty could see her own figure reflected.

What should she do? Could Miss Watson have overslept? Could she be ill? Either possibility seemed difficult to believe. In the twelve years since Miss Watson's coming, she had neither overslept nor had a day's indisposition. It would be very awkward if she called at the house and Miss Watson were just about to come over. It would look *officious,* poor Miss Fogerty told herself, and that could not be borne.

Miss Fogerty was a little afraid of Miss Watson, for though she herself had spent thirty years at Thrush Green School, she was only the assistant teacher and she had been taught to respect her betters. And Miss Watson, of course, really was her better, for she had been a headmistress before this, and had taught in town schools, so large and magnificent that naturally she was much wiser and more experienced. She was consistently kind to faded little Miss Fogerty and very willing to show her new methods of threading beads and making plasticine crumpets, explaining patiently, as she did so, the psychological implications behind these activities in words of three or, more often, four syllables. Miss Fogerty was humbly grateful for her goodwill, but would never have dreamt of imposing upon it. Miss Fogerty knew her place.

While she hovered on the threshold, patting

her wispy hair into place with an agitated hand and looking distractedly at her reflection in 'The Light of the World', a breathless child hurried into the lobby, calling her name.

'Miss Fogerty! Miss Fogerty!'

He rushed towards her so violently that Miss Fogerty put out her hands to grasp his shoulders before he should butt her to the ground.

The child looked up at her, wide-eyed. He looked awe-stricken.

'Miss Watson called me up to her window, miss, and says you're to go over there.'

'Very well,' said Miss Fogerty, calmly. 'There's no need to get so excited. Take off your coat and hang it up. You can go to your room now.'

The child continued to gaze at her. 'But, miss,' he blurted out, 'Miss Watson — she — she's still in her nightdress and the clock's struck nine.'

Miss Watson's appearance when she opened the side door alarmed Miss Fogerty quite as much as it had the small boy.

Her nightdress was decently covered by a red dressing-gown, but her face was drawn with pain and she swayed dizzily against the door jamb.

'What has happened?' exclaimed Miss Fogerty, entering the house.

Miss Watson closed the door and leant heavily against it. 'I've been attacked — hit on the head,' said Miss Watson. She sounded dazed and vaguely surprised. A hand went fumbling among her untidy grey locks and Miss Fogerty, much shocked, put her hand under her headmistress's elbow to steady her.

'Come and sit down. I'll ring Doctor Lovell. He'll be at home now. Tell me what happened.'

'I can't walk,' answered Miss Watson, leaning on Miss Fogerty's frail shoulder. 'I seem to have sprained my ankle as I fell. It is most painful.'

She held out a bare leg, and certainly the ankle was misshapen and much swollen. Purplish patches were already forming and Miss Fogerty knew from her first-aid classes that she should really be applying hot and cold water in turn to the damaged joint. But could poor Miss Watson, in her present state of shock, stand such treatment? She helped the younger woman to the kitchen, put her on a chair and looked round for the kettle.

'There's nothing like a cup of tea, dear,' she said comfortingly, as she filled it. 'With plenty of sugar.'

Miss Watson shuddered but made no reply. Her assistant switched on the kettle and surveyed her headmistress anxiously. Her usual feeling of respect, mingled with a little fear, had been replaced by the warmest concern. For the first time in their acquaintanceship, Miss Fogerty was in charge.

'The door-bell rang about half-past five, I suppose,' began Miss Watson hesitantly. 'It was still dark. I leant out of the bedroom window and there was a man waiting there who said there had been a car crash and could he telephone.'

'What did he look like?' asked Miss Fogerty.

'I couldn't see. I said I'd come down. I put on my dressing-gown and slippers and opened the front door —' She broke off suddenly, and took a deep breath.

Miss Fogerty was smitten by the look of horror on her headmistress's face.

'Don't tell me, my dear, if it upsets you. There's really no need.' She patted the red dressing-gown soothingly, but Miss Watson pulled herself together and continued.

'He'd tied a black scarf, or a stocking, or something over his face, and I could only see his eyes between that and his hat brim. He had a thick stick of some kind — quite short — in his hand, and he said something about this being a hold-up, or a stick-up or some term I really didn't understand. I bent forward to see if I could recognise him — there was something vaguely familiar about him, the voice perhaps — and then he hit me on the side of my head —' Poor Miss Watson faltered and her eyes filled with tears at the memory of that vicious blow.

The kettle's lid began rattling merrily and Miss Fogerty, clucking sympathetically, began to make the tea.

'I seem to remember him pushing past me.

I'd crumpled on to the door mat and I remember a fearful pain, but whether it was my head or my ankle, I don't really know. When I came round again, the door was shut and he'd vanished. It was beginning to get light then.'

'Why didn't you get help before?' asked Miss Fogerty. 'It must have been getting light at about seven o'clock. He will have got clear by now.'

'I was so terribly sick,' confessed Miss Watson. 'I managed to crawl to the outside lavatory and I've been there most of the time.'

'You poor, poor dear!' cried Miss Fogerty. 'And you must be so cold, too!'

'I couldn't manage the stairs, otherwise I should have got dressed. But I thought I would wait until I heard you arrive, and then I knew I should be all right.'

Miss Fogerty glowed with pleasure. It was not often, in her timid life, that she had been wanted. To know that she was needed by someone gave her a heady sense of power. She poured out the tea and put the cup carefully before her patient.

'Shall I lift it for you?' she asked solicitously, but Miss Watson shook her head, raising the steaming cup herself and sipped gratefully.

'The children —' she said suddenly, as their exuberant voices penetrated the quietness of the kitchen.

'Don't worry,' said Miss Fogerty with newly-found authority. 'I'll just speak to the bigger ones, then I'll be back to ring the doctor.'

'Don't tell them anything about this,' begged Miss Watson, with sudden agitation. 'You know what Thrush Green is. It will be all round the place in no time.'

Miss Fogerty assured her that nothing would be disclosed and slipped out of the side door.

The children were shouting and playing, revelling in this unexpected addition to their pre-school games' time.

Miss Fogerty leant over the low dry-stone wall which separated the playground from the school-house garden. She beckoned to two of the bigger girls.

'Keep an eye on the young ones, my dears. I'll be with you in a minute, then we'll all go in.'

'Is Miss Watson ill?' asked one, her eyes alight with pleasurable anticipation.

Miss Fogerty was torn between telling the truth and the remembrance of her promise to her headmistress. She temporised wisely. 'Not really, dear, but she won't be over for a little while. There's nothing for you to worry about.'

She hastened back to her duties.

Her patient had finished her tea and now leant back with her eyes closed and the swollen ankle propped up on another chair. She opened her eyes as Miss Fogerty approached, and smiled faintly.

'Tell me,' said Miss Fogerty, who had just remembered something. 'Did the man take anything?'

'He took the purse from my bag. There wasn't much in it, and my wallet, with about six pounds, I believe.'

Miss Fogerty was profoundly shocked. Six pounds was a lot of money for a schoolteacher to lose even if she were a headmistress.

'And I think he may have found my jewel box upstairs, but of course I haven't been up there to see. It hadn't much of value in it, except to me, I mean. There was a string of seed pearls my father gave me, and two rings of my mother's and a brooch or two — but nothing worth a lot of money.'

'We must ring the police as well as Doctor Lovell,' exclaimed Miss Fogerty.

'Must we?' cried Miss Watson, her face puckering. 'Oh dear, I do hate all this fuss — but I suppose it is our duty.'

Miss Fogerty's heart smote her at the sight of her patient's distress. It reminded her too that she should really get her into bed so that she could recover a little from the shocks she had received. She sprang to her feet, with new-found strength, and went to help her headmistress.

'Back to bed for you,' she said firmly, 'and then I'm going to the telephone. Up you come!'

Five minutes later, with her patient safely tucked up, Miss Fogerty spoke to Doctor Lovell and then to Lulling Police Station. That done, she went over to the school playground to face the forty or more children for whom she alone would be responsible that day.

Normally the thought would have made timid little Miss Fogerty quail. But today, fortified by her experiences, feeling six feet high and a tower of strength, Miss Fogerty led the entire school into morning assembly and faced a host of questioning eyes with unaccustomed composure and authority.

For the first time in her life Miss Fogerty was in command, and found she liked it.

[WINTER IN THRUSH GREEN]

Some time later, Dorothy suffered a more severe accident and broke a hip. She invited Agnes to share the school-house with her, and the two settled down together very happily. Agnes had no relations, and relished the companionship of her headmistress. Dorothy had a brother Ray, and did not always welcome his visits with his wife Kathleen, particularly when they were accompanied by their spoilt dog Harrison.

On one occasion they called at the school-house for tea, leaving the dog outside in the car. Conversation was carried on against a background of ear-splitting barking.

Agnes asked after Kathleen's health. At once, Ray's wife assumed a melancholy expression.

'I'm having some new treatment for my migraine attacks,' she told them, accepting a second cup of tea. 'It's terribly expensive, and I have to make two trips a week, but I think it may be doing me good.'

'I am so glad,' said kind Agnes.

'And I've been having attacks of vertigo,' volunteered Ray, with a hint of pride. 'Something to do with the middle ear. Very disconcerting.'

Agnes wondered if the dog's powerful voice could contribute to this discomfort, but thought it wiser to remain silent. Not once, she noticed, with rare warmth, had they enquired after poor Dorothy's broken hip — a much more serious business, surely!

'But there,' continued Kathleen, with sad recognition. 'I suppose we can't expect to be as spry as we were twenty years ago.'

'Indeed no!' agreed Dorothy, rising to cut the splendid sponge. She walked across to Kathleen, plate in hand. Was her limp rather more pronounced than usual, Agnes wondered? A little stiff from sitting perhaps, she decided.

'And how is the leg?' enquired Ray, somewhat tardily.

'I do my best to ignore it,' replied Dorothy. 'No one wants to hear about the troubles of the elderly.'

Kathleen greeted this pointed remark with a swiftly indrawn breath, and a meaning glance at her husband. He, man-like, pretended to be engrossed with his tea cup.

'And where are you proposing to go tomorrow?' asked Agnes hastily.

Before Ray could answer, Kathleen spoke. 'It's amazing how quickly people get over these hip operations these days. Why, a young curate we know was actually *dancing* six months after he fell from his bicycle.'

'He was fortunate,' said Dorothy.

'Oh, I don't know,' said Kathleen, shouting above the racket from the imprisoned dog. 'I'm sure it's just a matter of attitude of mind. He *intended* to get better just as quickly as possible. I think some people enjoy being invalids.'

Agnes noted with alarm that a pink flush was suffusing Dorothy's face, a sure sign of temper, and really, thought her loyal assistant, she had every right to be cross under the circumstances.

'I don't,' said Dorothy shortly.

'Of course not,' agreed Ray. 'It was exactly what I said to Kathleen when she was so worried about you in hospital.'

'Really?' replied his sister icily.

'Kathleen was a martyr to her migraine at

the time, as you know, otherwise we should have invited you to stay with us when you were discharged. But we knew you wanted to get home and pick up your normal life again. I said so at the time, didn't I, Kathleen?'

'You did indeed, dear,' said Kathleen, dabbing her mouth with a spotless linen napkin and leaving lipstick as well as jam upon it.

Before any civilised reply could be made, there was a rapping at the front door. Agnes, glad to escape, hurried to open it, and was confronted by Dotty Harmer with Flossie on a lead. A battered metal milk can dangled from the other hand.

Without being invited, Dotty pushed past Agnes and entered the sitting-room. She was in a state of considerable agitation, and burst into speech.

'Oh, Dorothy my dear, there is a poor dog *absolutely stifling to death* in a car outside. No window left open, and it is in a terrible state of anxiety. Aren't people thoughtless? Really they need a horse-whipping, and my father would have administered it, I assure you, if he had come across such fiends! Someone calling at The Two Pheasants, I suppose, or at the Shoosmiths.'

'The dog belongs to my brother here,' said Dorothy, with a hint of smugness in her tone. 'I'm sorry it upset you so, Dotty dear. I'm afraid it must have upset a great many people at Thrush Green during the past hour.'

Dotty was not the slightest bit abashed. 'I don't think I have had the pleasure of meeting you before,' she said, transferring Flossie's lead to her left hand and entangling it dangerously with the milk can, whilst proffering her right.

'My sister-in-law, Kathleen. My brother, Ray. My friend, Miss Harmer,' intoned Dorothy.

Ray bowed slightly. Kathleen gave a frosty smile. Outside, the barking changed to a high-pitched squealing, even more agitated than before. Ray began to make for the door.

'Excuse me, I'd better bring Harrison in,' he said. He was through the door before anyone could stop him.

Dorothy waved at the tea tray. 'Let me give you some tea, Dotty. Do sit down.'

'So kind of you, Dorothy, but I'm on my way to Ella's and mustn't delay.'

She began to make her way to the door. Flossie's lead was now hopelessly tangled round Dotty's wrinkled stockings.

At that moment, Ray's labrador, slavering at the mouth, burst into the room, gave a demented yelp, and rushed at Flossie.

The noise was indescribable. Flossie, the meekest of animals, screamed with alarm. Harrison charged into the table, knocking the sponge cake, chocolate biscuits, two tea cups, milk jug and a flurry of knives and teaspoons to the floor.

Dotty, pulled off balance, fell across Agnes's chair, driving her mother's cameo brooch painfully into her throat. Dorothy, ever quick-witted, sat down abruptly before her own precarious balance added to the confusion, and Kathleen, cowering in her chair, gave way to hysterics.

This scene of chaos confronted Ray when he regained the sitting-room. With commendable promptitude, he caught Harrison by the collar and held him firmly, while Agnes and Dotty recovered their balance. The milk can had rolled under Agnes's armchair and was dispersing a rivulet of goat's milk over the carpet.

'I apologise for this mess,' said Dotty. 'You must let me pay for any cleaning you have to have done. Goat's milk can be so very *pervasive*. I'd better return home and fetch some more for Ella. Luckily, Dulcie is giving a splendidly heavy yield at the moment.'

Quite in command of herself, she smiled politely in the direction of the hysterical Kathleen, now throwing herself about alarmingly in her chair, waved to Ray, and took the shaken, but now well-behaved Flossie into the hall. Agnes accompanied her, hoping that the blood on her throat from the brooch's wound would not stain her best silk blouse.

'Are you *sure* you would not like to rest for a little?' enquired Agnes. 'The dining-room has a most comfortable armchair, if you would like a few minutes' peace.'

'Thank you, my dear, but I am quite all right. The air will refresh me.'

Agnes watched her walk to the gate, as spry as a sparrow, and none the worse it seemed for her tumble. She returned, full of foreboding, to the scene of battle.

'Who *is* that interfering old busybody?' Ray was asking, as she returned.

'A dear friend of mine,' replied Dorothy, 'and a true animal lover. I absolutely agree with her that it was *monstrous* of you to leave that dog shut in the car.'

Kathleen's hysterics were now slightly muted, but had turned to shattering hiccups.

'If you remember,' she began, and gave a mighty hiccup, 'you yourself refused to have poor Harrison indoors.'

'I should have thought that even *you* knew better than to leave the car hermetically sealed. Calling yourselves animal lovers,' said Dorothy, with withering scorn. 'And the poor thing so badly trained that it cannot be brought into a Christian household.'

She bent down to retrieve the best china from the floor, whilst Ray picked up teaspoons with one hand and dabbed at the goat's milk with the other holding his handkerchief.

'*Please*, Ray,' said Dorothy, 'leave the mess to Agnes and me. We don't want it made worse by the use of your handkerchief.'

Agnes felt that, provoked though Dorothy might well be, such a slur on the cleanliness of her brother's personal linen was carrying things rather far.

'I will fetch some clean water and a cloth,' she said hastily, and made her escape.

A wild wailing noise followed her. Obviously, Kathleen was off again!

'I think,' Ray was saying, when Agnes returned with her cleaning materials, 'that we had better be going.'

'I whole-heartedly agree,' said Dorothy, standing facing him.

'You have thoroughly upset poor Kathleen,' he went on, 'and you know how she suffers with migraine.'

'When it suits her,' responded Dorothy.

'Are you implying,' cried her incensed brother, 'that Kathleen *pretends* to have these dreadful attacks?'

A terrible hiccup arrested Kathleen's wailing. She was now on her feet, eyes blazing.

'How dare you say such things? You know I'm a martyr to migraine! Not that I've ever had the slightest sympathy from you. You are the wickedest, most callous, unfeeling —'

Another hiccup rendered her temporarily speechless. Ray took the opportunity to put his arm about his wife, and to shepherd her and the panting Harrison to the door.

'Come along, my dear. We'll go straight back to The Fleece, and you must lie down with one of your tablets.'

'But poor Harrison hasn't had his tea,' wailed Kathleen. 'You know he likes it on the hearth-rug!'

'There is plenty for him,' observed Dorothy, 'wherever he looks on the carpet.'

It was Agnes who saw them to the door, and then into their car.

'I shall never come here again,' cried Kathleen, still hiccuping violently.

'We are deeply wounded,' said Ray. 'I don't think I shall want to see Dorothy — sister though she is — for a very long time!'

They drove towards Lulling, Harrison still barking, and Agnes returned to break the dreadful news that Dorothy might never see the pair again.

'What a relief!' said her headmistress, with infinite satisfaction. 'Now, we'll just get this place to rights, and have a quiet evening with our knitting, Agnes dear.'

[GOSSIP FROM THRUSH GREEN]

As it happened, the rift between Dorothy and her brother and his wife did not last long, much to Miss Fogerty's relief.

The two friends continued to live in harmony and, for Agnes in particular, the change from her lodgings was a lasting joy.

Miss Fogerty had never been so happy as she was now, living with Dorothy and next door to another old friend, Isobel Shoosmith, who had been at college with her years before. Although she had not realised it at the time, looking back she could see that her life at Mrs White's had been quite lonely. True, she had had a pleasant bed-sitting room, and Mrs White had cooked for her and always been welcoming, but on some cold summer evenings, sitting in her Lloyd Loom armchair by a gas fire, turned low for reasons of economy, Agnes had experienced some bleakness.

It was such a pleasure now to wake each morning in the knowledge that she was near to her friends, and had no need to make a journey, in all weathers, to the school. She was usually down first in the kitchen, happy to see to the kettle and the eggs and toast in readiness for Dorothy, who was still rather slow in her movements since breaking a hip.

It was that accident which had led to Agnes being asked to share the school-house, and she looked forward to several years together before retirement age. What happened then, Miss

Fogerty sometimes wondered? But time enough when that day loomed nearer, she decided, and meanwhile life was perfect.

Willie Marchant had brought two letters, one from the office obviously and one which looked as though it were from Dorothy's brother, Ray. Miss Fogerty sipped her tea whilst the headmistress read her correspondence.

'Ray and Kathleen are proposing to have a week or ten days touring the Cotswolds next month,' she told Agnes, as she stuffed his letter back into the envelope.

'How nice,' said Agnes. 'Are they likely to call here?'

'A call I should like,' said Dorothy, with some emphasis, 'but Ray seems to be inviting himself and Kathleen to stay here for a night or two.'

'Oh!' said Agnes, somewhat taken aback. The school-house had only two bedrooms. The one which had once been the spare room she now occupied permanently. Before then, she knew, Ray had sometimes spent the night there on his travels as a commercial salesman. Since Dorothy's accident, however, things had been a little strained. She had confidently expected to convalesce with her brother and his wife, but they had made no offer, indeed nothing but excuses. If it had not been for Agnes's willingness to help, poor Miss Watson would have been unaided in her weakness. It was quite plain to Miss Fogerty that she had not forgiven or forgotten.

'I could easily make up a bed in the sitting-
room,' offered Agnes, 'if you would like to have
mine. Then they could have the twin beds in
your room.'

'It won't be necessary, Agnes dear,' said Dorothy, in the firm tones of a headmistress. 'We
are not going to put ourselves out for them.
They have quite enough money to afford a hotel.
They can try The Fleece if they must come and
stay here. Frankly, it won't break my heart if
we don't see them at all.'

'Oh Dorothy!' begged gentle little Miss
Fogerty, 'don't talk like that! He is your own
flesh and blood — your own brother!'

'No fault of mine,' said Dorothy, briskly, rolling up her napkin. 'I didn't choose him, you
know, but I do choose my *friends!*'

She glanced at the clock. 'Better clear up, I
suppose, or we shall be late for school. I really
ought to look out some pictures for my history
lesson this morning.'

'Then you go over to school, dear,' said Miss

Fogerty, 'and I'll see to the breakfast things.'

'You spoil me,' said Miss Watson, limping towards the door.

And how pleasant it was to have someone to spoil, thought Agnes, running the tap. More often than not, she did stay behind to do this little chore but never did she resent it. Looking after others, children or adults, was little Miss Fogerty's chief source of pleasure.

Miss Watson, making her way carefully across the playground, thought fondly of her assistant. She was the soul of unselfishness, as her ready offer to vacate her bedroom had shown yet again. But Miss Watson was determined that Agnes should now come first. She had been a loyal colleague for many years, respected by parents and children alike, and since the accident had proved a trusted friend and companion.

All that stuff about blood being thicker than water, thought Miss Watson robustly, was a lot of eyewash! She had had more help and affection from her dear old Agnes than ever Ray and Kathleen had shown her. It had to be faced, they were a selfish pair, and she had no intention of upsetting Agnes's comfort, or her own, to save them a few pennies.

'You can come and help me to carry some pictures, George dear,' she said to young Curdle, who was skipping about the playground. It was by way of being a royal command.

She swept ahead to enter her domain, followed

by one of her willing subjects.

[GOSSIP FROM THRUSH GREEN]

Next door, at eleven o'clock, stood a fine Edwardian house which for many years was called Quetta. When we first hear of it, the house had been empty for some time, and Albert Piggott deplored its neglect.

Mr Piggott straightened his aching back, clasped his hands on top of the broom, and surveyed Thrush Green morosely. Behind him lay the bulk of the church, its spire's shadow throwing a neat triangle across the grass. To his right ran the main road from the Cotswold hills down into the sleepy little market town of Lulling, which Thrush Green adjoined. To his left ran a modest lane which meandered northward to several small villages.

Within fifty yards of him, set along this line, stood his cottage, next door to The Two Pheasants. The village school, now quiet behind its white palings in the morning sunshine, was next in the row, and beside it was a well-built house of Cotswold stone which stood back from the green. Its front windows stared along the chestnut avenue which joined the two roads. The door was shut, and no smoke plumed skywards from its grey chimneys.

The garden was overgrown and deserted. Dead black roses drooped from the unkempt bushes growing over the face of the house, and the broad flagged path was almost hidden by unswept leaves.

Mr Piggott could see the vegetable garden from his vantage point in the churchyard. A row of bean poles had collapsed, sagging under the weight of the frost-blackened crop. Below the triumphant spires of dock which covered the beds, submerged cabbages, as large as footballs, could be discerned. Onions, left to go to seed, displayed magnificent fluffy heads, and a host of chirruping birds fluttered excitedly about the varied riches of the wilderness.

Mr Piggott clicked his false teeth in disapproval at such wicked waste, and shook his head at the 'FOR SALE' board which had been erected at the gate the week before.

'Time someone took that over,' he said aloud. 'What's the good weeding this 'ere if all that lot's coming over all the time?' He cast a sour look at the leaves which still danced joyously in his path. Everlasting work! thought Mr Piggott gloomily.

The clock began to whirr above him before striking ten. Mr Piggott's face brightened. Someone came out of The Two Pheasants and latched the door back to the wall hospitably. The faint clinking of glasses could be heard and a snatch of music from the bar's radio set.

Mr Piggott propped his broom against the church railings and set off, with unaccustomed jauntiness, to his haven.

[WINTER IN THRUSH GREEN]

Fortunately, Quetta was bought a few months later by a retired man, Harold Shoosmith. Conjectures about the newcomer were many and various.

Ella's lively interest in Harold Shoosmith was shared by the rest of Thrush Green. It was said that he was retired from the army, the navy, the civil service and the BBC. He had been a tea-planter in Ceylon, a cocoa-adviser in Ghana, and a coffee-blender in Brazil. It also appeared that he had owned a sugar plantation in Jamaica, a rubber plantation in Malaya and a diamond mine — quite a small one, actually, but with exceptionally fine diamonds — in South Africa.

Thrush Green was sorry to hear that he had never been married, had been married unhappily and was now separated from his wife, had been happily married and lost his wife in child-birth, and (disastrously) still married, with a wife who would be coming to live with him at the corner house within a few days.

The inhabitants of Thrush Green were able to gaze their fill at the stranger on the first Sunday after his arrival, as he attended morning service in a dove-grey suit which was far better cut, everyone agreed, than those of the other males in the congregation. The rector and one or two other neighbours had called upon him already and pronounced him 'a very nice man' or 'a decent sort of fellow' according to sex.

To the rector's unfeigned delight, the new-comer was among the very few communicants at the altar rail at the eight o'clock service on the following Sunday. About half a dozen faithful female Christians kept the rector company at early service usually. It did the rector's heart good to see a man among his small flock, and he hoped that others might follow his example.

Betty Bell was the chief informant about Harold Shoosmith for she had been engaged for three mornings and three evenings a week. The morning engagements Thrush Green could readily understand, for a man living alone could not be expected to polish and clean, to cook and scrub, and to wash and iron for himself; though, as Ella pointed out, plenty of women lived alone and did all that with one hand tied behind them, and often went out to work as well into the bargain, and no one considered it remarkable.

The evening engagements were readily explained by Betty Bell herself. She went for an hour and a half to give him a hot cooked dinner, which she had prepared in the morning, and to wash up afterwards.

'He's a very clever kind of man,' said Betty to her other employer, Dotty Harmer, one morning. 'He wants to learn to cook for himself. Being out in those hot countries, you know, he's never had a chance to learn. The kitchen's full of black people falling over themselves to do the work, and he's never been allowed to see his own dinner cooking, so I hear.'

[WINTER IN THRUSH GREEN]

Before long though, Harold meets his future wife Isobel, who had been at college with Agnes Fogerty, and they live happily ever after.

And this brings us to the end of our clockwise tour of Thrush Green and our brief meetings with the chief inhabitants. But there are two more establishments, a little farther away, whose inmates play their parts in Thrush Green's gentle dramas.

Dotty Harmer, a spinster and stout friend of all animals, lived some quarter of a mile westward towards Lulling Woods. Her schoolmaster father had been a disciplinarian who firmly believed that sparing the rod spoilt the child and whose memory caused many a local male heart to tremble.

Dotty Harmer was an eccentric old maid who lived alone in a ramshackle cottage in one of the meadows which bordered the path to Lulling Woods. Her father had been a history master at the local grammar school and Dotty had kept house for the old man until his death, when she sold their home, bringing some of the furniture, all the books, four cats, two dogs and a collection of medicinal herbs to her new home. The herbs flourished in her tiny garden, with roses, peonies, lilies and carnations which were the envy of all the gardeners in Lulling.

Dotty concocted alarming potions from the herbs and these she pressed upon her unwilling neighbours and friends if they were unwary enough to admit to any slight ailment in her presence. So far, she had killed no one, but the vicar of St Andrew's had once had to call in Doctor Bailey as he was in agony with severe stomach pains, and had had to admit that he had taken tea and sandwiches with a peculiar and pungent filling, at Dotty Harmer's a few hours before. The doctor had dismissed his troubles airily, diagnosing 'Dotty's Collywobbles', a fairly common Lulling complaint, and had warned him about accepting further hospitality at that lady's hands.

[THRUSH GREEN]

Dotty's way of life sometimes alarmed her

friends. Ella Bembridge, exhausted by Christmas shopping, called into the local tea shop, The Fuchsia Bush, in Lulling High Street and encountered her old friend.

'Well, Dotty, expecting anyone?' boomed Ella, dragging back the only unoccupied chair in the tea shop.

'No, no,' replied Dotty, removing a string bag, a cauliflower and a large paper bag labelled 'LAYMORE' from the seat. 'Bertha Lovelock was here until a minute ago. Do sit down. I'm just going through my list once more. I think I've got everything except whiting for my cat. It's usually rock salmon, you know, but I think she's expecting again and whiting must lie less heavily on the stomach, I feel sure.'

'Tea, please,' said Ella to the languid waitress who appeared at her side.

'Set-tea–toasted-tea-cake–jam-or-honey–choice-of-cake-to-follow–two-and-nine,' gabbled the girl, admiring her engagement ring the while.

'No thanks,' said Ella. 'Just tea.'

'Indian or China?'

'Indian,' said Ella. 'And strong.'

The girl departed and Ella unwound the long woollen scarf from her thick neck, undid her coat and sighed with relief.

'Wonder why it's "Indian or China"?' she remarked idly to Dotty. 'Why not "Indian or Chinese"? Or "India or China"? Illogical, isn't it?'

'Indeed, yes,' agreed Dotty, breaking a digestive biscuit carefully in half. 'But then people *are* illogical. Look at Father's man trap.'

Ella looked startled. Sometimes Dotty's conversation was more eccentric than usual. This seemed to be one of her bad days.

'What's your father's man trap got to do with it?' demanded Ella.

'I just want it back,' said Dotty simply. She popped a fragment of biscuit into her mouth and crunched it primly with her front teeth. The back ones had been removed. She had the air of a polite bespectacled rabbit at her repast.

'Oh, come off it!' begged Ella roughly. 'Talk sense!' Dotty looked vaguely upset.

'You know Father gave his valuable man trap to the museum. It was quite a fine working model used in the eighteenth century by Sir Henry — a great-great-grandfather of the present Sir Henry. Father used to demonstrate it to the boys at the grammar school when he was teaching history there.' She paused to sip her tea, and Ella, fuming at the delay, began to wonder if that were all Dotty would say.

Dotty replaced her cup carefully, patted her mouth with a small folded handkerchief, and continued.

'Well,' she said, 'now I could do with it.'

Ella made a violent gesture of annoyance, nearly capsizing the tea tray which the languid girl had now brought.

'What on earth do you want a man trap for?' expostulated Ella.

Dotty looked at her in surprise. 'Why, to catch a man!' she explained.

Ella made a sound remarkably like 'Tchah!' and began to pour milk violently into her cup.

'I suspect,' continued Dotty, unaware of Ella's heightened blood pressure, 'that someone is stealing my eggs. I could set the man trap at dusk and let the police interview him in the morning.'

'Now, look here, Dotty,' said Ella, in a hectoring tone, 'don't you realise you'd probably break the chap's leg in one of those ghastly contraptions — ?'

'Naturally,' replied her friend coolly, 'a man trap works on that principle, and ours was in excellent condition. Father saw to that. He would be quite safe in it till morning. I get up fairly early, as you know, so he wouldn't be in it more than a few hours.' She spoke as though she would be acting with the most humane consideration, and even Ella was nonplussed.

'But man traps are illegal,' she pointed out.

'Fiddlesticks!' said Dotty firmly. 'So are heaps of other traps, but they're used, more's the pity, on poor animals that are doing no wrong. This wretched man knows quite well he is doing wrong in taking my eggs. He deserves the consequences, and I shall point them out to him — from a safe distance, of course — as soon as I've trapped him.'

There was a slight pause.

'You know what?' said Ella. 'You're absolutely off your rocker, Dot.'

Dotty flushed with annoyance. 'I'm a lot saner than you are, Ella Bembridge,' she said snappily. 'And a lot saner than those chits of girls at the museum who won't let me have Father's property back. I very much doubt if they are legally in the right about refusing my request. After all, Father left all his property to me, and as I say, that man trap is exactly what I need at the moment.'

'You forget it,' advised Ella, rolling a ragged cigarette. 'Pop up to the police station instead and get Sergeant Stansted to keep his eyes skinned. And, what's more,' she added, for she was fond of her crazy friend, 'don't tell him you want the man trap back, or you're the one he'll be keeping his eye on.'

She drew a deep and refreshing inhalation of strong cigarette smoke. This was an occasion, she thought to herself, when a woman could do with a little comfort.

[WINTER IN THRUSH GREEN]

The second establishment was located halfway down Lulling High Street and was occupied by the Misses Lovelock — Ada, Bertha and Violet. It was a handsome Georgian house, with a white-painted front door, approached by three steps and two elegantly curved iron handrails. We meet them here at a party given by Ella and Dimity.

Ella made her way to the ladies' end to re-plenish Violet Lovelock's glass. The three

Miss Lovelocks had seated themselves on the window-seat, their silvery heads nodding and trembling, and their glasses, as Ella was not unsurprised to see, quite empty.

These three ladies, now in their seventies, lived in a Georgian doll's house in Lulling's High Street. There they had been born, their wicker bassinette had been bumped down the shallow flight of steps to the pavement by their trim nursemaid, young men had called, but not one of the three tall sisters had emerged from the house as a bride. They lived together peaceably

enough, busying themselves with good works and their neighbours' affairs, and collecting *objets d'art* for their overcrowded gem of a house with a ruthless zeal which was a byword for miles around.

Many a hostess had found herself bereft of

a lustre jug or a particularly charming paper-weight when the Misses Lovelock rose to leave, for they had brought the art of persuasive begging to perfection. Continuously crying poverty, they lived nevertheless very comfortably, and the inhabitants of Lulling and Thrush Green were wary of these genteel old harpies. Tales were exchanged of the Lovelocks' exploits.

One told of their kind offer to look after her garden while she was away and how she came back to find it stripped of all the ripe fruit and the choicest vegetables. 'Such a pity, dear, to see it going to waste. We knew you would like us to help ourselves, and it does keep the crop growing, of course. We must let you have a bottle of the raspberries — so delicious.'

Neighbours who were unwary enough to let the Misses Lovelock look after the chickens in their absence rarely found any eggs awaiting them on their return, and in some cases a plump chicken had died. 'Terribly upsetting, my dear! It was just lying on its poor back with its legs stuck up and a dreadfully resigned look on its dear face! We buried it in our garden as we didn't want to upset you.'

The ladies now smiled gently upon Ella as she retrieved their glasses. All three were drinking whisky, barely moistened with soda water, with a rapidity that had ceased to startle their friends. Ella noticed, with some alarm, that their eyes were fixed upon the silver basket which Dimity was proffering.

'Do you like salted nuts, Bertha?' asked Dimity anxiously of the youngest Miss Lovelock. Bertha, Ada and Violet took two or three daintily in their clawlike hands. Their eyes remained appraisingly upon the gleaming little dish.

'What a charming little basket!' murmured Violet.

'We have its brother at home,' said Ada, very sweetly. 'I believe this should be one of a pair.'

[WINTER IN THRUSH GREEN]

And so, from 1958 onwards, these characters became my dolls, and their way of life and the houses they inhabited became so real to me that it was quite a shock when I occasionally returned to the place which had started it all, Wood Green, near Witney.

Where was the village school? Why had Witney Urban District Council taken over Harold Shoosmith's house? Where was the statue to Nathaniel Patten which had caused such consternation at Thrush Green? And how had my chestnut avenue suddenly dwindled to one or two trees?

This clash of reality and imagination was disturbing. I had no such problem with the village of Fairacre, about which I also wrote, for that was entirely my own creation. Nevertheless, I grew fonder of Thrush Green with every book I wrote about it, and I liked the characters as they developed.

I found it interesting to take one person, say the rector, Charles Henstock, and make him the chief character in one book and follow his fortunes, as

I had in the first book about the great Mrs Curdle. Naturally, the other people appeared and something would crop up which made me plan to give their adventures an airing in a future book. Thus it was that I decided to give Edward Young a greater part to play in *At Home in Thrush Green* for, having burnt down the rectory in an earlier book, it seemed only right that I should hand over the job of replacing my act of arson to the architect I had created.

Now that I had my dolls and their dolls' houses, I set about playing with them with the greatest pleasure, and when I visited Wood Green I shut

The Butter Cross, one of the sights of Witney

my eyes to some of the realities. I didn't look down the footpath which led to the buttercup fields where Dotty Harmer lived, for they were there no more, and I ignored the traffic which came down the New Yatt Road.

But there was still enough to enchant me. The Three Pigeons stood as comfortably as The Two Pheasants, and the major houses round the green endured in all their Cotswold serenity.

There was no doubt about it. Thrush Green was an ideal place to play, and I set about moving my dolls along their allotted paths during the next few years.

The High Street, Witney

What Happened to Them

AS YOU CAN imagine, the dozen or so habitations, and their inmates, became very dear to me over the years, and gradually took over from reality. After more than forty years, strangers now dwelt in the houses I knew at Wood Green. To go back to our first port of call, the Youngs' lovely house (at twelve o'clock). When I knew it, during the war years, it was occupied by an elderly bachelor who was one of the several mill owners in Witney, the town famed world-wide for its blankets since the seventeenth century.

I only once went into his garden, a beautifully kept one, even in war-time, when he kindly picked a bunch of tulips for me and showed me some new potatoes he was growing in pots in the greenhouse. There were some splendid Cotswold-stone outbuildings and these I turned into a retirement cottage years later for the elderly Bassetts. On my last visit to Wood Green, I saw that an attractive house had been built on that part of the garden. I am not sure if this is a case of Nature following Art, or the other way round, but the result is most satisfactory.

Joan Young, her architect husband Edward, and their young son Paul, grew clearer to me with every Thrush Green book that emerged. Joan and her sister Ruth appeared early in the saga, and young Paul opened the very first book of the series.

As soon as he opened his eyes the child remembered, and his heart soared. This was the day he had waited for so long — the day of the fair.

He lay there for a minute, beneath his tumbled bedclothes, savouring the excitement. His mind's eye saw again, with the sharp clarity of a six-year-old, the battered galloping horses with flaring nostrils, the glittering brass posts, twisted like giant barley sugar sticks, the dizzy red and yellow swingboats and the snakes of black flex that coiled across the bruised grass of Thrush Green waiting to ensnare the feet of the bedazzled.

His nose tingled with the remembered scent of the hot oily smell which pulsed from the blaring roundabout and the acrid odour of his own hands, faintly green from clutching the brass post so tightly. In his head rang the music of the fair, the raucous shouting, the screams of silly girls in swingboats, the throbbing of the great engine which supplied the power, and over all, the head-hammering mammoth voice which roared old half-forgotten tunes from among the whirling horses of the roundabout.

At last — at last, Paul told himself, it was the first day of May! And at this point he sat up in bed, said 'White Rabbits!' aloud, to bring luck throughout the coming month, and looked eagerly out of the window into the dewy sunshine which was beginning to shimmer on Thrush Green.

[THRUSH GREEN]

Molly Piggott, later Ben Curdle's wife, was general help in the Youngs' house, and Paul liked nothing better than to watch her cook.

One of his favourite cakes was a sticky gingerbread which she made frequently in the cold days of winter. He watched her putting the ingredients into two vessels, the dry ones in a large bowl on the kitchen table, and the rest into a saucepan on the massive Aga cooker.

When the winter wind whistled through the bare branches, the fragrance of this spicy cake was comforting. But when the chestnut avenue outside the Youngs' house was making 'a tunnel of green gloom' in high summer, Molly made bottles of lemon essence to quench the thirst of Paul and his friends.

It gave Molly great pleasure to bake for Paul and his young friends, and these are a few of their favourites.

Sticky Gingerbread

250 g (8 oz)
 plain flour
pinch of salt
1 level teaspoon
 bicarbonate of soda
1 level teaspoon
 cinnamon
3 level teaspoons
 ground ginger
125 g (4 oz)
 dried fruit

2 eggs
4 tablespoons milk
90 g (3 oz) lard
125 g (4 oz) dark
 sugar
1 heaped tablespoon
 black treacle
1 heaped tablespoon
 golden syrup

Put all the ingredients in the first column into a mixing bowl. Then in a small bowl, beat up the eggs with a little milk. Melt the lard, sugar, treacle and golden syrup, and add to the dry ingredients. Tip in the egg and milk mixture and beat well.

Pour the mixture into a 7-inch square tin. Molly cooked her gingerbread in the Aga; in the oven, cook at Gas mark 3/160°C/325°F for about an hour.

Chocolate Brownies

There is a nice crunchiness about these unusual little cakes.

60 g (2 oz) walnuts
60 g (2 oz) plain
  chocolate
90 g (3 oz) butter
60 g (2 oz) caster
  sugar

1 egg
125 g (4 oz) flour
¼ teaspoon baking
  powder
¼ teaspoon salt
milk to mix

Chop the walnuts, and melt the chocolate in a basin over hot water. Cream together butter and sugar, and add the well-beaten egg. Sift in the flour, baking powder and salt, and mix well. Now add the nuts, melted chocolate and a very little milk, just enough to bring it to a soft consistency.

Spread the mixture into a greased baking tin and dredge a little sugar on top. Bake in the oven at Gas mark 3/160°C/325°F for about 30 minutes. Cut into neat squares or fingers whilst still warm.

Flapjacks

250 g (8 oz) caster
 sugar
175 g (6 oz) butter
150 g (5 oz) porridge
 oats

90 g (3 oz) desiccated
 coconut
125 g (4 oz) plain
 chocolate for
 covering, if liked

Cream the sugar and butter, and mix in the oats and coconut. Stir well together and press into a large shallow tin, to a depth of about 1.5 cm (½ inch). Cook in the oven at Gas mark 3/160°C/325°F for about 25 minutes, or until golden brown.

To make this doubly delicious and fattening, melt some plain chocolate and spread over the cooked flapjack. Make curly squiggles with a fork and, when cold, cut into neat fingers.

Idiot Biscuits

So-called, so my friend tells me,
because any idiot can make them.
I feel sure young Paul would have
managed them without Molly's help.

125 g (4 oz) butter
60 g (2 oz) caster
  sugar
½ teaspoon vanilla
  essence

125 g (4 oz)
  plain flour
1 tablespoon cocoa
  powder

Cream the butter and sugar together, and add the essence. Stir in the flour and cocoa. Roll into small balls and place on a greased baking sheet. Press down a little with a fork dipped in hot water, and bake in the oven at Gas mark 3/160°C/325°F for about 25 minutes.

Lemonade

3 lemons
750 g (½ lb) white sugar
30 ml (1 fl oz) citric acid
1.7 litres (3 pints) boiling water

Pare the lemons, halve and squeeze them, putting the rind, juice, sugar and citric acid into a large china bowl. Add the boiling water, stir, and leave to cool. Strain and bottle.

Dilute according to taste, usually one part lemon with about five parts of cold sparkling water to make a refreshing summer drink.

Edward and Joan Young remained on excellent terms with John and Ruth Lovell, the two sisters meeting almost daily. All four were fond of playing cards, and they met occasionally for whist or bridge, either at the Youngs' or the Lovells' newer house along the road to the north.

Both men had arduous jobs, and were conscientious. John Lovell coped with his admirably, and seldom worried his wife with any problems connected with it. But Edward, more volatile and moody, was often in need of his wife's comfortable common-sense.

When the Victorian vicarage at Thrush Green burnt down, it was replaced by a set of one-storey retirement homes for old people. Edward was

given the contract and threw himself into it with vigour, aided no doubt by his life-long abhorrence of the building which he was now about to replace.

Everyone agreed that the result was most successful. It was practical and in harmony with the surroundings. But there was one fault in the design which did not escape the sharp eyes of the Thrush Green neighbours, and John Lovell was one who pointed out the weakness to his brother-in-law.

Edward Young, as architect, took a keen interest in the residents' reactions to his work, and on the whole was gratified. All agreed that the houses were light, warm, well-planned and easy to run.

The main objection came from John Lovell one day when he met his brother-in-law by chance, as he returned from a visit to the Cartwrights, the wardens at the new homes.

'All going well there, Edward?'

'No great problems so far,' said the architect.

'There will be,' replied John.

Edward looked taken aback. 'How d'you mean?'

'Well, those outside steps, for instance. You've been extra careful to have no steps inside, but that flight outside could be a menace, particularly in slippery weather.'

'I don't see,' said Edward frostily, 'how you can overcome a natural incline except by steps — and these are particularly shallow ones — or a ramp. As it happens, I've provided both. And an adequate handrail.'

'No need to get stuffy!'

'I'm not getting stuffy,' retorted Edward, 'but I do dislike outsiders criticising something they don't understand. You don't seem to realise the difficulties that confronted us when facing the problems that this site gave us.'

'I'm not such an outsider that I can't see what a mistake you made with those steps —'

'*Mistake?* What rubbish! You stick to your job, John, and leave me to mine.'

'Unfortunately, I shall have to patch up the results of your mistakes! Mark my words, a few slippery leaves, or later on some snow and ice, and I shall have some old people in my surgery with sprains and breaks. It could all have been avoided with proper planning.'

'Are you suggesting that I'm a bad architect?'

'Not always. But to design an old people's home with a hazard like that, is not only stupid, it's downright criminal.'

By this time, both men were flushed with anger. They took their work seriously, and were sensitive to criticism. The fact that normally the two brothers-in-law got along very peaceably made this present exchange particularly acrimonious.

'The steps are perfectly safe,' said Edward, with considerable emphasis. 'You're getting a proper old woman, John, seeing danger where there is none. I shan't come criticising your healing methods, though I gather that some of them leave much to be desired, so I'd be obliged if you left well alone in my field.'

He strode off across the green to his home, leaving John fuming.

'Pompous ass!' said John to the retreating back. 'You wait till I get my first casualty from the homes! I shan't let you forget it!'

[AT HOME IN THRUSH GREEN]

The two men said nothing at the time to their wives, but a day or two later, the question of an evening of cards cropped up.

The tiff between John and Edward still made itself felt. The two couples frequently had an evening together playing cards, but when Joan broached the subject to her husband, she was surprised at his response.

'Oh, skip it for a bit! John's in one of his awkward moods. Let him simmer.'

'How do you mean?'

'Oh, he was rather offensive to me the other day.'

'John? Offensive? I can't believe it.'

Edward began to fidget up and down the room. 'Nothing too personal, I suppose, but he was throwing his weight about over the steps at the old people's place.'

'Well, he may be right. Mr Jones mentioned them to me the other morning. He hoped the residents there wouldn't slip on them.'

'Oh, don't you start! There's absolutely nothing wrong with those steps,' exploded Edward. 'The point is I don't particularly want to spend a whole evening in John's company at the moment.'

'Well, calm down,' begged Joan, taken aback at such unaccustomed heat. 'You'll have a seizure if you get into such a state, over such a silly little thing.'

'It isn't a silly little thing to me,' almost shouted her incensed husband. 'It's a criticism of my work, and I'm not standing for it.'

At that Joan shrugged her shoulders, and went out, without comment, to do her shopping.

Ruth Lovell, Joan's sister, was also perplexed by her husband's moodiness. She knew from experience that he took everything seriously. It was one of his qualities which his patients appreciated. He was willing to give time, as well as his medical expertise, to their troubles and this they warmly appreciated.

Such dedication frequently exhausted him,

and Ruth did her best to provide a relaxing atmosphere in their home. Their occasional evenings at the card table with the Youngs were one of John's few outside pleasures.

But he too, it seemed, did not want to spend an evening with his brother-in-law, but said less about his reasons than the voluble Edward.

'Perhaps later on,' he said when Ruth suggested a card-playing evening. 'I'm rather tired these days, and Edward can be a bit overpowering, I find.'

'Just as you like,' answered Ruth. 'And if you're feeling tired, what about a dose or two of that tonic you make up for the patients?'

'That stuff?' exclaimed her husband. 'Not likely! It tastes appalling.'

[AT HOME IN THRUSH GREEN]

It so happened that the first person to come a cropper on the steps was the warden Jane Cartwright, who was a good deal younger and more agile than those in her care.

Across the green, Doctor Lovell heard for the first time about the accident at the old people's homes, and was magnanimous enough not to make any comment about Edward Young's steps in front of his partners.

Nevertheless, he felt a certain satisfaction in hearing that his fears were not groundless, although he had every sympathy for poor Jane Cartwright's mishap.

'I hope all the old dears over there will hold tight to the handrail,' was his only remark when he was told the news, but he said more to Ruth when he went home at lunch time.

'Well that's the first casualty at Edward's famous edifice. And won't be the last, as far as I can see!'

'What's happened?' asked Ruth, soup spoon suspended in mid-air.

'Jane Cartwright's broken a leg on those idiotic steps. Asking for trouble to put steps like that where there are old people. I told Edward so months ago.'

'But Jane isn't old,' protested Ruth.

'Oh, don't quibble!' snapped her husband. 'I know she's not! All I'm pointing out is that those steps are a hazard, and one which any sane architect would have omitted from his plan from the start.'

Ruth continued to sip her soup in silence. When John was so short-tempered, it hardly seemed possible to conduct a civilised conversation.

However, by the time the apple tart stage had been reached, Ruth spoke.

'I'm taking the children to watch the bonfire just after six. Paul is home and Jeremy Prior's going to be there as well. Joan suggests we have a drink with them, before or after, just which suits you best.'

'I suppose Edward is attending this bean feast?'

'Naturally.'

'Well, I'll come along for a little while to the bonfire, but don't accept for me later. I'm on surgery duty tonight.'

'Fair enough. We won't be late back. Mary will be tired out with all the excitement.'

'You'll be a lot tireder, I surmise,' said John with a smile. He pushed back his chair, kissed his wife, and went back to his duties.

Well, he seemed to have cheered up, thought Ruth, clearing the table. But if only he would try some of his own tonic!

[AT HOME IN THRUSH GREEN]

The coolness between the two men, but not between the sisters, continued until one day when Edward was obliged to seek medical advice.

He, poor fellow, was being driven to distraction by the pain in his right shoulder. It seemed to have spread to his neck and down the right side of his back.

Joan, over the last week, had applied calamine lotion, witch hazel, petroleum jelly, and had even contemplated using a sinister looking ointment concocted by Dotty, but did not take this final drastic step. Nothing seemed to alleviate the torment, and Edward grew more fractious daily.

When, at last, some nasty little spots began to appear, and he had spent the last night of the year sitting up in bed and holding his pyjama jacket away from his afflictions, Joan put her foot down.

'I'm calling John in to have a look at you,' she said firmly.

'Oh, don't fuss! Anyway, I suppose I'd better go to the surgery, if I must see him.'

'Not with those spots. You may have something infectious.'

'Thanks. Very reassuring, I must say. What's your guess? Leprosy?'

'Don't be childish. You'll stay there in the morning, and I shall ask John to come after surgery. No arguing now. You need some expert treatment.'

Edward grunted, but forebore to argue. He knew when he was beaten, but it was clear to his wife that he was still reluctant to be obliged to his brother-in-law.

Joan Young was as good as her word, and later John Lovell called to see his brother-in-law.

'Let's have a look at this rash,' said the doctor, helping Edward off with his shirt.

He surveyed the spots in silence, whilst the patient awaited the worst.

'Well,' he said at last. 'You know what you've got, I expect?'

'Far from it! That's why you're here!'

'Shingles. I don't think it will be too bad a dose, but it's a beast of a complaint.'

'I'll endorse that,' said Edward. 'I wonder where I got it?'

'Lots of chickenpox about. It's connected, you know. Have you been in contact with anyone particularly?'

Edward thought, as he did up his shirt buttons.

'Young George Curdle's got it, of course, and I've visited him now and again. Playing snakes and ladders and draughts and other thrilling games.'

'Sounds as though that's it.'

'Am I infectious?'

'No, no! It's one of those things that we think lies dormant, and can flare up if the patient has been under strain or run down. Or, of course, in contact with chickenpox.'

'Well, to tell the truth, John, I am having a devil of a time with a contract in Cirencester. Have had for weeks now. Might be that partly.'

'Quite likely.' He smiled at his patient. 'We all worry too much,' he went on. 'I've had a few guilty twinges about ticking you off about those steps. No business of mine really.'

'Oh, forget it, John,' said Edward. 'Can you give me something to stop this plaguey itching?'

'Yes. I'll write you a prescription for a lotion and some tablets. And off work for a week at least. Lots of drink — not spirits, old boy — nice healthy stuff like water and orange juice!'

'Thanks a lot!'

'An evening's card-playing might help. Take your mind off your troubles. Come to us on Thursday. It's my evening off surgery.'

Within five minutes he had gone, leaving Edward to try and decipher the hieroglyphics of his prescriptions.

'Why do doctors have such terrible handwriting?' he asked the cat, who had wandered in. But, rather naturally, there was no reply.

[AT HOME IN THRUSH GREEN]

Across the road at Tullivers, Phyllida Prior and Jeremy soon became friendly with the older residents of Thrush Green. The girl's solitary state occasioned a good deal of sympathy, and in some cases, even stronger feelings.

Harold Shoosmith, the bachelor who had retired to live at Quetta, the corner house, was one whose kind heart was moved by this newcomer. He admired her efforts to make a little money by freelance writing, whilst awaiting a divorce from the husband who had deserted her.

He returned thoughtfully to his quiet house and sank into an armchair. What exactly was happening to him? He didn't mind admitting that he was attracted to Phil Prior, but then he had been attracted to many girls in the past. He had always enjoyed the company of intelligent women, and if they were pretty, then so much the better. This protective feeling for Phil Prior, he told himself, was the result of her unfortunate circumstances. Anyone with a spark of humanity would want to help a poor girl left defenceless and hard up, especially when she had to cope with the rearing of a young child, single handed.

Harold rose from the chair and walked restlessly about the room. Was he really becoming fonder of the girl than he realised? Dammit all, this was absurd! He was a steadfast bachelor and intended to remain so. He was old enough to be Phil's father. Well, nearly —

He walked to the end of the room and studied his reflection in the handsome gilt-framed mirror which lay above the little Sheraton side-table.

He was tall and spare, his eyes bright, and his hair, although silver, still thick. As a young man, he had been reckoned good-looking. He supposed now, trying to look at himself dispassionately, he still had a few good points — but he was old, old, old, he told himself sternly. No young woman would consider him now, and quite right too!

He returned to his chair, dismissing these foolish thoughts, and opened the paper. It was as inspiring and exhilarating as ever. Four young men were appearing on charges of peddling drugs, an old lady had had her hand chopped off whilst attempting to retain her purse, containing just two and eightpence, and a motorway to end all motorways was proposed which would wipe out particularly exquisite villages and several hundred miles of countryside.

Harold threw it to the floor, leant back and closed his eyes. How pleasantly quiet it was! The fire whispered. The clock ticked. Somewhere, across the green, a car changed gear as it moved towards Lulling, and hummed away into nothingness. This was what he had looked forward to throughout those long hard years of business life in Africa. He would be mad to try and change his way of life now.

And yet Charles Henstock had found a great deal of happiness in later life since his marriage to Dimity. Charles, Harold pointed out to himself, had nothing to lose when he married. Ruled by that dreadful old harridan Mrs Butler, that desiccated Scotswoman who half-starved the poor rector, enduring the chilly discomfort of that great barn of a rectory all alone — of course marriage would be attractive! Besides, Charles was the sort of man who *should* be married: he was not. That was the crux of the matter.

He took up the poker and turned over a log carefully. Watching the flames shoot up the chimney, he told himself firmly that marriage was out of the question. Once that poor girl's divorce was through, he hoped that some decent kind

126

young man would appear to make her happy, and take some of her present burdens from her.

Meanwhile, he would do what he could to help her, and would frankly face the fact that her presence gave him enormous pleasure. But for her sake, he must guard his feelings, he reminded himself. Thrush Green was adept at putting two and two together and making five, and she had enough to contend with already, without being annoyed by foolish gossip.

'Avuncular kindness!' said Harold aloud, and was immediately revolted by the phrase. He hit the flaring log such a hefty thwack that it broke in two. He dropped the poker and went to pour himself a much-needed drink.

[NEWS FROM THRUSH GREEN]

Later, Winnie Bailey's nephew, Richard Bailey, was also to become an admirer of her young neighbour.

Winnie's nephew Richard arrived the following week. He seemed genuinely grateful for his aunt's hospitality, and set himself out to be exceptionally charming to Doctor Bailey.

To Winnie's eye, he looked very fit and lively, having acquired a fine tan in America which set off his pale hair and blue eyes. But it was not long before symptoms of the hypochondria which had always been present showed themselves in strength.

Two small bottles of pills stood by his plate

at the first evening meal, and naturally excited the professional interest of his uncle.

'I find them indispensable,' said Richard. 'Otto — Professor Otto Goldstein, you know, the dietician — prescribed them for me. The red ones take care of the cholesterol, and these yellow and black torpedoes check acidity and act as a mild purge. Constipation is a terrible enemy.'

'You need a few prunes,' said the doctor, 'and a bit of roughage.'

'Donald!' protested Winnie. 'Must you? At table?'

'Sorry, my dear, sorry,' said her husband.

'Too bad of me,' apologised Richard. 'Living alone such a lot makes one over-interested perhaps in one's natural functions.'

Winnie felt that this could lead to somewhat alarming disclosures which might be regretted by all. She changed the subject abruptly.

'You must meet our new neighbour,' she said brightly, passing her nephew Brussels sprouts.

He held up a stern denying hand. 'Not for me, Aunt Winnie. Not *cooked* greens, I fear. Quite forbidden by Otto because of the gases. You haven't two or three raw ones, by any chance?'

'Not washed,' replied Winnie shortly, passing the rejected dish to her husband. She was keenly aware of the smile which hovered round the old doctor's lips.

'A pity,' murmured Richard, tackling pork

chops *en casserole* with faint distaste.

'She plays bridge and whist, and is a very nice person to talk to. She writes.'

'Really?' replied Richard vaguely. Clearly his mind was concerned with his digestive tract.

'Will you have any spare evenings?' pursued Winnie.

Richard gave a gusty sigh, the sigh of one who, overburdened with work, still enjoys his martyrdom.

'I very much doubt it. I shall be writing the notes on my experiments, of course, and I intend to spend as much time as I can refuting Carslake's idiotic principle. An obstinate fellow, if ever there was one, and a very elusive one too. I must thrash things out with him during the next few months.'

Winnie felt a wave of pity for the absent Professor Carslake. Richard, on the rampage, must be an appalling bore. She decided to put aside the idea of arranging Richard's social life at Thrush Green. Richard obviously did not want it, and was it really fair to her friends to inflict her nephew on them, she added reasonably to herself?

She watched him swallow a red pill and then a yellow and black one. It was quite apparent that he enjoyed them far more than the excellent dinner which Winnie had spent hours in preparing.

'Coffee?' she asked, rising from the table. 'Or does Professor Goldstein forbid that too?' There was an edge to her tone which did not escape her observant husband.

'No, indeed,' replied Richard, opening the drawing-room door politely. 'He approves of coffee, provided that the berries are really ripe, well roasted and coarsely ground. He doesn't agree with percolators, though. He always strains his through muslin. Do you?'

'Not with Nescafé,' said his aunt, with a hint of triumph, leading the way.

[NEWS FROM THRUSH GREEN]

Luckily, Phil Prior found a market for her work with an editor friend of Harold's, called Frank Hurst. Both men were fond of the girl, and when her husband — from whom she was estranged — was killed in a car crash, their sympathy was great, and shared by the rest of Thrush Green. For the girl herself it was a sad time.

Christmas, for Phil Prior and for her young son, was made less painful by the kindness of her neighbours. Jeremy's natural joy in the festivities found fulfilment at the Youngs' house, where a children's party and innumerable presents helped to put his father's tragedy into the background. The arrival of the long-awaited kitten added to his excitement. But, inevitably, it was more difficult for his mother. Memories of past Christmases were inescapable.

She saw again John lighting the red candles on the Christmas tree, with wide-eyed two-year-old Jeremy gazing with wonder at each new flame. John pulling crackers, and showing Jeremy the small fireworks inside — setting fire to the 'serpent's egg', waving a minute sparkler, making a flaming paper balloon rise to the ceiling, whilst Jeremy applauded excitedly. John wrapping her in a scarlet cashmere dressing gown, which she considered madly extravagant but adorable of him. John had always been at his best at Christmas, gay, funny, sweet, considerate. It was more than Phil could bear to think that he would never again be there to make Christmas sparkle for her.

It was strange, she thought, how the bitterness of the last year was so little remembered. The humiliation, the misery, the wretched effort of keeping things from Jeremy, were all submerged beneath the remembrances of earlier shared happiness. She marvelled at this phenomenon, but was humbly grateful that her mind worked in this way. When the subject of his father cropped up, which was not very often, Phil found that she could speak of him with true affection, keeping alive for the little boy his early memories of a loving father.

She was relieved when the New Year arrived and things returned to normal. Jeremy started school during the first week in January, and she was glad to see him engrossed in his own school affairs and friendships again. Meanwhile, she set herself to work with renewed determination.

It was plain that she must work doubly hard.

John's affairs had been left tidily, with a will leaving his wife everything unconditionally. But when all had been settled, it seemed that Phil could expect a sum of only about six thousand pounds. There was no doubt about it — things were going to be tight if she decided to continue to live at Tullivers.

But she was determined to stay there. She loved the little house and she loved Thrush Green. The friends she had made were the dependable, kindly sort of people whose company would give her pleasure and support in the years to come, as their affection towards her, in these last few terrible weeks, had shown so clearly. She had settled in Thrush Green as snugly as a bird in its nest, and so had Jeremy. Whatever the cost, Tullivers must remain their home.

[NEWS FROM THRUSH GREEN]

Jeremy loved it at Thrush Green, and as well as the kitten, hoped to add to his pets. He was a regular visitor at Dotty Harmer's, glorying in the variety of animals to be found there.

One spring Saturday morning he bounded down the path by Albert Piggott's cottage and gained the path leading to Dotty's and finally to Lulling Woods. The air was balmy, his spirits high, and he carried a large bunch of grass and greenery from the hedges as a present for Daisy, the milker, and Dulcie, the younger goat.

Charles Henstock privately thought that Dul-

132

cie was poorly named — neither sweet nor gentle, and very quick to use her horns on unsuspecting visitors, as he had found to his cost one wet day. His clerical grey trousers had never completely recovered from their immersion in the puddle in which Dulcie's sly butting had landed him. Jeremy, however, was rather more alert to Dulcie's wiles, and his passion for her was unclouded.

On this particular morning he found Dotty in a somewhat agitated mood. She was having difficulty in fixing a chain to Dulcie's collar. Daisy, taking advantage of the disturbance, was adding gleefully to the chaos by bleating continuously, and rushing round and round in cir-

cles so that her tethering chain was soon short-
ened to a couple of feet. This gave her the opportunity to bleat even more madly, puffing
noisily between bleats to prove how sorely she
was being tried.

Dulcie, unduly skittish, kicked up her heels
every time that Dotty approached her. Dotty,
red in the face, greeted Jeremy shortly.

'Get Daisy undone, boy, will you? And give
her some of that stuff you've brought to stop
her row.'

Jeremy obediently accomplished this task. In
the comparative peace that followed, Dotty cap-
tured the younger goat, mopped her brow and
sighed noisily with relief.

'Where's Dulcie going?' asked Jeremy.

'To be mated,' said Dotty flatly.

'What d'you mean — *mated?*' queried Jeremy.

'Married, then,' said Dotty, hitching up a
stocking in a preoccupied way.

'*Married?* But only *people* get married!' exclaimed Jeremy.

'I know that,' said Dotty, nettled. Dulcie
began to tug powerfully at her lead.

'But you said —'

'Here, you clear off home,' said Dotty forth-
rightly. 'I'm up to my eyes this morning, as
you can see.'

The boy retreated very slowly backwards.

'Will she have baby goats when she's been
mated?'

'*Kids,* you mean,' said Dotty pedantically.

'Do use the right expressions, child.'

'Well, will she?'

'What?' said Dotty, stalling for time.

'Have baby goats. Kids, I mean?'

'Maybe,' said Dotty, with unusual caution. Difficult to know how much children knew about the facts of life these days, and anyway it wasn't her business to enlighten this one.

'Can I have one when they come, Miss Harmer?' begged Jeremy longingly. '*Please,* can I?'

Dotty's slender stock of patience suddenly ran out at her heels like gunpowder. Her voice roared out like a cannon.

'Look, boy! I don't know *if* she'll have kids, *when* she'll have kids, or if your mother would let you have one if she *did* have kids! You're far too inquisitive, and a confounded nuisance. Get off home!'

She raised a skinny, but powerful arm, and Dulcie, sensing joyous combat, lowered her head for action. In the face of this combined attack, Jeremy fled, but even as he ran determined to come again as soon as things at Dotty's had returned once more to their usual chaotic normality.

Meanwhile, he decided, slackening his pace as the distance between Dotty's and his own breathless form increased, he must set about persuading his mother that a little kid would be very useful for keeping Tullivers' grass down. But, somehow, he sensed that that would be an uphill battle.

[NEWS FROM THRUSH GREEN]

It was some months later that Harold and Richard realised that Phil Prior had found a husband elsewhere.

'I've some wonderful news,' said Phil, 'and I want you to be the first to know. Can you guess?'

Harold looked at her. He had always thought that poets grossly overstated things when they talked of eyes like stars. Now he began to understand.

'I was never good at guessing,' he confessed. 'I only knew myself yesterday. Frank has asked me to marry him. Say you're pleased.'

Harold took a deep breath. If he felt a pang

136

of jealousy, it vanished at once. Wholeheartedly, he congratulated her.

'He's the luckiest devil in the world,' he told her sincerely, taking her hands in his.

'He's coming here tomorrow to arrange things with the rector,' said Phil. 'We had the longest telephone talk ever known to the Lulling exchange last night. We shall get married this summer.'

She leant forward and kissed Harold on the cheek.

'And will you give me away?' she asked.

'It's like asking me to part with my heart,' replied Harold, half-meaning it, 'but since you ask me, I shall count it an honour, my dear.'

They stood up and gazed across the garden.

'Will you leave Thrush Green?' asked Harold.

'We haven't got that far,' smiled Phil, 'but I don't think I could ever leave Tullivers. We could build on, I suppose.'

She looked about her vaguely, trying to envisage the future, and suddenly became conscious of the wonder of a life which contained such a precious element as sure joy to come.

[NEWS FROM THRUSH GREEN]

Next door to Tullivers stood the Baileys' house. As I have said already, it was in just such a position that the doctor who attended us in wartime lived. Not that I ever went into the house, for the doctor's surgery, which he shared with one other, stood in Witney High Street where it widened into the market place.

Fortunately, we seldom needed to call upon the doctor, but our daughter, as an infant, was obliged to submit to various injections, and usually responded with great violence to these administrations. The doctor was so used to being called in a second time to cope with the results of his first visit that eventually he dug in his heels and advised against another jab dealing with whooping-cough.

When the child caught this later and went off her food, I found that tiny Marmite sandwiches handed over whilst I pushed the pram round Wood Green and along the New Yatt Road, seemed to be acceptable to the invalid. Our perambulations were interrupted now and again when other young friends with babies, hove in sight and, being infectious, we had to wave from a distance and hurry away from each other. Luckily, this leprous condition did not last long, and the doctor's visits grew less frequent as the child thrived.

This real doctor was a much younger man than the Doctor Bailey I created to live in his old house. In fact, we only meet this good man in the last few months of his life.

Before nightfall, the news that Doctor Bailey was sinking was common knowledge at Thrush Green.

There was general sadness. Even Albert Piggott had a good word to say for the dying man, as he drank his half-pint of bitter at The Two Pheasants.

'Well, we shan't see his like again,' he commented morosely. 'He done us proud, the old gentleman. I s'pose now we has to put up with young Doctor Lovell dashing in and out again before you can tell him what ails you.'

'There's the new chap,' said the landlord. 'Seems a nice enough young fellow.'

'Him?' squeaked Albert. 'Nothing but a beardless boy! I wouldn't trust my peptic ulcer to him, that I wouldn't. No, I'll put me trust in strong peppermints while I can, and hope Doctor Lovell can spare a couple of minutes when I'm real hard-pressed. You mark my words, we're all going to miss the old doctor at Thrush Green.'

It was the older people who were the saddest. Doctor Bailey had brought their children into the world, and knew the family histories intimately. He had not been active in the partnership for some years now, so that the younger inhabitants were more familiar with Doctor Lovell, who had married a Thrush Green girl, and was accepted as a comparatively worthy successor to Doctor Bailey.

But it was the old friends and neighbours, the Youngs, the Henstocks, Ella Bembridge, Dotty Harmer, Phil Prior and the comparative newcomer, Harold Shoosmith, who were going to miss Donald Bailey most keenly. Most of them had visited the invalid often during the past few months, marvelling at his gallant spirit and his unfailing good temper.

Now, as the day waned, their thoughts turned to that quiet grey house across the green. The rector had called during the afternoon and found Winnie Bailey sitting by her husband's bedside.

He was asleep, his frail hands folded on the white sheet. A downstairs room, once his study, had been turned into a bedroom for the last few months, and his bed faced the french windows leading into the garden he loved so well. Propped up on his pillows, he had enjoyed a view of the flower beds and the comings and goings at the bird table all through the summer.

His particular joy was the fine copper beech tree which dominated the scene. He had watched it in early May, as the tiny breaking leaves spread a pinkish haze over the magnificent skeleton. He had rejoiced in its glossy purplish midsummer beauty which had sheltered the gentle ring-doves that cooed among its branches. And now, in these last few days, he had watched its golden leaves fluttering down to form a glowing carpet at its foot, as the autumn winds tossed the great boughs this way and that.

For once, the boisterous wind was lulled. Wisps of high grey cloud scarcely moved behind the copper beech. The garden was very still, the bird table empty, the room where the dying man lay as quiet and tranquil as the grave to which so soon he would be departing.

Charles Henstock sat beside his old friend for a short time, his lips moving in prayer. After a little he rose, and Winnie went with him into the sitting-room. She was calm and dry-eyed, and Charles admired her control.

'He's very much in our thoughts and prayers, as you know,' said Charles. 'I know that Ella and Dimity — everyone in fact — will want to know how he is and would like to call, but they don't wish to intrude at a time like this. Shall I tell them the latest news? Or would you like one of us to sit with you?'

Winnie smiled.

'You tell them, please. Doctor Lovell says it is only a matter of hours now. I shall stay by him. He has a few lucid moments every now and again. Why, he's even doing the crossword, bit by bit, but I think visitors would tire him too much. I know that they will understand.'

Charles nodded.

'Jenny is with me,' continued Winnie. 'She insisted on staying today, and I'm grateful to have someone here to answer the door. I will keep in touch, Charles dear, and I'll tell Donald you called.'

The sun was setting as the rector set off homeward. Long shadows stretched across the grass from the chestnut avenue and the houses round the green. Above The Two Pheasants, a curl of blue smoke hung in the still air. The bar fire had been lit ready for the customers.

Willie Bond, the postman, was pushing his

bicycle along the road to Nidden, at the end of his last delivery, and in the distance the rector could see Ella vanishing down the alley that led to Lulling Woods and Dotty Harmer's house. No doubt, she was off to collect her daily pint of goat's milk.

Sad though he felt, there was a touch of comfort in these manifestations of life going on as usual. Donald Bailey, he knew, would agree with him. He remembered his philosophy so clearly. We are born, we live our little lives, we die. Our lives are cut to the same pattern, touching here, overlapping there, and thus forming rich convolutions of colour and shape. But at the end, we are alone, and only in the lives and memories of our children, our friends and our work can we hope to be remembered.

Charles Henstock, whose belief in an after-life was absolute, had never been able to persuade his old friend to share his convictions, and he had once told Donald, after an amicable exchange of views on the subject, that he considered the doctor to be the finest unbeliever he had been privileged to meet.

In some ways, thought the rector, observing the cock on St Andrew's spire gilded with the setting sun, one could have no better epitaph.

[BATTLES AT THRUSH GREEN]

The subject of an after-life was also being discussed by those two indomitable ladies Ella Bembridge and Dotty Harmer in the latter's cluttered kitchen near Lulling Woods. Ella had called for the goat's milk.

'Jolly sad,' boomed Ella, 'snuffing it like that. The end of everything, I suppose.'

Dotty, scrabbling for change in a jar which, long ago, had held Gentlemen's Relish, gave a snort.

'If you were a true Christian, Ella, you would look upon it as a new beginning.'

'But who's to know?' Ella's voice was almost a wail.

Dotty looked at her friend sharply. 'Well, I for one, know! If my dear father believed in the hereafter, and all the good and intelligent clergymen we have met in our lives do so too, then I am *quite confident*.'

'But what do you think happens, Dotty?'

'We are simply translated,' said Dotty briskly. She looked at the coins in her hand.

'Are you giving me five pence or five peas for the milk? I quite forget.'

'It started at sixpence, if you remember, but now things have got so out of hand I thought you ought to have five peas.'

'But isn't that a shilling? That's far too much.'

'The milkman charges more than that for his homogenised muck, so take the bob, Dotty dear, and we'll all be content.'

'It's more than generous. And I shan't have to bother with change, shall I?'

'No. And now, how do you mean *translated?*

Drift off into other new babies, d'you mean, or daffodils, or wireworms? Some other form of life, as it were?'

Dotty grew scarlet with impatience.

'Of course not. I've no time for all that wishy-washy muddled thinking! When you die you simply leave your worn-out body behind, and your spirit takes off. Don't you ever pay attention to the teachings of the Church?'

'But takes off to *where*, Dotty?'

'To heaven, of course,' said Dotty tartly, seizing an enormous wooden spoon and advancing upon an iron saucepan which had been rumbling and grumbling to itself throughout the conversation.

'And don't fuss any more about such things,' said Dotty, 'I really haven't time to explain it all when the chickens are waiting to be fed.'

'Quite,' agreed Ella, taking up the goat's milk. 'It makes me sad, though, to think that we shan't see Donald Bailey again.'

144

'Speak for yourself,' replied Dotty, stirring furiously. 'I have every expectation of seeing the dear man again, in a better world.'

'That must be a comfort,' rejoined Ella, as she shut the kitchen door behind her.

'But not for me,' she added sadly to herself, setting off homeward through the twilight.

[BATTLE AT THRUSH GREEN]

After Donald's death, his widow Winnie did her best to come to terms with her new and sad circumstances.

She was lucky, she realised, that her financial situation remained much as it was in Donald's life time. For many widows, the sudden drop in income was the greatest worry they had to face, and that she was spared, although steeply rising costs, in fuel and rates alone, meant that the old house would be expensive to run. Repairs too, would be another hazard to face, but the structure was sturdily built and had always been well maintained. With any luck, it should not need much doing to it over the next few years.

The thing was, of course, that it was really too big for one woman. Winnie felt guilty, sometimes, when she read of people crowded into tenements, and thought of her own empty bedrooms.

On the other hand, she loved the house, and could not bear to leave it. Its sheltering walls had enclosed their happy life together. The furniture, the pictures, the loved knick-knacks, all told their story of a lifetime spent together in this small community where both had played useful parts.

No, the house was not the main problem. She intended to stay there, and was willing to retrench in other ways so that she could continue to live in Thrush Green among her friends, and also have room to entertain more distant friends who would be invited to stay.

The worry which most perturbed Winnie was one of which she was deeply ashamed. She had found, since her return to the house, that she was horribly nervous of being alone in it at night.

She tried to reason with herself about this. After all, she argued, poor Donald could not have protected either of them if burglars had broken in. They never had been so unfortunate as to have intruders, and were unlikely to start now. What would there be, of any value, for a thief to find? There were far more profitable houses to burgle within a stone's throw of her own modest establishment.

But such sweet reasoning did not comfort her. As soon as nightfall arrived, she found herself locking doors, shutting windows, and finding strange solace in being barred and bolted.

She made up her mind never to open the doors after dark to people knocking. Stupid though it might appear, she went upstairs and spoke to them from an upper window. There were far too many accounts in the papers, of unsuspecting women who opened doors and were hideously attacked by those waiting. As far as lay in her power, Winnie took precautions against violence. Nevertheless, her feelings worried her. She tried to analyse them as she took an afternoon walk along the road to Nidden one winter's day. The wind was fresh, and although there was no rain, there were puddles along the length of the chestnut avenue, and water lay in the furrows of the ploughed fields. A pair of partridges whirred across the road in front of her, and Winnie remembered that Ella had told her that they mated for life. What happened, she wondered, to the survivor of such a devoted couple? Was it too as bereft as she now was?

Things were not too bad during the day. There were so many little jobs to do, and trips into Lulling for shopping when she met friends and had company.

And Jenny, of course, was a constant comfort. Winnie grew to look forward to Jenny's mornings more and more. She was deft and quiet, with the rare gift of speaking only when something needed to be said, but her friendliness warmed the house for Winnie, and the knowledge that Jenny would do anything, at any time, to help her, was wonderfully comforting.

She supposed that she must face the fact that she was run down after the years of nursing and the final shock of Donald's death. She refused to look upon herself as an invalid, but it might be sensible to take a tonic, say, during the coming winter months, and to catch up with the loss of sleep she had so cheerfully endured. With returning strength, these unnatural fears might vanish.

It was natural too, she told herself, to feel vulnerable now that Donald had gone. For years now, she had been the protector, taking decisions, fending off unwelcome visitors, sparing Donald all unnecessary cares. It was understandable that there should be some reaction.

She had reached the new housing estate by now, which stretched away to the left, and covered the fields she so well remembered that overlooked Lulling Woods.

The houses were neat and not unpleasing in design, though to Winnie's eyes they appeared to be built far too close together, and the low wire fences gave no privacy. Washing blew on most garden lines, and a number of toddlers played together in the road, jumping in a big puddle to the detriment of their clothes and their obvious delight.

Winnie smiled at them and walked on by.

'Who's that old lady?' asked one child, in a shrill treble that carried clearly through the winter air.

Old lady, thought Winnie, with sudden shock! Well, she supposed she was. But how surprising! An old lady, like that ancient crone who lived in the cottage she had just passed, who had a hairy mole on her chin and squinted hideously. Or like Jenny's mother, whose grey head trembled constantly, so that she reminded Winnie of a nodding Chinese doll she had owned as a child.

An old lady, an old lady! The houses were behind her now, and the lane stretched ahead bounded by high bare hedges. On her right stood an empty cottage, fast becoming derelict. She stooped to lean on the stone wall and rest.

The house stood forlorn and shabby, shadowed by a gnarled plum tree. Ivy was growing up its trunk and the recent gales had wrenched some of it from the bark. It waved in the wind, bristly as a centipede's legs.

The garden was overgrown, but the shape of submerged flower beds could still be seen, and the minute spears upthrusting by the house wall showed where there remained a clump of snowdrops.

Behind the house, a rotting clothes line stretched, a forked hazel bough still holding it aloft. Bird droppings whitened a window sill, and from the bottom of the broken front door Winnie saw a mouse scurry for cover in the dead grass by the door step. Neglected, unloved, slowly disintegrating, the house still sheltered life, thought Winnie.

Although no children played, no parent called, no human being opened and shut the door, yet other creatures lived there. Spiders, beetles, mice and rats, many birds, and bats, no doubt, found refuge here from the cruelty of wind and weather. It was, she supposed, simply a change of ownership.

She looked kindly upon the old quiet cottage. An old cottage! An old lady! She smiled at the remembrance.

Well, in many ways they were alike. They had once been cherished, had known warmth and love. Now they were lonely and lost. But the house was still of use, still gave comfort and shelter. There was a lesson to be learnt here.

She must look about her again, and try to be useful too. There were so many ways in which she could help, and by doing so she might mitigate the fears which crowded upon her when dusk fell.

It was growing colder. The wintry sun was sinking. The sky was silver-gilt, against which the black trees threw their lacy patterns.

She turned and made her way homeward, feeling much refreshed.

[BATTLES AT THRUSH GREEN]

Winnie's natural nervousness about living alone continued, until one happy day when Jenny, her friend and daily help, arrived looking excited.

'Had good news, Jenny?' asked her mistress.

'Yes. Willie Bond brought a letter for the old folks. They've got a new house at last. One of those old people's homes the council built.'

Jenny's honest plain face glowed with pleasure.

'How wonderful! Just what they've always wanted. And when can they move in?'

'About a month's time. There's got to be an inspection or something, to make sure everything works. As soon as that's done, they can go in.'

'And what about your present house, Jenny?'

'Well, that'll come down. All our row will, and a good thing too. It's been condemned for years now. We knew it would happen one day.'

'So what will you do?'

'I'll face that when the time comes,' said Jenny cheerfully. 'I'll find a room somewhere I expect. Might even go nursing — I did a bit once — and I could live in the hostel.'

'Would you want to do that?'

'Not really,' said Jenny. 'Besides, I'm a bit old. I don't know if they'd have me. But I shall find something all right. Just get the old folks settled, and I'll start thinking.'

She went humming upstairs to clean the bathroom, while Winnie turned over in her mind a plan which had been lurking there for some time.

It continued to engage her thoughts as she sat knitting that afternoon. Her dislike of being alone after dark had certainly diminished as the weeks went by, but she could not honestly say that she was completely carefree. She had wondered if it would be sensible to let two rooms upstairs. She would still have a spare bedroom, quite enough for the modest entertaining she proposed to do in her widowed state.

The two rooms adjoined. Both had wash-basins, one of which could be changed to a kitchen sink. There would be plenty of room for an electric stove and for cupboards, and it would convert easily into a comfortable kitchen.

The room next door was larger and would make an attractive bed-sitting room. Both rooms overlooked the green and were light and sunny.

The difficulty was, who would be acceptable? Winnie did not want a married couple, and such a minute flat would not be suitable for people with babies or pets. A single man might be useful for attacking the marauders that Winnie feared, but then he might expect his washing and ironing to be done, and his socks darned, and Winnie was beginning to feel rather too old for such mothering.

No, a pleasant single woman was the answer! One with a job during the day, who enjoyed looking after her small domain, and who did not demand too much attention from her land-lady. The financial side was something of a problem to Winnie, who had not the faintest idea what should be charged. Nor did she know if there should be some legal document setting out the terms upon which landladies and lodgers agreed.

And then, supposing they did not get on? It was common knowledge that one really had to live with people before one knew them properly. Look at that terrible Brides-in-the-Bath man! No, thought Winnie, don't look at him, with dusk already beginning to fall!

She rose to draw the curtains and to switch on the lamp. Across the green, she saw the rector marching purposefully toward The Two Pheasants. Unusual, thought Winnie. Perhaps he was calling on his sexton, Albert Piggott, or on Harold Shoosmith nearby.

But the rector was opening the wicket gate at the side of the public house, and vanished from sight.

Winnie resumed her seat and her knitting. Over the past few weeks she had come to the conclusion that the person she would most like to share her home was quiet, devoted Jenny. That is, of course, if she would come.

And now, with this morning's news, it looked as though there were a chance. She would await her opportunity, and put the proposition before Jenny. How lovely, thought Winnie, letting her knitting fall and looking at the leaping flames, if she agreed! The bogey of loneliness would be banished and the tiresome business of trying to find out what would be a fair rent would also be solved, for Jenny would live there rent-free.

Winnie allowed herself to indulge in happy daydreams for some five minutes, and then pulled herself together sharply. It was no good getting too hopeful. Jenny might well have other plans, besides the vague ones she had mentioned and, in any case, a shared home at Thrush Green might be abhorrent to her.

Well, time would show. Winnie picked up her knitting again, determined to remain cool-headed over the whole affair. But hope warmed her throughout the evening.

[BATTLES AT THRUSH GREEN]

And so it happened that Jenny came to live with Winnie Bailey, rejoicing in her new flat and the modern kitchen where she had full scope for her passion for cooking.

One of Thrush Green's favourite confections was a dish of Jenny's hot cheese scones, and here is her recipe.

Cheese Scones

60 g (2 oz) butter
  or margarine
180 g (6 oz)
  self-raising flour
pinch of salt

60 g (2 oz) grated
  cheddar cheese
sour or fresh
  milk to mix

Rub the fat into the flour and salt until the mixture is like breadcrumbs. Add the grated cheese and mix to a dough with the milk. Roll out to a depth of about 2 cm (¾ inch). Cut into small circles, and bake in a very hot oven (Gas mark 7-8/220-230°C/425-450°F) for 10-15 minutes.

Split and butter, and eat them whilst warm.

If you walk up the steep hill from Witney to Wood Green on the main Woodstock road, on your right you will notice an attractive building on a high bank.

It was once the Friends' Meeting House, and a flight of stone steps led to it when I first knew it. Here, during the war, a nursery playgroup met one or two mornings a week. In charge was a vivacious Viennese lady who had fled from danger, and who now put her outstanding skills in child welfare to good account. Accompanied by our daughter, I spent many happy hours helping there.

It was a lively place and did good work. I always felt that it was typical of the Quakers' practical Christianity to allow their building to be so used. I liked too to see the toddlers playing happily in the small grassy graveyard which adjoined it, their blue and white checked overalls gay against the sober grey of the simple tombstones. Here the living and the dead were in harmony.

It was near here, at roughly four o'clock on the green, that I placed the small house where the two friends Ella and Dimity lived amicably together for a number of years. Although it was generally believed in Thrush Green that 'poor Dimity was put upon by Ella', it was not the case. It was true that Dimity appeared to fall in readily with any of Ella's demands, but if it came to a matter of principle, then Dimity was unshaken.

This Ella knew. Her gruff mannish exterior hid a sensitive and complex nature. Those large and lumpish hands could produce exquisitely fine work when required, and she relished the thoughts of others. She kept a commonplace book unknown to all but Dimity, who sometimes pointed out a passage in her reading which she felt might appeal to her friend.

One of them was an extract from the prayer of St Theresa of Avila.

Teach me the glorious lesson that occasionally it is possible that I may be mistaken. Keep me reasonably sweet. I don't want to be a saint; some of them are hard to live with, but a sour old woman

156

is one of the crowning works of the devil.

Help me to extract all possible fun out of life. There are so many delightful things around us, I don't want to miss any of them.

Ella was a great admirer of Anthony Trollope, partly because she was impressed with the industry and perseverance of the man. Another of her private heroes was Isambard Kingdom Brunel, for the same reason. She admired few men, considering them selfish, lazy and weak, so that the one or two who won her respect by sustained endeavour were doubly honoured.

Doggedness was one of the virtues which Ella prized. Loyalty was another. It came to the fore most strongly when she faced the fact that one day Dimity might marry. It was Harold Shoosmith she had in mind then, mistakenly thinking that Dimity was attracted to him.

She went for a walk one spring afternoon to think things out.

It was one of those clear mild days which come occasionally in mid-winter and lift the spirits with their hint of coming springtime. Catkins were already fluttering on the nut hedge behind Albert's house and the sky was a pale translucent blue, as tender as a thrush's egg-shell.

Two mottled partridges squatted in the grass not far from the pathway, like a pair of fat round bottles. Ella looked upon them with a kindly eye. She knew they mated for life, and though she did not think much of married bliss, yet she approved of constancy.

Her mind turned from the partridges, naturally enough, to the possibility of Dimity marrying. Nothing had been said between the two friends, and Ella often wondered if she had imagined a situation which did not, in fact, exist. But ever since the day when she had faced her own fears she had held fast to her principles. If Dimity chose to leave her, then she must wish her all the happiness in the world and make her going easy for her. It was the least one could do in gratitude for so many years of loyal friendship, and the only basis on which that friendship could continue.

[WINTER IN THRUSH GREEN]

Ella's thoughts that day did, in due course, become reality. It was at the little house that she shared with Ella that Dimity received the proposal of marriage which was to change her life.

158

The rector, as he had intended, found Dimity alone at the house, for he had observed Ella striding towards Lulling Woods, basket in hand, and had remembered that this was the day on which the eggs were collected.

'Why, Charles!' cried Dimity. 'How lovely to see you! I didn't know you were allowed out yet after that wretched flu.'

'This is my first walk,' admitted the rector. 'But I wanted to come and thank you properly for all that you have done.' How convenient, at times, thought the rector, was the English use of the second person plural!

'Ella's out, I'm afraid,' said Dimity, leading the way to the sitting-room. 'But I don't think she'll be very long.'

The rector felt a little inner agitation at this news, but did his best to look disappointed at Ella's temporary absence. He handed Dimity the flowers with a smile and a small bow.

'Freesias!' breathed Dimity with rapture, thinking how dreadfully extravagant dear Charles had been, and yet how delicious it was to have such treasures brought to her. 'How very, very kind, Charles. They are easily our favourite flowers.'

The rector murmured politely while Dimity unwrapped them. Their fragrance mingled with the faint smell of wood smoke that lingered in the room and the rector thought, yet again, how warm and full of life this small room was. Ella's book lay face downward on the arm of a chair, her spectacles lodged across it. Dimity's knitting had been hastily put aside when she answered the door, and decorated a low table near the fire. The clock ticked merrily, the fire whispered and crackled, the cat purred upon the window sill, sitting four-square and smug after its midday meal.

A feeling of great peace descended upon the rector despite the preoccupations of the errand in hand. Could he ever hope, he wondered, to have such comfort in his own home?

'Do sit down,' said Dimity, 'while I arrange these.'

'I'll come with you,' said Charles, with a glance at the clock. Ella must have reached Dotty's by now.

He followed Dimity into the small kitchen which smelt deliciously of gingerbread.

'There!' gasped Dimity, 'I'd forgotten my cakes in the excitement.'

'Could you pass that skewer, Charles?' she asked, intent on the oven's contents. Obediently, the rector passed it over.

'Harold is coming to tea tomorrow,' said Dimity, 'and he adores gingerbread.' She poked busily at the concoctions, withdrew the tins from the oven and put them on the scrubbed wooden table to cool.

The rector leant against the dresser and watched her as she fetched a vase and arranged the freesias. His intentions were clear enough in his own mind, but it was decidedly difficult to make a beginning, particularly when Dimity was so busy.

'I must show you our broad beans,' chattered Dimity, quite unconscious of the turmoil in her old friend's heart. 'They are quite three inches high. Harold gave us some wonderful stuff to keep the slugs off.'

Fond as the rector was of Harold Shoosmith, he found himself disliking his intrusion into the present conversation. Also the subject of slugs, he felt, was not one which made an easy stepping-stone to such delicate matters as he himself had in mind. The kitchen clock reminded him sharply of the passage of time, and urgency lent cunning to the rector's stratagems.

'I should love to see them sometime,' said Charles, 'but I wonder if I might sit down for a little? My legs are uncommonly feeble after this flu.'

Dimity was smitten with remorse. 'You poor dear! How thoughtless of me, Charles! Let's take the freesias into the sitting-room and you must have a rest.'

She fluttered ahead, pouring out a little flow of sympathy and self-reproach which fell like music upon the rector's ears.

'Have a cushion behind your head,' said Dimity, when the rector had lowered himself into an armchair. She plumped it up with her thin hands and held it out invitingly. The rector began to feel quite guilty, and refused it firmly.

'Harold says it's the final refinement of relaxation,' said Dimity, and noticed a wince of pain pass over the rector's cherubic face. 'Oh dear, I'm sure you're over-tired! You really shouldn't have ventured so far,' she protested.

'Dimity,' said Charles, taking a deep breath, 'I want to ask you something. Something very important.'

'Yes, Charles?' said Dimity, picking up her knitting busily, and starting to count stitches with her forefinger. The rector, having made a beginning, stuck to his guns manfully.

'Dimity,' he said gently, 'I have a proposal to make.'

Dimity's thin finger continued to gallop along the needle and she frowned with concentration. Inexorably, the little clock on the mantelpiece ticked the precious minutes away. At length she reached the end of the stitches and looked with bright interest at her companion.

'Who from?' she asked briskly. 'The Mothers' Union?'

'No!' said the rector, fortissimo. 'Not from the Mothers' Union!' His voice dropped suddenly. 'The proposal, Dimity, is from me.' And, without more ado, the rector began.

'Oh, Charles,' quavered Dimity when he had ended. Her eyes were full of tears.

'You need not answer now,' said the rector gently, holding one of her thin hands in his own two plump ones. 'But do you think you ever could?'

'Oh, Charles,' repeated Dimity, with a huge

happy sigh. 'Oh, yes, please!'

When Ella came in, exactly three minutes later, she found them standing on the hearthrug, hand in hand. Before they had time to say a word, she had rushed across the room, enveloped Dimity in a bear-hug and kissed her soundly on each cheek.

'Oh Dimity,' said Ella, from her heart. 'I'm so happy!'

'Dash it all, Ella,' protested Charles, 'that's just what *we* were going to say!'

[WINTER IN THRUSH GREEN]

Thrush Green Rectory, standing at six o'clock, was Charles and Dimity's first home and here they settled very happily — apart from the draughts. The ugly rectory is a figment of my imagination, for there was never such a building on Wood Green. However, I quite enjoyed describing the horrors of my creation, and shared with Edward Young, the architect, his revulsion for the hideous house, covered in peeling stucco, as chilling within as without.

It was with great relish that I prepared to burn it down — while Charles and Dimity were conveniently away for a few days. Harold Shoosmith discovered the fire and promptly summoned the fire brigade.

Within five minutes, a little knot of helpers was gathered at the blaze. The sight was awe-inspiring. The collapse of part of the roof had let in air which intensified the conflagration. Flames were now shooting skyward, and the upstairs windows showed a red glow. Smoke poured from the main bedroom window, and there were terrifying reports as the glass cracked in the heat.

Mr Jones, the landlord of The Two Pheasants, was organising a chain of water carriers from the tap in his bar, and Albert Piggott, stomach pains forgotten, had trundled out an archaic fire-fighting contraption which had been kept in the vestry since the Second World War and had never been used since the time when a small incendiary bomb had set light to the tassels of the bell ropes, and an adjacent pile of copies of Stainer's 'Crucifixion', in 1942.

This relic, when attached to a nearby hydrant well-hidden in nettles in the churchyard, spouted water at a dozen spots along its perished length and saturated several onlookers.

'Get the damn thing out of the way!' yelled Harold Shoosmith. 'We'll have someone falling over it!'

He and several other men, including Edward Young and Ben Curdle, were busy removing furniture, books and papers, and anything they could grab downstairs, before the inevitable happened and the whole top floor collapsed. These were being piled, well away from danger, by willing hands. Ella Bembridge, for once without a cigarette in her mouth, worked as stoutly as the men, and would have forced her way into

the building to collect some of Dimity's treasures if she had not been forbidden to do so
by Harold, who had taken charge with all the
ready authority of one who had spent his life
organising others.

The welcome sound of the fire brigade's siren
sent people scattering to allow its access across
the grass to the blazing house. It was a joy to
see the speed and economy of effort with which
the hoses were turned on.

'This started some hours ago, by the look of
things,' said the captain to Harold. 'I can't think
how it went undetected for so long.'

Harold explained that the house was empty,
and at that moment a second fire engine arrived
from Nidden, and started work at the side of
the building where the flames seemed thickest.

A terrible roaring sound began to emanate
from the doomed building, and the bystanders
were ordered to get well away. With a thun-

derous rumbling the top floor of the rectory now collapsed. Sparks, smoke and flames poured into the air, and the heat became intense. People began to cough in the acrid air, and to rub eyes reddened with smoke and tears.

Now it was quite obvious that nothing more could be rescued. The rector's modest possessions which were still inside the house must be consumed by the fire. It was a tragedy that few could bear to witness, and Winnie Bailey, in dressing-gown and wellingtons, led the redoubtable Ella away to her own house across the green. It was the only time she had seen her old friend in tears.

[GOSSIP FROM THRUSH GREEN]

Harold Shoosmith undertook the unenviable task of ringing Charles and Dimity in Yorkshire where they were on holiday, and breaking the news to them.

Luckily, it was Charles who answered the telephone. Harold had already rehearsed what he should do if Dimity had lifted the receiver. Charles would have to be summoned. This was the sort of thing the men must cope with, thought Harold, true to his Victorian principles.

'Nice to hear you,' was the rector's opening remark. 'You're up early. Everything all right at your end?'

'I'm afraid not. Charles, I have to tell you some bad news. Are you sitting down?'

'Sitting down?' came the bewildered reply.

'Because this is going to be a shock,' continued Harold doggedly. 'There was a bad accident here last night.'

'No! Not anyone hurt! Not *killed*, Harold, don't say that!'

'Nothing like that. Perhaps *accident* was the wrong word. The fact is your house has been badly damaged by fire.'

There was a brief silence.

'Hello!' shouted Harold. 'You there, Charles?'

'Yes, yes. But I can't have heard right. The house damaged by fire? How badly?'

'I hate to tell you — but it is completely gutted. I think it is quite beyond repair, Charles, as you will see.'

'I can't take it in. I really can't,' said the poor rector. 'How could it have happened? We switched off everything, I'm sure, and we hadn't had a fire in the grate for days. Surely no one would be so wicked as to set fire to the place?'

'I'm sure it wasn't that,' said Harold. 'I just felt you should know that our spare room is waiting for you and Dimity when you return.'

'We'll be back during the day, Harold, and our deepest thanks for offering us shelter tonight. What a terrible affair. I must go and break it to dear Dimity, and then we must clear up things here, and set off for Thrush Green without delay.'

'We shall look forward to seeing you,' said Harold.

'And Harold,' said Charles in a firmer tone, 'I very much appreciate your telling me the news so kindly. It couldn't have been easy. You have prepared us to face whatever awaits us there, quite wonderfully.'

He rang off, and Harold thought how well he had taken it.

No one saw Charles and Dimity arrive, and for that they were grateful. They halted the car on the edge of the battered and rutted grass which was still sprinkled with the ash and trodden cinders of last night's activities.

Dimity covered her face with her hands and her thin shoulders shook. Charles's face was stony as he gazed unwinking at the scene. He put his arm round his grieving wife, but was quite unable to speak. They sat there, silent in their distress, for five terrible minutes.

Then, sighing, Charles opened the car door and stepped into the desolation of what had once been Thrush Green rectory.

He stirred the damp black ashes of the study floor with his foot. He could scarcely see for the blur of tears behind his spectacles, but he bent to investigate a glint of metal among the dust.

Turning it over in his hand, he recognised it. It was the silver figure of Christ which had been mounted on the ivory cross behind his desk. It was distorted and blackened by the heat, but Charles knew immediately what it was. He slipped it into his pocket, and turned to help

Dimity over a low sooty wall which was all that was left of her kitchen.

[GOSSIP FROM THRUSH GREEN]

Of course, all their Thrush Green friends rallied round them, and Joan and Edward Young gave them comfort and a meal that evening. Later the Youngs accompanied them to Harold and Isobel Shoosmith's house where they were to spend the night.

The Youngs took a turn around the green before returning home.

They walked on together, past the silent school and the public house, until they rounded the bulk of St Andrew's church and stood facing the ruins.

The acrid stench which had hung over Thrush Green all day was almost unbearable here. Joan looked with pity and distaste at the mess which had once been the rectory.

She caught a glimpse of Edward's face in the dying light.

'Edward!' she said accusingly. 'You're *pleased!* How can you be so *heartless!*'

Edward hastened to explain himself. 'My darling, three-quarters of me grieves for dear old Charles and Dim, just as much as you do. But the other quarter — the professional bit — is so relieved to see the end of that ghastly place that it can't help rejoicing in a perverse sort of way.'

Joan gazed at him with disgust, but then began to smile. She took his arm, and they turned their backs upon the wreckage, and set off towards their home.

'I suppose you are already planning a new house, monster that you are,' she observed.

'How did you guess?' asked Edward.

[GOSSIP FROM THRUSH GREEN]

The Henstocks were lucky enough to find lodgings in the village while they awaited a new home. But fortune favoured them when Charles was summoned to meet his Bishop.

The Bishop lived in a fine red-brick house at the end of a long drive bordered with lime trees.

Charles parked his car in as unobtrusive a spot as possible beside a flourishing prunus tree, and tugged at the wrought-iron bell pull by the white front door.

A very spruce maid welcomed him and showed him into the Bishop's drawing-room.

'I'll tell the Bishop you are here,' said the girl. 'At the moment he is telephoning.'

She departed, leaving Charles to admire the silver cups on a side table, and the oar hanging above the fireplace. The Bishop was a great oarsman, Charles remembered, a true muscular Christian. Perhaps that contributed to his good looks, thought Charles, and bent to pull up his wrinkled socks as Dimity had told him.

The solemnly ticking grandfather clock by the door said two minutes to the half hour when Charles heard the Bishop approaching.

He stood up as the door swung open.

'My dear fellow! I hope I haven't kept you waiting. You are wonderfully punctual. Come into my study. We'll be unmolested there.'

He strode through the hall, followed by the good rector who admired the clerical grey suit which clothed those broad shoulders and neat waist.

He certainly was a handsome fellow.

But at least, thought Charles, I remembered to pull up my socks.

[GOSSIP FROM THRUSH GREEN]

Later that afternoon he and Dimity stop for tea on their way home. It was one of their favourite cafés, renowned for its tea cakes.

'And how did you find the dear Bishop?'
'As upstanding as ever. He inquired most

171

kindly after you. Ah! Here comes the girl!'

The girl was approximately the same age as the rector, must have weighed thirteen stone, and was dressed in a rather tight flowered overall.

'Could we have some of your delicious toasted tea cakes? And a pot of China tea for two?'

The waitress wrote busily on a little pad.

'Any jam, honey or other preserve? We have our home-made apricot, mulberry and quince.'

'How lovely that sounds!' cried Dimity. 'Like a list of jams from Culpeper!'

'We only keep our own, madam,' said the girl with some hauteur.

'Then shall we try mulberry, dear?' asked Dimity. 'I don't think I've ever had it.'

The waitress added MJ to her pad and departed.

'And now tell me, what happened, Charles?'

The rector began to look quite shy. 'Did you know that Anthony Bull is leaving Lulling?'

'Really? Now you come to mention it, I believe Bertha Lovelock said something about it.'

The rector's look of shyness was replaced by one of startled exasperation. 'But how on earth could she know? It isn't general knowledge yet!'

'Well, you know how things get about in a small community,' said Dimity soothingly. 'Anyway, where's he going? Not retiring, surely?'

'Far from it. He's been appointed to a splendid living in one of the Kensington parishes.

Rather High Church, I gather, and a most beautiful building. Anthony will be just the man for it, the Bishop said. I'm so glad he has got preferment. I always felt that Lulling was only a stepping-stone to greater things for Anthony.'

The waitress reappeared with the tray and set out the teapot, milk jug, hot water container and a large dish covered with a silver lid.

A small bowl containing a wine-coloured confection aroused Dimity's interest.

'And this is the mulberry jam? What a beautiful colour.'

'We make it on the premises,' replied the waitress, thawing in the face of Dimity's enthusiasm. 'We have a tree in the garden. It is reputed to be a hundred and fifty years old.'

'How wonderful!'

The waitress made off again, and Dimity applied herself to pouring out the tea.

'But what about us, darling? Did he mention anything about our new house?'

'He did indeed. I think two of those sugar lumps. They seem rather small.'

'They're called *fairy* lumps, I believe,' said Dimity. 'Well, go on.'

'I'm afraid there won't be a new house, my dear.'

Dimity dropped the sugar tongs in her dismay. 'Not a new house? Then where on earth are we to go?'

Her husband had now bent down to retrieve the tongs from beneath the table. When he reappeared his face was very pink.

'To an old one, Dimity. I have been offered the living of the four merged parishes, and we should live at Lulling Vicarage.'

Dimity gazed at him open-mouthed.

'Charles!' she croaked at last. 'I can't believe it! That lovely, lovely house!'

'Don't cry, Dimity! Please don't cry,' begged Charles. 'Aren't you pleased?'

Dimity unfolded a snowy handkerchief and wiped her eyes.

'Of course I'm pleased. I'm just completely overwhelmed, that's all. Oh, Charles dear, this is an honour you so richly deserve. Won't it be wonderful to have our own home at last?'

'I'm glad you are pleased. It means we shall still be among our friends, and I shall still be able to take services at St Andrew's.'

'And when do you take over?'

'Probably before Christmas. Anthony expects to be inducted in October or November.'

'And then we shall be able to move in,' said Dimity happily. She spread mulberry jam in reckless bounty upon a slice of tea cake. 'What a blessing I didn't fall for some curtaining remnants this afternoon. They would never have done for the vicarage windows.'

She looked with surprise at the jam dish. 'Oh dear, Charles! I seem to have taken all the mulberry preserve.'

'I think we might be able to afford some quince as well,' said Charles. 'By way of celebration, you know.'

And he raised a plump hand to summon the girl.

[GOSSIP FROM THRUSH GREEN]

Wood Green stands at the northern end of Witney. Better known, and much more photographed, is the larger Church Green which is at the southern end and is dominated by the fine church of St Mary the Virgin. It was in this splendid wool church that our daughter was christened.

When I began writing the Thrush Green books, I changed the name of St Mary's of Witney to St John's of Lulling, and here Charles Henstock became vicar when he was appointed after the fire at Thrush Green. When I described the vicarage, I had in mind the lovely one at Chieveley, the village in Berkshire where we had lived for some years.

Charles Henstock awoke with a start. He must have overslept, it was so light in the bedroom.

He turned his head and squinted sideways at the bedside clock. To his relief, the hands stood at twenty past seven.

Still bemused, he gazed above him, relishing the warmth of his bed and the elegant swags of plasterwork which decorated the vicarage ceiling. Those skilful workers some two hundred years ago certainly knew how to delight the eye, thought the present incumbent of the parish of Lulling.

Not that Lulling was the only parish in his care. A mile to the north lay his old parish of Thrush Green, and north and west of that delectable spot were those of Nidden and Lulling Woods. It was a large area to care for, with four splendid churches, and Charles Henstock constantly prayed that he might fulfil his responsibilities with diligence.

His wife Dimity lay curled beside him, still deep in sleep. They had started their married life together at Thrush Green, in the bleak Victorian rectory which had been burnt to the ground some two years earlier. The general opinion was that the fire was a blessing in disguise. The hideous building had stood out like a sore thumb among the beautiful stone-built Cotswold houses round the green.

But Charles still mourned his old home. He had known great happiness there, and even now could scarcely bear to look at the empty site where once his home had stood.

A pinkish glow was beginning to spread over the ceiling. The sun must be rising, but still that strange luminosity which had roused him hung about the room. More alert now, the good rector struggled upright, taking care not to disturb his sleeping partner.

The ancient cedar tree was now in sight, its outspread arms holding thick bands of snow. The telephone wire sagged beneath the weight it was bearing, and the window sill was heavily encrusted.

Very carefully the rector slipped out of bed and went to the window to survey the cold February scene. Since his early childhood he had delighted in snow. Now, looking at his transformed garden, his heart beat faster with the old familiar excitement.

The snow covered everything — the paths, the flower beds, the tiny snowdrops which had so recently braved the bitter winds and tossed their little bells under the hedges. It lay in gentle billows against the summerhouse door and the tall yew hedge.

Beyond the garden, St John's church roof glistened under its snowy canopy against a rose-pink cloud and, high above, the golden weathercock on the steeple caught the first rays of the winter sun.

The beauty of it all enraptured Charles. He caught his breath in wonderment, oblivious of the chilly bedroom and his congealing feet. What enchantment! What purity! An overnight miracle!

'Charles,' said Dimity, 'what has happened?'

'It's been snowing,' said her husband, smiling upon her. 'It's quite deep.'

'Oh dear,' said Dimity, getting out of bed. 'What a blessing I brought the spade indoors last night! No doubt we'll have to dig ourselves out.'

Dimity had always been the practical partner.

[AFFAIRS AT THRUSH GREEN]

177

Witney is blessed with several open spaces of singular beauty. Church Green is to the north of St Mary the Virgin's church and leads towards the Butter Cross and the crossroads there.

South of the church is an even larger grassy space called the Leys. Here the ancient Mop Fair is held in September each year, there is a children's playground, and room for all manner of games. I think it was here, or in a field adjoining the Leys, that I took our daughter to see a display of riding by a team which called itself the Cossacks. Heaven alone knows if they had any Russian connections, but in 1944 it was good to have any innocent excitement.

Their costumes were shabby, but their exploits on horseback were notable. They galloped, they cleared great hurdles decorated with coloured paper, they waved swords, they yelled, they were indomitable. We sat entranced, my daughter's passion for horses increasing every moment, while the hooves pounded and the battered grass gave forth its scent.

Overhead, strangely incongruous, a stream of aeroplanes towing gliders made its slow way eastward. It was going to the sad battle of Arnhem, but of that we knew nothing on that fateful afternoon. The adults around that makeshift arena told each other that Something Was Up, and our attention was divided between earth and sky. The children, used to warfare all around them, concentrated on the afternoon's entertainment on the ground before them.

For Jill, our daughter, the sight of so many horses was absolute rapture, and during the next few years she was to become one of the thousands of pony-mad little girls suffered by even more thousands of parents. At the height of her infatuation, some time later, I was driven to writing the following verses expressing, I believe, the feelings of many hard-pressed parents.

Hippomaniac

My daughter's conversation
Is exclusively of horse:
Of snaffle-bit and saddle-soap,
Of leading-rein and lunging-rope,
Of sickle-hock and pastern-slope —
And Foxhunter, of course.

My daughter's bookshelves overflow
With books about the beast:
She Loved Her Pony, Saddle Lore,
Gymkhana Jane, The Horse Next Door,
Matilda Never Rode Before —
Three score of them, at least.

My daughter's bedroom walls are crammed
From ceiling to the floor:
With Palaminos, Arab Bays,
With Lippizaners, Windsor Greys,
With Quaggas, Cobs and Dziggetais —
And half a hundred more.

I like the horse, I love my child,
But — this is where it's sad —
The two together, night and day,
Will drive me mad.

But to return to September 1944. I was invited
to tea by one of the hospitable Witney ladies a
week or two after the Cossacks' entertainment. A
young soldier was there, and was introduced by
my hostess with the unforgettable words:

'This is James. He is just back from Arnhem,
and he's got the *most dreadful cold!*'

Some forty years later we find Charles and Dimity Henstock happily settled in Lulling Vicarage
only a hundred yards or so from the field where
the Cossacks thundered and the slow aeroplanes
droned above, many never to return.

'I must pay a visit to Thrush Green this afternoon,' said Dimity to her husband.

They were breakfasting in the kitchen of Lulling Vicarage. Charles buttered a slice of toast carefully.

'I can drive you there before two, my dear, but I have this meeting in Oxford at three.'

'Don't worry, I shall walk. Ella is clean out of light blue tapestry wool for her lovers' knots, and I have some here.'

'Her lovers' knots?' echoed Charles, toast poised.

'Round the edge of the chair seat,' explained Dimity.

She rose and began to clear the table. Charles, still looking bewildered, chewed the last mouthful of toast.

'I must get on, dear,' said Dimity. 'Mrs Allen comes today, and I like to get things cleared up.'

'I always thought that we employed Mrs Allen for the express purpose of clearing up for us.'

'Yes, one would think that in theory, but in practice, of course, it really makes more work to do.'

'Then I will go and water the greenhouse,' said the vicar of Lulling.

He stepped out of the back door into the dewy freshness of a fine June morning, and made his way happily through the vicarage garden.

[AT HOME IN THRUSH GREEN]

In the later Thrush Green books, Charles Henstock is priest in charge of Lulling, Thrush Green, Nidden and Lulling Woods. The churches at Nidden and Lulling Woods are scarcely mentioned, but the one at Thrush Green, called St Andrew's, figures largely in the novels. In reality, there is a church called Holy Trinity on Wood Green. It is the only building to stand on the green itself. The habitations, both real and imaginary, stand on the road which surrounds the green.

Holy Trinity is a sturdy Victorian building with a well-kept graveyard containing some varied trees, lime, fir, laburnum and others. The grass is mown regularly, the graves are cared for. It is not a bit like the imaginary churchyard of St Andrew's which is sadly neglected by Albert Piggott, sexton, caretaker, gravedigger and general factotum.

One fine September morning, Harold Shoosmith made his way to the rectory and passed St Andrew's church.

The church stood at the south-western corner of Thrush Green, and Albert Piggott's house was placed exactly opposite it and next door to The Two Pheasants. Albert divided his time, unequally, between the two buildings.

The sunshine and serenity of the morning were not reflected in Albert's gloomy face. Hands in pockets, he was mooching about among the tombstones, kicking at a tussock of grass now and again and muttering to himself.

'Good morning, Piggott,' called Harold.

'A good morning for some, maybe,' said Albert sourly, approaching the railings. 'But not for them as 'as this sort of mess to clear up.'

Harold leant over the railings and surveyed the graveyard. Certainly there were a few pieces of paper about, but to his eye it all looked much as usual.

'I suppose people throw down cigarette boxes and so on when they come out of the pub,' he remarked, 'and they blow over here. Too bad when there's a litter box provided.'

'It's not the paper as worries me,' replied Albert. 'It's this 'ere grass. Since my operation, I can't do what I used to do.'

'No, no. Of course not,' said Harold, assuming an expression of extreme gravity in deference to Albert's operation. Thrush Green was learning to live with Albert Piggott's traumatic experience, as related by him daily, but it was finding it a trifle exhausting.

'Take a look at it,' urged Albert. 'Take a proper look! What chance is there of pushin' a mower up these 'ere paths with the graves all going which-way? One time I used to scythe it, but Doctor Lovell said that was out of the question. "Out of the question, Piggott," he said to me, same as I'm saying to you now. "Out of the question." His very words.'

'Quite,' said Harold.

'And take these railings,' went on Albert, warming to his theme. 'When was they put up, eh? You tell me that. When was they put 'ere?'

'A good while ago,' hazarded Harold.

'For Queen Victoria's Golden Jubilee, that's when,' said Albert triumphantly. 'Not 'er Diamond one, but 'er *Golden* one! That takes you back a bit, don't it? Won't be long before these railings is a 'undred year old. Stands to reason they're rusted. 'Alf of 'em busted, and the other 'alf ought to be pulled out. There was always this nice little stub wall of dry stone. That don't wear too bad, but these 'ere railings 'as 'ad it!'

Harold looked, with more attention, at Albert Piggott's territory. To be sure, he had some grounds for grumbling. Tall rank weeds grew inside the stub wall, nettles, the rusty spires of docks, cow-parsley with skeleton umbels turning papery as the summer waned, with convolvulus entwining all and thrusting its tentacles along the railings.

The tombstones stood among hillocks of grass which had grown beyond a mower's powers, as Albert had said. Here and there, a few grassy mounds, neatly shorn, paid tribute to the loving hands of relatives who did their best to honour the resting places of their dead. But these islands of tidiness only served to throw the neglected whole into sharp contrast.

Albert was right about the railings too, Harold observed. Several had splintered with rust and would be dangerous to handle.

'Is there any need for the railings, I wonder!' said Harold, musing aloud.

'There's need all right,' responded Albert. 'That's why they was set 'ere. In the old days there used to be cows and that, grazing on the green, and they could get over this liddle ol' wall as easy as kiss your 'and. And the kids too. You gotter keep people and animals out of a churchyard, stands to reason.'

'You won't keep people out for ever,' pointed out Harold, preparing to go on his way. 'We'll all be in there together before long.'

'Some sooner than others,' retorted Albert, with a morose sniff, as Harold departed.

[BATTLES AT THRUSH GREEN]

It was Harold who later took Charles Henstock to see a graveyard which had been tidied and made easier to keep neat. He had come across it when he stopped for tea on one of his afternoon drives in the Cotswolds.

Harold navigated a bend in the village street, and drew up by a grass verge. To their left stood a square-towered church of golden stone, set in a large graveyard.

The two men got out and went to the wall which bordered the verge. It was a little more than waist-high, and was sprinkled with dots of green moss and orange and grey lichens.

The two rested their arms on the top and gazed before them. Around the other three sides stood tombstones, placed upright just inside the wall. Some were of weathered local stone, some of marble, some of slate or granite, with here and there an iron cross of the late Victorian era. They made a dignified array, in their muted colours and varied shapes, set so lovingly around the noble church which sheltered them.

The churchyard was a completely flat close-cut lawn. The stripes of a fresh cutting showed how easily a mower could keep the large expanse in order. Only one or two cypress trees, and a cedar of great age, broke the level of the grass, and the whole effect was of space and tranquillity.

'Beautiful!' whispered the rector. 'Simple, peaceful, reverent —'

'And dead easy to keep tidy,' broke in Harold practically. 'We could do the same at Thrush Green.'

'I wonder,' pondered Charles. 'You notice, Harold, that there are no modern graves here. I take it that there is a new burial ground somewhere else in the village?'

'I suppose there is. But I don't see that that should pose a problem. After all, the new addition to Thrush Green's churchyard is quite separate. When was that piece purchased?'

'Just before the war, I believe. They intended to plant a hedge between the old and new graveyards, but war interfered with the work and, in any case, the feeling was that it should all be thrown into one.'

'Would it matter?'

The rector stroked his chin thoughtfully.

'We should have to get a faculty, of course, a licence from the ecclesiastical authorities, and I've a feeling that it would be simpler if we only had the old graveyard to deal with as, obviously, they have had here. But I must go into it. I shall find out all I can as soon as we return.'

'So you like the idea?'

'Like it?' cried Charles, his face pink with enthusiasm. 'Like it? Why, I can't wait to get started!'

He threw his arms wide, as though he would embrace the whole beautiful scene before him.

'It's an inspiration, Harold. It's exactly what I needed to give me hope. If it can be done here, then it can be done at Thrush Green. I shall start things moving as soon as I can.'

Harold began to feel some qualms in the face of this precipitate zeal.

'We can't rush things, Charles. We must have some consultations with the village as a whole.'

'Naturally, naturally,' agreed Charles. 'But surely there can be no opposition to such a scheme?'

'I think there's every possibility of opposition.'

The rector's mouth dropped open. 'But if that is so, then I think we must bring the doubters to see this wonderful place. We could hire a coach, couldn't we? It might make a most inspiring outing —'

Harold broke in upon the rector's outpourings. 'Don't go so fast, Charles. We must sound out the Parochial Church Council first. I must confess that I didn't think you would wax so enthusiastic when I suggested this trip.'

'But why not? It's the obvious answer to our troubles. Even Piggott could keep the grass cut once the graves were levelled. A boy could! Why, even young Cooke could manage that! And we could get rid of those appalling railings at the same time as we put the stones against the wall. It's really all so simple.'

'It may seem so to you, Charles, but I think you may find quite a few battles ahead before you attain a churchyard as peaceful as this.'

Charles turned his back reluctantly upon the scene, and the two men returned to the car.

[BATTLES AT THRUSH GREEN]

As it happened, Harold's fears were realised. It was plain to him that there was bound to be hostility to the idea. Any disturbance to the churchyard would be looked upon as desecration by some

188

of Charles's parishioners. Harold had a much shrewder knowledge of his fellow men than the guileless rector.

A week or so later, a meeting of the Parochial Church Council took place in the rector's dining-room. The evening was so cold and windy that even Charles Henstock became conscious that the icy room was not very welcoming, and suggested to Dimity that they should light a fire.

The meeting was at seven-thirty (thus successfully interfering with most people's meal arrangements), and the fire was alight by six. Even so, the lofty room was barely warm, despite Dimity's efforts, for the fire had smoked when first lit, and the windows had had to be opened for a time.

Nevertheless, it looked quite cheerful to see a fire in the grate, and when the curtains were drawn and some chrysanthemums set centrally on the table, Dimity was pleased with the result.

[BATTLES AT THRUSH GREEN]

The trouble began when Charles Henstock reached the item on the agenda 'The Future of the Churchyard'. The Parochial Church Council listened attentively.

He began to expound it with clarity and enthusiasm. The difficulties of its present main tenance and the sadness which the community felt at its dilapidated condition were put forward admirably, and there were murmurs of agreement as the rector made his points.

When he reached the proposal, however, the murmurs grew less noticeable, and Harold Shoosmith saw signs of restlessness among one or two members.

Oblivious of the drop in the temperature of the meeting, Charles described the visit to the churchyard in the west which had done so much to arouse his ambitions for their own.

'The place is an inspiration,' declared the rector. 'And I feel sure that Mr Shoosmith will bear me out.'

Harold nodded.

'It can be done here,' he went on, 'and I don't think there would be any difficulty in getting permission.'

He paused and looked hopefully at the faces round the table.

Percy Hodge was the first to speak. 'Mr Chairman, sir, I don't altogether like the idea. This tampering with graves will upset people. It does me, for that matter.'

'Me too,' said Mrs Cleary with some indignation. 'My husband and I spent a lot on that cross and kerb for his mother, and now his name is engraved under hers, and I just don't want the stones shifted. Our nearest and dearest are there, in that spot — I may say, that *hallowed* spot — and to have the memorial stones put elsewhere is downright misleading, not to say sacrilegious!'

She was quite pink in the face after this outburst, and poor Charles gazed at her in dismay.

'But they would not be *disturbed,* my dear Mrs Cleary, simply removed to the perimeter of the churchyard. It would all be most reverently done, I assure you. The graves themselves would not be touched.'

'I still think it's wrong,' said Mrs Cleary forcefully, slapping her gloves on the table.

'I must say that I agree,' said Percy Hodge. 'All my family are there from 1796 onward, as near the yew tree as they can cluster, and I'm only sorry there's no room for me, except in the new part. I shall definitely oppose any move to shift the headstones, kerbs and any other memorials.'

Charles's chubby face began to pucker like a hurt child's, and Harold hastily intervened.

'Mr Chairman, I think this is a very natural reaction to the suggestion, and one with which we can sympathise. I'm sure that other parishes who have faced this problem have also had to overcome some misgivings. There is the other proposition, you remember, about the sheep.'

'*Sheep?*' squeaked Miss Watson.

'I can remember sheep in the churchyard,' quavered her elderly neighbour, one of the churchwardens.

'Thank you, thank you,' said Charles. 'It was suggested by someone that if the churchyard stayed as it is now, then a few sheep might graze there and help to keep it tidy.'

'That's even worse!' exclaimed Mrs Cleary. 'Sheep indeed!'

'Wouldn't be practical with all the yew there is there now,' said Percy Hodge. 'Fencing alone would cost a small fortune.'

'What about Miss Harmer's goats?' suggested someone, half-jokingly.

Harold saw that Charles was beginning to get distressed as well as dismayed.

'Not goats,' said the rector. 'I don't think either sheep or goats are a good idea myself.'

At this point, Miss Watson spoke up bravely. 'I think the rector's first suggestion is a good one, and we ought to consider it. Those railings are a downright danger, and the state of the churchyard is a positive disgrace. What's the use of my telling the children to keep the place tidy, with that muddle facing them every time they go out on the green?'

'Quite right,' said Harold.

'And to my mind,' continued Miss Watson,

'it's far more irreligious to neglect the dead as we are doing at the moment than to rearrange things so that the place can be a fitting memorial to those who have gone before us.'

There were murmurs of assent for this point of view, and Charles began to look a little happier.

'That is exactly my feeling,' he said. 'It is quite impossible to get help, either paid or voluntary, to keep the churchyard as it should be. We can put several matters on the one faculty when we apply. The railings should certainly go. The headstones — er, rearranged — and the turf levelled so that a mower can keep the whole space beautifully cut. I do urge you to visit the church which I mentioned. It would be inspiring, I assure you.'

'Know it well,' said Mrs Cleary. 'Looks like a children's playground.'

'I really think,' piped the very old churchwarden tremulously, 'that Miss Watson's point about the churchyard's untidiness being a bad example for her pupils is one of the most telling. I should like to see this other place. To my mind, the idea is sound.'

There was general discussion, some against, but more for the proposal, and the hideous black marble clock on the black marble mantelpiece struck nine before the rector could restore order.

'It seems to me that we should take a vote on this project,' he said at last. 'Those for?'

Eight hands were raised.

'And against?'

Three hands went up.

The rector sighed.

'Later on there will be a notice on the church door. Any objections, I believe, must be sent to the Diocese. Meanwhile, I will find out more about applying for a faculty, giving us permission to go ahead. Thank you, my dear people, a most interesting meeting.'

Mr Hodge and Mrs Cleary were two of the last to leave. Their faces were stern as they shook the rector's proffered hand at the front door.

'You'll see my name among the objectors, sir, I'm afraid,' said Percy.

'And mine *most certainly*,' said Mrs Cleary, sweeping out.

Harold and Charles watched them depart beneath the starry sky.

'Dear, oh dear!' cried the rector. 'Would you have thought it?'

'Yes,' said Harold simply, and began to laugh.

[BATTLES AT THRUSH GREEN]

Of course, the battle about St Andrew's churchyard raged beyond the confines of the Parochial Church Council.

As is so often the case, those most vociferous were the people who had the least to do with the church. Several stalwart chapel-goers, whose parents and friends lay peacefully beneath the tussocky grass of the graveyard, were among the first to put their names on the list of objectors to the scheme. Percy Hodge's name, of course, was there, in company with Mrs Cleary's.

'I've been tending the graves of my old grandpa and grandma since I was big enough to hold shears,' he said fiercely to Joan Young who had been unfortunate enough to meet him on Thrush Green.

'And then my dad's and mum's. Four graves I've seen to every other week, and four nice green vases I've paid for and put up respectful.'

'It isn't such people as you,' said Joan, in a placatory manner, 'that the changes are being made for. It's dozens of graves that are neglected that make the place such an eyesore.'

'Maybe, maybe! Nevertheless, there's some as adds to the ugliness simply by tending the graves without real taste. Take that one next door to old Mrs Curdle now. I'm not mentioning names —'

Joan Young knew it was a relation of the Cooke family whose grave was under discussion, but let the old man continue.

'— but that woman has put five jam jars along her husband. *Five jam jars,* mark you, and every one full of dead asters for month after month, not to mention stinking water. Now, there *is* an eyesore! With what she spends in cigarettes she could well afford a nice green vase like mine.'

At The Two Pheasants, the debate went on night after night. Albert Piggott, with proprietorial rights, as it were, over the plot in question, found his opinion sought in the most flattering way, and very often a half-pint of beer put into his welcoming hand as well.

He adopted a heavily impartial attitude to the subject. He found he did better in the way of *pourboires* by seeing both sides of the question. He saw himself as a mixture of the Man-on-the-Spot, Guardian-of-Sacred-Ground and One-Still-Longing-to-Work but regretfully laid low by Mr Pedder-Bennet's surgical knife.

'No one who ain't done it,' he maintained, 'can guess how back-breaking that ol' churchyard can be! If I 'ad my strength, I'd be out there now, digging, hoeing, mowing, pruning.'

'Ah! That you would, Piggy-boy,' said one old crone, and the others made appreciative noises of agreement, although every man-jack of them knew that Albert Piggott had skrimshanked all his life, and that the churchyard had never been kept in such a slovenly fashion until it fell into his hands.

'Well, I call it desecration,' said the landlord, twirling a cloth inside a glass. 'Plain desecration! What, flatten all them mounds containing the bones of our forefathers? It's desecration, that's my opinion. Desecration!'

'I'm with you,' said a small man with a big

196

tankard. 'And not only bones! Take a newish grave now, say, old Bob Bright's, for instance. Why, he hasn't even got to the bones stage! He must —'

Someone broke in. 'Them mounds don't have bones or anything else in 'em!'

'What are they, then?'

'Earth, of course. What the coffins displaced. The body has to be a proper depth. That's right, ain't it, Albert?'

Albert drained his glass quickly and put it in a noticeable position on the counter.

'That's right. So many feet, it's all laid down proper, or there'd be trouble. And hard work it is too. Specially in this 'ere clay. But that's what them mounds are, as Tom 'ere says. Simply earth.'

'Another half, Albie?' queried Tom, gratified at being supported by authority.

'I could manage a pint,' said Albert swiftly.

'Right. A pint,' agreed Tom.

'I don't agree about the desecration,' said a large young man with a red and white bobble hat. 'It's more of a desecration to see it full of weeds and beer cans, to my mind. I'm all for straightening it up. It's the living we've got to think of, not the dead.'

'That's sense!' said the small man who had feared more than bones in the mounds.

'Ah!' agreed Albert. 'It's the living what has to keep it tidy, and the living what passes by and has to look at it.'

He took a long swig at the freshly-drawn pint.

'I'm backing the rector,' said bobble-hat. 'He wouldn't do anything what wasn't right, and I reckon his idea's the best one.'

'A good man, Mr Henstock,' said Albert, wagging his head solemnly. 'Wants to do right by the dead and the living.'

'Well, he's not flattening my Auntie May without a struggle,' announced the landlord, still twirling the glass cloth madly.

'We all respect your feelings,' said bobble-hat, 'but they're misplaced, mate.'

Albert put his empty glass on the counter. It rang hollowly.

'You got a thoughtful mind,' he said to bobble-hat, with a slight hiccup. 'A mind what thinks. I can see that. I'm a thinking man myself, and I recognise a man as thinks. A man as has thoughts, I mean. You understand me?'

'Yes,' said the thoughtful one. 'Want another?'

'Thanks,' said Albert simply.

[BATTLES AT THRUSH GREEN]

Poor Charles Henstock suffered greatly in the months that followed. It grieved him to see the warfare among his parishioners, and it was even more difficult to bear when he knew that he was the cause of such bitterness.

However, as time passed, he was able to persuade the objectors to withdraw their criticisms, a faculty was applied for, and the rector waited anxiously.

One blue and white March morning, Willie Marchant, one of the postmen at Thrush Green, tacked purposefully up the hill from Lulling, causing alarm to various drivers going about their lawful business on the right side of the road.

Willie ignored their shouted protestations, as usual, and dismounted from his bicycle at the rectory. A stub of cigarette exuded pungent fumes, killing temporarily the fragrance wafting from a clump of early narcissi.

He opened the door of the rectory and collected half a dozen letters left there, and put the one he was carrying in their place.

'Only one this morning,' called Dimity, when she went to collect the post. Charles was coming down the stairs.

'But it is the one we've been waiting for,' said the new Rural Dean.

He opened it hastily, and his pink face creased into a beam.

'It's granted!' he said, with a gusty sigh of

relief. 'The precious faculty itself . . . to be deposited in the Church Chest. Now, at last after all our battles, we can go ahead!'

[BATTLES AT THRUSH GREEN]

Charles Henstock has always been one of my favourite characters, a kindly modest man who took all his parishioners' troubles to heart. The fact that I had shifted him to Lulling did not remove him from Thrush Green, for he was still rector of that parish and of the neighbouring parishes of Nidden and Lulling Woods.

Always a conscientious visitor, he took particular interest in the old people who lived in the new Rectory Cottages built on the site of his old home. Typical of the man is this encounter with his friend Tom Hardy, one of the home's inmates, on a freezing afternoon.

During the cold weather Jane Cartwright took extra care of the old people in her charge. The health of old Tom Hardy, in particular, caused her some concern, and she mentioned her worries to Charles Henstock one afternoon when he paid a visit to his old friends at the home.

The rector promised to do his best, and made his way to Tom's little house, bending against the vicious wind which whipped his chubby cheeks.

He found the old man sitting by a cheerful fire, fondling the head of his much-loved dog.

To Charles's eye, old Tom seemed much as

usual as he greeted his visitor warmly.

'Come you in, sir, out of this wind. I took Poll out this morning, just across the green, but I reckon that's going to be enough for today.'

'Very wise, Tom. And how are you keeping?'

'Pretty fair, pretty fair. I never cease to be thankful as I'm here, and not down at the old cottage. Jane Cartwright looks after us all a treat.'

Polly came to the rector and put her head trustingly upon his knee. The rector stroked her gently. She was an old friend, and had stayed at Lulling vicarage when her master had a spell in hospital.

Charles wondered whether to mention Jane's concern, and decided that it could do no harm. 'She's a marvellous woman, but I think she worries rather too much about you all. She certainly said just now that she hoped that everything was right for you.'

Tom did not reply.

'She said you seemed pretty healthy, which was good news, but she had the feeling that something was troubling you. Is it anything I can help with?'

Tom sighed. 'It's Polly. I frets about her.'

'But let's get the vet then.'

'It's not that. It's nought as the vet can do. She's got the same trouble as I have, sir. We be too old.'

'We're all getting old,' replied Charles, 'and have to face going some time. But what's wrong otherwise with Polly?'

He looked at the dog's bright eyes, and felt her tail tap against his legs as she responded to her name. 'It's what happens to her when she goes,' said Tom earnestly. 'All the dogs I've had, I've buried in my garden. There's two graves now down at my old place by the river.'

'So what's the difficulty?'

'There's nowhere to bury poor old Poll when her time comes. It grieves me.'

The old man's eyes were full of tears, much to Charles's distress.

'Then you can stop grieving straightaway,' he said robustly, leaning across Polly to pat his old friend's knee. 'If it makes you happier, let Polly be buried in the vicarage garden at Lulling. There are several pets buried there and Polly was well content when she stayed with us.'

Tom's face lit up. 'That's right good of you, sir. It'd be a weight off my mind.'

'And if you go ahead of her, Tom,' said the rector smiling, 'she can come to the vicarage anyway and be among friends. So now stop fretting.'

Tom drew in his breath gustily. 'I wish I could do something to repay you.'

'You can, Tom. What about a cup of tea?'

He watched the old man go with a spring in his step to fill the kettle. He was humming to himself as he went about setting a tray.

If only all his parishioners' troubles could be settled so simply, thought Charles!

[THE SCHOOL AT THRUSH GREEN]

It was no wonder that Dimity's marriage, late in her life, had been so contented. She was as devout and as hard-working as Charles, and together they made a strong team.

During our wartime walks round Wood Green, my daughter and I were often encumbered by a diminutive dolls' pram.

I wish now that we had kept this ancient vehicle. It was very high, very narrow, and decidedly wobbly, but dolls' prams were virtually unobtainable in those dark days, and a kind friend had dug this one from her loft and given it to Jill.

Other small friends had much more modern prams, either their mothers' or bought second-hand, but our antiquated model was the one they all fought over. It was black, rather spidery in appearance, and the battered hood was far from weatherproof, but it was dearly loved.

I tried to dissuade our child from pushing it erratically and energetically in Witney High Street, for people who have been struck smartly in the back of the knee are understandably vexed, and I grew tired of making endless apologies whilst attempting to guide child and pram when bent double.

Wood Green was a safer venue when the dolls' pram was with us. Sometimes we met another of Jill's friends who lived there. Pat's pram was far superior, but she was more than willing to exchange, and the two would push each other's dolls along the New Yatt Road.

In Witney, at that time, most prams, dolls' or otherwise, had beautiful little blankets made from pieces of the local woollen cloth. Even in wartime, it was possible to buy these offcuts of fine quality blankets from the local mills and even lengths of satin ribbon to bind them. It was a joy to handle such rare treasures as everything grew scarcer as the war years rolled on.

It was Pat's father, also in the RAF, who unwittingly gave me a most embarrassing time, and all done through kindness.

He was a great fisherman — and still is. He told me one sunny day that he was going pike fishing on the morrow, and if he caught several he would give me one.

Now, I don't know a great deal about fish, but

Looking north up the High Street towards Wood Green, my Thrush Green

I did know that pike are great scavengers, tucking into old boots, ailing frogs, unwary moorhens, and any dead bodies lying in their waters. The thought of eating pike revolted me, but as I was too cowardly to say so, I thanked him, and prayed that he would not catch one.

I was to rue my politeness because he did catch one, of course. He arrived the next afternoon bearing a long damp parcel swathed in newspaper, and wearing a justifiable air of triumph.

We put it in the shade of the porch. It was a boiling hot day, and when he had gone I knew that I must dispose of the corpse without delay. But how? My landlady assured me that neither she nor her chickens would face pike, even in wartime. I rang various friends. Nothing doing.

I began to realise how difficult it must be for murderers to get rid of their victims. Even a grave for my pike would take some digging. The river Windrush flowed at the end of the garden, but I disliked the idea of polluting that limpid stream, and anyway I didn't want to handle the parcel.

At last inspiration came.

At that time there was a first-class restaurant in the High Street, called The Home Maid. (Later it became The Fuchsia Bush in my Thrush Green novels.)

It was run by a handsome and very competent woman who was an excellent cook. I knew her pretty well. If anyone could cope with a pike she would be the one.

'I'd love it,' she said when I rang. 'I have six

Polish officers coming to supper and I shall give them pike cutlets with a tomato and basil sauce.'

Transporting the pike a hundred yards or so was now the next problem, but after rolling it in more pages of newspaper, I settled it on a mackintosh in the pram. I put up the hood against the scorching sun and Jill and I delivered it thankfully to The Home Maid, and returned home.

It was then that my conscience began to torment me. What should I say if I were asked if I had enjoyed it? Should I tell the truth? Should I simply say 'Delicious!' and hope that that would be the end of the affair? And why on earth hadn't I had the sense to say from the start that I did not eat pike?

I had a wakeful night torturing myself. The next morning, Peggy, Pat's mother, came to see us.

'Did you eat the pike?' she asked.

Faced with this sensibly direct question, I said 'No!'

'Thank heavens!' she said, looking greatly relieved. 'Ours was definitely off.'

My brief respite from guilt was immediately followed by a wave of horror. Those Polish officers!

Had I caused the death of six of our gallant allies? Within minutes I saw them in the Radcliffe Infirmary, or possibly Brize Norton's medical quarters, writhing in their last agonies while letters were being composed in Polish to their next of kin.

By now, completely undone, I babbled out the whole story.

'Let's ring The Home Maid,' suggested Peggy, with admirable calm.

'Nothing to worry about,' said the owner over the telephone. 'I realised it was off when I undid the parcel, so they had scrambled eggs instead.'

I wished that I had a Polish flag to run up.

As it was, Peggy and I celebrated with a cup of wartime coffee before taking our daughters for their walk.

And the moral of this sad, but true, story?

SPEAK THE TRUTH!

But to return to the tour of Thrush Green. The next house, at seven o'clock, beyond the rectory, stood opposite St Andrew's church and was the home of Albert Piggott.

As I have described, Albert is a widower when we first meet him, with Molly, his daughter, doing her best to look after him. But after Molly's marriage to Ben Curdle, he lived alone for a time until Nelly Tilling became his wife, cleaned his house, and cooked him meals which were far too rich for his sorely-tried stomach.

It was hardly surprising that his habitual gloominess was increased by an incipient ulcer, and that Nelly grew more and more impatient with his grumblings. The attentions of the visiting oilman who called every Tuesday at Thrush Green were of great comfort to Nelly at this

207

time, and it was not long before Albert put two and two together.

Albert surveyed the cold November day through his cottage window. It was going to be proper bleak tugging up them old railings. Been stuck there, in Cotswold clay, for a hundred years. They'd take some shifting.

He said as much to Nelly who was whirling about behind him with a tin of polish and a duster. He got short shrift from her.

'A good day's work won't hurt you, Albert. Make a nice change,' she puffed, rubbing energetically at the top of the table. 'Do that liver of yours a power of good.'

Fat lot of sympathy she ever gives me, thought Albert morosely, lifting his greasy cap from the peg behind the door. He dressed slowly, watching his buxom wife attacking the furniture with zest.

All right for some, Albert grumbled to himself, crossing to the windy churchyard. She'd never had a day's illness in her life — strong as a horse, she was — and still game to make eyes at that oilman.

The pain which gnawed intermittently at Albert's inside seemed worse today. Doctor Lovell's pills helped a little, but Nelly's food was too rich, no doubt about it, and he was that starved with hunger when it came to meal times, he ate whatever she provided, dreading too the lash of her tongue if he refused to eat.

He set about the broken railings and found the job as difficult as he had feared. As he tugged, he contemplated his marriage. What a fool he'd been! A clean house and good cooking was no exchange for peace and quiet, and that was what he missed. The only times he had the house to himself were Tuesdays and Fridays when Nelly took herself to Bingo at Lulling.

Or did she? A sudden suspicion made Albert straighten his back and look across Thrush Green. Come to think of it, Bingo was on Saturday night. It dawned, with horrible clarity, on Albert's dull mind, that Nelly must be meeting the oilman on Tuesdays and Fridays.

That was it! Tuesdays was the oilman's half-day, he remembered, and Friday was his payday. It all fitted together.

He bent to his task again, half relishing the scene when he confronted Nelly with his discovery. The pain in his stomach seemed worse, and there was a tight feeling across his chest which he had not suffered before, but he continued tugging with the vigour born of righteous indignation.

He saw Nelly whisk out of the cottage, a basket on her arm, bound for the butcher's down the hill. He gave her no greeting, but watched sourly as her ample back vanished in the distance.

'You wait, my gal,' said Albert grimly. 'You just wait!'

[NEWS FROM THRUSH GREEN]

Hostilities began a few days later at the Piggotts' establishment. Albert's suspicions had grown stronger the more he thought about that oilman. Nelly had certainly seemed unusually happy on Tuesdays and Fridays. There must be some connection.

International crises always seem to occur at weekends. Domestic crises appear to follow the same pattern.

Certainly, there was a crisis at Albert Piggott's home on the Sunday. Nelly had dished up a boiled hand of pork, broad beans, onions and plenty of parsley sauce. She had also excelled herself by providing a Christmas pudding for the second course with a generous helping of brandy butter.

'I made six full-size ones,' said Nelly, surveying the pudding fondly, 'but this little 'un was for a try-out before Christmas. What d'you think of it?'

210

'All right, if your stummick's up to it,' replied Albert dourly, turning his spoon about in the rich fruitiness.

'Lord love old Ireland!' cried Nelly, in exasperation. 'Ain't you a misery? Small thanks I get for slaving away over the stove day in day out. Wouldn't do you no harm to have bread and water for a week.'

'You're right there,' agreed Albert sarcastically. 'You knows full well the doctor said I was to go easy on rich food. I believes you does it apurpose to upset me.'

Nelly rose from the table with surprising swiftness for one of her bulk. She whisked round the table behind her husband, and before he knew what was afoot, she had thrust his head sharply into his plate of pudding.

'*You besom!*' spluttered Albert emerging with a face smothered in the brown mess, and with a badly-bumped nose. He picked up the plate and threw it at his wife. It clattered to the floor, puddingside down, but miraculously did not break.

Nelly, who had dodged successfully, now broke into peals of hysterical laughter as she watched her husband grope his way to the sink to wash off his dessert.

'You wait till I gets my hands on you,' threatened Albert. 'I'll beat the living daylights out of you, my gal! Pity I never done it before. You and that oilman!'

Nelly's shrieks of laughter stopped suddenly.

'You can leave him out of this, Albert Piggott. He knows how to treat a lady.'

'Humph!' grunted Albert, from the depths of the roller-towel on the door. 'I'll bet he knows! I could have the law on him, if I'd a mind, carrying on with another man's wife.'

Nelly adopted a superior aloofness. 'I'm not stopping here to listen to your filthy insinuations,' she said loftily. 'I shall go and have a lay-down, and you can clear up this mess you've made with your tantrums.'

'That I won't!' shouted Albert to her departing back. 'I'm due at church at 2.15 for christenings, and you can damn well clear up your own kitchen!'

The door, slamming behind Nelly, shook the house, and a minute later Albert heard the springs of the bed above squeak under his wife's considerable weight.

Growling, he flung himself into the chair by the fire, picked up the *News of the World*, and prepared to have a quarter of an hour's peace before going across to St Andrew's for his duties.

Hostilities were not resumed until the early evening. Nelly remained upstairs, but ominous thumps and door-bangings proclaimed that she was active. When she re-appeared, she was dressed in her best hat and coat, and was carrying a large suitcase which she set upon the table, taking care to miss the dirty dinner plates and cutlery with which it was still littered.

'Well, Albert, I've had enough,' said Nelly flatly. 'I'm off!'

If she expected any pleading, or even surprise from her husband, she was disappointed. Albert's morose expression remained unchanged.

'Good riddance!' said Albert. 'You asked yourself here and you can go for all I care. But don't come here whining to be took back when that fancy-man of yours has got fed up with you.'

Nelly drew in an outraged breath.

'Come back here? Not if you went down on your bended knees, Albert Piggott, and begged of me! No, not if it was with your dying breath! You've seen the last of me, I can tell you. I'm going where I shall be appreciated!'

She hoisted the case from the table and struggled to the door. Albert remained seated by the fire, the newspaper across his knees, his face surly and implacable.

He remained so for several long minutes, listening to his wife's footsteps dying away as she walked out of his life for ever. He had no doubt that Nelly spoke the truth. Their ways had parted.

He looked at the kitchen clock. Time he went to ring the bell for Evensong.

But when he came to stir himself, the pain across his chest seared him like a red-hot knife. He fell to his knees, his head pillowed on the *News of the World* on the hearthrug, and was

213

unable to move. The last thing he saw, before the blackness engulfed him, was the remains of the Christmas pudding spattered, dark and glutinous, across the kitchen wall.

[NEWS FROM THRUSH GREEN]

Luckily for Albert, help soon arrived. Alarmed at Albert's absence, the rector called in, Harold Shoosmith and Doctor Lovell were summoned, and the rescue began.

'We've got an ambulance on the way for you, Albert,' said Doctor Lovell. 'I want to have a proper look at those innards of yours. Where's your wife?'

'Gorn,' said Albert, in a whisper. 'For good.'

None of the three men tried to dispute the statement. The signs of a fight downstairs, the empty clothes cupboard in the bedroom, and the general disorder, were plain enough. There had been plenty of talk about the Piggotts' differences, and about the oilman's advances. Albert, they knew, was speaking the truth.

'We'd better let her know anyway,' said the doctor. 'Know her address?'

'No,' said Albert shortly. 'Nor want to.' He closed his eyes.

An hour later he was asleep between the sheets at Lulling Cottage Hospital, and Harold and Charles were telling Dimity what had happened.

'She's bound to come back,' she said. 'She

wouldn't leave him just like that — not in hospital, not when she hears that he's ill!'

'I agree that most women would bury the hatchet when they heard that their husbands had been taken ill, but somehow,' said Harold, admiring his whisky against the light, 'I don't think Nelly will return in a hurry.'

'But what will he do?' asked the rector, looking distressed. 'He must have someone to look after him when he comes out of hospital!'

'I know,' said Dimity suddenly. 'I'll write to Molly, his daughter. She married Ben Curdle, the man who owns the fair,' she told Harold. 'She left here just before you came to live here. A dear girl — we all liked her so much. She should know anyway, and perhaps she will come and look after him.'

'He wasn't very nice to her when she did live with him,' ventured the rector doubtfully. 'And now she has Ben and the baby to look after, I really can't see —'

'Never mind,' said Dimity firmly. 'I shall let her know what has happened, and it is up to her to decide. I must ring Joan Young for her address. I know she keeps in touch. They were such friends when Molly used to be nursemaid to Paul.'

She made her way briskly to the study, and the two men heard her talking to Joan.

The rector gave a loud yawn and checked himself hastily.

'I'm so sorry. I'm unconscionably tired. It's

the upset, I suppose. Poor Albert! I feel very distressed for him.'

'You'd feel distressed for Satan himself,' replied Harold affectionately. 'Poor Albert, indeed! I bet he asked for it. I don't blame Nelly for leaving that old devil.'

'I married them myself,' said the rector sadly, gazing at the fire. 'I must admit, I had doubts at the time.'

Dimity returned, a piece of paper fluttering in her hand.

'I've got the address. If I write now, then Willie can take it in the morning.'

'Well, I must be off,' said Harold rising. 'Many thanks for the drink.'

'I've just thought,' cried Dimity, standing transfixed. 'Did you see Albert's cat? I'd better go across and feed it.'

'You leave it till the morning,' advised Harold, patting her thin shoulder. 'It won't hurt tonight. There's plenty of Christmas pudding lying about the kitchen to keep it going.'

[NEWS FROM THRUSH GREEN]

On Albert's return from hospital, he muddled along on his own with some help from Molly, who was now married and living nearby in the Youngs'

house. The fair had been sold, Ben had found work in Lulling, and Molly was happy to be back in her old job. She was also near to her irritable old father.

Molly confronted her incensed father across a zinc bath half full of steaming water.

The kitchen was snug and steamy. The kitchen range was alight, and on its gleaming top stood a large kettle and the biggest saucepan the cottage could boast.

'Never!' shouted Albert, his face suffused with wrath. 'I ain't gettin' in there, and that's flat.'

'You are,' replied Molly. 'You're plain filthy. You smell somethin' chronic, and you can get them rags off of your back for me to wash, or burn maybe, and get soaping. I'll be upstairs, sorting things out, so nobody's going to stare at you.'

'Never!' shouted Albert again. 'Never 'eard such cheek!'

Molly looked at him grimly. 'D'you want me to get the *District Nurse*?'

Albert's bravado cracked a little.

'You wouldn't dare! Besides, it's not decent. That young woman? Why, she ain't even married!'

'She's coming tomorrow if you don't do as I says. Then we'll both get you into the tub. So take your choice.'

Slowly the old man fumbled with the greasy

217

scarf about his scrawny neck. He was muttering crossly to himself.

'That's right,' said Molly, reaching for the kettle. 'I'll just top up the water, and you can have a good soak in front of the fire. See here, I'll spread the towel over the back of the chair. Warm it nice, that will, and keep the draught off of you.'

Her ministrations done, she mounted aloft, leaving the staircase door ajar in order to hear that the old man attended properly to his ablutions. Once he was in, she intended to return to scrub his neglected back, modesty or not. Heaven alone knew when Albert's body had last seen soap and water! Not since his last trip to hospital, Molly suspected.

Albert stepped out of the last of his dilapidated underwear. He put one toe reluctantly into the steaming water.

'Women!' muttered Albert, and braced himself for semi-immersion.

[RETURN TO THRUSH GREEN]

Far away, Nelly Piggott was discovering that Charlie, the oilman, was not only mean with money, but also unfaithful. With some trepidation she decided to return to Albert and life at Thrush Green.

When Nelly Piggott finally arrived at her own doorstep, she dropped her heavy case and grocery carrier and paused to take breath.

The brass door handle, she noticed, was badly tarnished, the step itself thick with footmarks. Behind the sparse wallflowers was lodged a collection of crisp bags, ice-lolly sticks and cigarette cartons which had blown there from the public house next door, and which Albert had failed to remove.

Time I was home, thought Nelly to herself, and opened the door.

'What's going on?' growled Albert thickly. 'Who's that, eh? Get on off!'

There was the sound of a chair being shifted, and Albert still muttering, approached. Nelly swiftly heaved her luggage inside and followed it nimbly, shutting the door behind her.

Albert confronted her. His eyes and mouth were round Os of astonishment, but he soon found his voice.

'None of that, my girl! You're not comin' back here, I'm tellin' you. Clear orf! Go on, you baggage, clear orf, I say!'

He began to advance upon her, one threatening fist upraised, but Nelly took hold of his thin shoulders, and guided him swiftly backwards towards the chair. He sat down with a grunt, and was immediately overtaken by a prolonged fit of coughing.

Nelly stood over him, watching until the paroxysm spent itself.

'Yes, well, you see what happens when you lose your temper,' she said calmly. There was a hint of triumph in her voice which enraged

Albert. He struggled to rise, but Nelly put him down again with one hand.

'Just you be reasonable, Albert Piggott.'

'*Reasonable!*' choked Albert. 'You walks out! You comes back! You expects me to welcome you, as though nothink 'as 'appened? You can go back to that so-and-so. Or 'as he chucked you out?'

'Certainly not,' said Nelly, putting the carrier bag on the table, and feeling for the chops. 'I came of my own accord.'

'Oh, did you? Well, you can damn well go back of your own accord.'

Nelly changed her tactics. 'You may not like it, Albert Piggott, but you'll have to lump it. Here I am, and here I stay, at least for the night, and you can thank your stars as I've brought you some nice chops for your supper. From the look of you, you can do with a square meal.'

Albert lay back. Exhaustion kept him from answering, but the thought of a return to Nelly's cooking, however brief, was a pleasant one.

Nelly began to busy herself about the kitchen, and Albert watched her through half-closed eyes.

'And when did this place last get a scrub up?'

'Molly done it lovely,' whispered Albert, defending his family.

'And not been touched since,' said Nelly

tartly, filling the kettle. 'This frying-pan wants a good going over before it's fit for use.'

She whisked about, unpacking the chops, and some tomatoes and onions. For all his fury, Albert could not help feeling some slight pleasure at the sight of her at her old familiar ploys. He roused himself.

'Seein' as you've pushed yourself in, you'd best stay the night, I suppose. But it'll have to be the spare bed. You ain't comin' in with me.'

'Don't flatter yourself,' said Nelly shortly, investigating dripping in a stone jam jar.

She scoured the pan, and then set the food into it. Once the cooking had begun to her satisfaction, she took up the heavy case and began to mount the stairs.

Albert heard her thumping about above. The fragrant smells of frying onion and chops wreathed about the kitchen, and Albert settled back in his chair with a happy sigh.

[RETURN TO THRUSH GREEN]

Pork Hot-Pot

1 large potato
1 kg (2 lb) lean
    pork
1 apple
1 onion

1 teaspoon chopped
    or dried sage
salt, pepper
stock or water
    to cover

Peel the potato, slice fairly thickly and place in the bottom of a casserole. Cut the meat into decent sized pieces, and arrange in layers with sliced apple and onion; add a sprinkling of sage and seasoning between each layer. Just cover with stock or water.

Place a lid on the casserole, and simmer for 2 hours in a slow to moderate oven (Gas mark 2-3/155-160°C/310-320°F).

This is very good with haricot beans or braised celery.

(Serves 4)

The two settled down together in a state of armed neutrality. It suited Nelly and it suited Albert up to a point. At least he did not have to bother about the house and feeding the cat, or locking up at night. Not that he had taken any of these duties even perfunctorily in Nelly's absence, but he knew that she would cope with all the domestic arrangements, leaving him to grumble about his work in the church opposite.

It was not long before Nelly decided that she wanted a job. She needed the interest as well as the money. For a time she had cleaned Thrush Green school but then she heard that there was a post vacant at the Misses Lovelock.

Nelly Piggott lost no time in calling upon the Misses Lovelock in Lulling High Street.

The sun was still warmly bathing Thrush Green in golden light when she set out from her home. It was half past six, and Albert was already next door at The Two Pheasants, despite Nelly's protestations.

From berating him, Nelly had turned to more womanly tactics, and on this particular evening, dressed in her finery for the forthcoming interview, and fragrant with attar of roses, she bestowed a rare kiss upon Albert's forehead.

'Just to please me, Albert dear,' she said in her most seductive tones.

But Albert was not to be wooed. 'That soft soap,' he told her, shaking her off, 'don't cut any ice with me.'

With this splendid mixed metaphor as farewell, he then departed next door, leaving Nelly to collect her handbag and go off in the opposite direction.

She was not particularly upset by her failure to wean Albert from his beer. Nelly took a philosophical view of marriage. All men had their little weaknesses. If Albert's had not been liquor, it might have been wife-beating, or even infidelity, although Nelly was the first to admit that, with Albert's looks, a chance would be a fine thing.

She sailed down the hill and along Lulling High Street, relishing the evening sunshine and her own aura of attar of roses.

The three Misses Lovelock lived in a beautiful Georgian house halfway along the main street. Here they had been born, and the outside and the inside of their home had altered very little, except that there was far more *objets d'art* crowded inside than in their childhood days.

The Misses Lovelock were inveterate collectors, and rarely paid much for their pieces of porcelain, glass and silver. Older inhabitants of Lulling and Thrush Green knew this, and were always on their guard when the sisters called.

Nelly pulled lustily at the old-fashioned iron bell pull at the side of the door, and Bertha opened it.

'I've come about the place, miss,' said Nelly politely.

Bertha's mind, somewhat bewildered, turned to fish. Had they ordered plaice? Perhaps Violet . . .

'I heard you was needing help in the house,' continued Nelly. 'But perhaps you're already suited?'

'Oh, *that* place!' exclaimed Bertha, light dawning. 'No, not yet. Do come in.'

She led the way into the dining-room which,

despite the heat of the glorious day, struck cold and dark.

'If you'll sit down, Mrs Er?'

'Mrs Piggott,' said Nelly, sitting heavily on a delicate Sheraton chair. It creaked ominously, and Bertha felt some anxiety, not only for the chair's safety, but also at her visitor's identity. For, surely, this was the sexton's wife whose conduct had been so scandalous? Hadn't she run away with another man? Oh dear! What would Ada say?

'I will just go and tell my sisters that you are here. You do undertake homework, I suppose?'

'Yes'm. And cooking. I fairly loves cooking.'

'Yes, well — I won't be a moment.'

She fluttered off, leaving Nelly to cast a disparaging eye on the gloomy oil paintings, the heavy velvet curtains and the huge sideboard laden with half a hundredweight of assorted silver. The work the gentry made for themselves!

Bertha, breaking in upon Ada's crochet and Violet's tussle with *The Times* crossword puzzle, gave a breathless account of their visitor.

Her sisters lowered their work slowly, and surveyed her with disapproval.

'But why invite such a person into the house?' asked Ada.

'But can she undertake housework?' asked Violet, more practically.

'Because I didn't know who she was,' cried Bertha, answering Ada, 'and she can certainly do housework. I remember Winnie Bailey telling me what a marvellous job she made of Thrush Green school,' she went on, turning to Violet.

The three sisters exchanged glances of doubt and indecision.

'And another thing,' continued Bertha, 'I've just remembered that she is a first-class cook. It was Winnie who told me that too.'

Ada sighed.

'Well, I suppose we'd better see this person now that she's here.'

She rolled up her crochet work in an exquisite silk scarf, and put it on one side. Violet placed *The Times* on the sofa.

Together the three sisters advanced upon the dining-room. Nelly struggled to her feet as they entered, the chair creaking with relief.

'Do sit down,' said Ada graciously. The three sisters took seats on the other side of the table, and Nelly lowered herself again into the long-suffering chair, and faced them.

'Let me tell you what we require,' said Ada. 'Our present helper is looking after her daughter who is just about to be confined. She will probably be home again in six weeks or so.'

'Yes'm,' said Nelly, surveying the three wrinkled faces before her. Never seen three such scarecrows all together before, she was thinking. Why, they couldn't weigh twenty stone between 'em!

'Two mornings a week, one of them a Friday, but any other morning which would be convenient for you would be quite in order with us.'

She glanced at her sisters, who nodded in agreement.

'Tuesday would suit me best,' said Nelly, thinking of washing day on Monday.

'And I hear that you are an excellent cook, Mrs Piggott.'

Nelly smiled in acknowledgement.

'Perhaps, very occasionally, you might prepare luncheon for us?'

'I'd be pleased to,' said Nelly. She waited to hear about payment.

'Have you brought any references?' inquired Ada.

'Well, no,' confessed Nelly. 'But Miss Watson would speak for me, and the Allens at The Drover's Arms.'

There was a whispered consultation between the three sisters, and much nodding of trembling heads.

'Very well,' said Ada. 'As this will be only a temporary arrangement, we will waive the references. When can you start?'

Nelly decided that she must take a firm stand.

'I should like to know the wages, ma'am, before saying "Yes" or "No".'

'We pay fifty pence an hour, Mrs Piggott, and should like three hours each morning. You would receive three pounds a week.'

Fifty pence! thought Nelly. It was the least she had ever been offered, but it would be useful, and the job looked like being one after her own heart.

Ada, seeing the hesitation, added swiftly: 'You would be paid extra, of course, if you prepared a meal while you were here. Another fifty pence, Violet? Bertha?'

'Oh, yes, indeed,' they quavered obediently.

Nelly rose.

'Then I'll come next Tuesday,' she said. 'Nine o'clock?'

'I think nine-thirty,' said Ada. 'We breakfast a little late, now that we are approaching middle age.'

She rose too, and the three sisters ushered Nelly out of the front door into Lulling High Street.

'Approaching middle age,' repeated Nelly to herself, as she set off for Thrush Green. 'That's a laugh! They must be over eighty, every one of them! Well, I shan't make a fortune there, but it'll be a nice change from cleaning Albert's place.'

[RETURN TO THRUSH GREEN]

But the job with the Lovelock sisters proved most unsatisfactory, as Nelly found before many days had passed.

It was the *meanness* of the three ladies which infuriated Nelly. It was one thing to find that the dusters provided consisted of squares cut from much-worn undergarments, but quite another to be denied the tin of furniture polish.

Miss Violet had undone the lid, selected one of the deplorable squares, and scooped out about a teaspoonful of the polish upon it.

'That,' she told Nelly, 'should be *quite* enough for the dining-room.'

Seeing Nelly's amazed countenance, she had added swiftly: 'Come to me again, Nelly, if you need more, although I hardly think you will find it necessary.'

She had swept from the room, tin in hand, leaving Nelly speechless.

All the cleaning equipment was handed out in the same parsimonious style. A small puddle of Brasso in a cracked saucer was supposed to cope with the many brass objects in the house. Vim was handled as though it were gold-dust. Washing-up liquid was measured by the thimbleful. It was more than Nelly could stand, and she said so.

Her complaints brought very little improvement, and Nelly retaliated by cleaning all that she could, and leaving the rest as soon as the rations for the day ran out. But she resented it bitterly. She *liked* to see things clean, and never stinted cleaning agents in her own home.

However, she comforted herself with the thought that it was only for six weeks, maybe less. Surely, she could stick it out for that time, especially as nothing else had cropped up to give her alternative employment?

The memory of the lunch she had been obliged to cook made her shudder. Nelly respected food, and always chose the best when shopping. It was no good being a first-class cook, as she knew she was, if the materials were poor. You might just as well try to paint a portrait with creosote.

When Miss Bertha had fluttered into the kitchen that morning, and had asked her to cook that day's luncheon, Nelly's spirits had risen. She had visions of rolling out the lightest of pastry, of whipping eggs and cream, of tenderising steak or skinning some delicate fish cooked in butter.

'And you will stay to have some too, Nelly, I hope.'

'Thank you, ma'am,' said Nelly, envisaging herself at the kitchen table with a heaped plate of her own excellent cooking. Albert had been left with a cold pork-pie, some home-made brawn, strong cheese and pickled shallots, so Nelly had no qualms on his behalf. She had told him that she intended to shop in the afternoon. Really, things had worked out very well, she told herself, and this would save her going to The Fuchsia Bush for a cup of coffee and a sandwich, as she had planned.

Miss Bertha vanished into the larder and appeared with a small piece of smoked fillet of cod. It was the tail end, very thin, and weighed about six ounces. To Nelly's experienced eye it might provide one rather inferior helping, if eked out with, say, a poached egg on top.

'Well, here we are,' said Bertha happily. 'If you could poach this and share it between three, I mean, *four*, of course.'

'Is this all? inquired Nelly flabbergasted. 'Why, our cat would polish that off and look for more!'

Miss Bertha appeared not to hear, as she made her way back to the larder, leaving Nelly gazing at the fish with dismay.

'You'd like poached eggs with this, I take it?' said Nelly.

Bertha put two small eggs carefully beside the fish. 'We prefer scrambled eggs, Nelly. These two, well beaten, should be ample for us all.'

'There won't be enough,' said Nelly flatly.

'We add a little milk.'

'Horrible!' protested Nelly. 'Should never be done with scrambled eggs. Butter's all you need, and a little pepper and salt.'

'Not *butter!*' gasped Bertha. 'We always use margarine in cooking. *Butter* would be *most* extravagant!'

Nelly began to see that she would certainly need to visit The Fuchsia Bush to supplement the starvation diet being planned.

'Vegetables?' she managed to ask.

'Plenty of spinach, Nelly, in the garden, and I thought some rhubarb for pudding. There is still some growing by the cold frame. I will leave out the sugar for you.'

'Very well, ma'am,' she said as politely as her outraged sensibilities would allow.

She finished drying the breakfast things, and went, basket in hand, to fetch the spinach and rhubarb. On her return, she found half a cupful of granulated sugar awaiting its union with the rhubarb, and about half an ounce of margarine.

Nelly left the spinach to soak, and wiped the thin sticks of rhubarb. They were well past their best, and showed rusty marks when she chopped them.

For the rest of the morning Nelly seethed over the appalling ingredients which were to make a lunch for four people.

'Not enough for a sparrow,' she muttered to herself, as she went about her chores. 'And all windy stuff too. If those old scarecrows is doubled up this afternoon, it won't be my fault, and that's flat!'

She cooked the food as best she could. It grieved her to be using margarine instead of butter, but there was nothing else to use, and mighty little of that.

Miss Violet had set the table. The heavy Georgian silver gleamed, the glasses sparkled, and handmade lace mats lay like snowflakes on the polished mahogany.

Nelly carried in the dish of fish and scrambled egg and placed it before Miss Ada at the head of the table.

'I took the liberty, ma'am,' said Nelly, 'of picking a sprig of parsley to garnish it.' Her face expressed scorn.

Miss Ada inclined her head graciously.

'You did quite rightly,' she said. 'It all looks delicious.'

Nelly returned to the kitchen and surveyed the teaspoonful of food upon her plate. At that moment, the cat leapt through the window.

'Here,' said Nelly, handing down the plate, 'try your luck with that.'

Delicately, with infinite caution, the cat sniffed at the food. A rose petal tongue emerged

233

to lick the fish tentatively, then the cat shuddered slightly, and turned away.

'And I don't blame you,' said Nelly. She threw the scraps out of the window, and watched a gaggle of sparrows descend upon them.

'What I could do to a nice fillet steak!' mourned Nelly, preparing to carry in the dish of sour rhubarb, unadorned by any such rich accompaniment as cream or custard.

Later, when Nelly had washed up and had been complimented upon her cooking by the three old ladies, Nelly tried to forget the whole shocking experience. Never again, she told herself, never again! Not if they went down on their brittle old bended knees would she be party to such a travesty of cooking! It was more than flesh and blood could stand. Nevertheless, she was determined to stick out the six weeks.

It was hardly surprising that Albert found her exceptionally snappy that evening. Nelly had suffered much.

[RETURN TO THRUSH GREEN]

Smoked Haddock and Sweet Corn

750 g (1½ lb)
  smoked haddock
  (smoked fillet of
  cod can be used,
  if preferred)
500 g (1 lb) sweet
  corn, frozen or
  canned
30 g (1 oz) butter
seasoning

For white sauce
30 g (1 oz) butter
30 g (1 oz) flour
300 ml (½ pint)
  milk
seasoning

Put a generous layer of drained sweet corn into a casserole. Cut the fish into squares or strips and arrange on the corn, dotting with a little butter, and sprinkling lightly with salt and pepper. Put the rest of the sweet corn over the fish.

Make 300 ml (½ pint) white sauce and pour over the ingredients in the casserole. Cover, and cook gently for 30-40 minutes in a moderate oven (Gas mark 3-4/160-190°C/320-370°F). Remove lid about 5-10 minutes before serving so that the top browns a little.

Spinach or pureed tomatoes go well with this dish, and if a more substantial meal is needed then poached eggs, or *oeufs mollet* can be served with it.

(Serves 4)

Rhubarb Fluff

1 kg (2 lb) forced
  rhubarb
150-175 g (5-6 oz)
  caster sugar
  (preferably vanilla-flavoured)

200 ml (7 fl oz)
  double cream

There is usually plenty of forced rhubarb about at the beginning of the year. Chop it into short pieces and simmer until soft with the sugar and 3 tablespoons of water. Whisk to a puree or put into a blender.

Whip the cream, not too stiffly; fold it into the rhubarb, and serve very cold.

(Serves 4)

Nelly completed her time in the Lovelocks' employment and later found her true vocation next door at The Fuchsia Bush. It came about because of an accident to Mrs Jefferson, an old-timer there. Mrs Peters, who owned the restaurant, told Ella Bembridge and Dimity Henstock the sad tale, and it was they who suggested that Nelly might help.

That same evening, as soon as The Fuchsia Bush closed, weary Mrs Peters climbed into her little car and turned its nose towards Thrush Green.

She had spent the day trying to deputise for

the absent Mrs Jefferson, and at the same time attempting to galvanise her lethargic staff to greater efforts.

Really, thought Mrs Peters, it was much simpler to do the job oneself, rather than urge such lumps as Rosa and Gloria to give a hand. Mrs Jefferson had been one of the old school, punctual, hard-working and taking a pride in all her kitchen creations.

The two women had much in common and had grown to admire and respect each other. Both were widows, and both had been obliged to work to bring up their children single-handed. They were equally energetic, willing to put in many hours of work, and both deplored the slackness of the younger generation.

Mrs Peters drove up the steep hill to Thrush Green, mourning the temporary loss of her old colleague. She did not know Nelly Piggott, as far as she could recall, but it was worth seeing her from what Miss Bembridge and Mrs Henstock had said, although she was not particularly hopeful.

She drew up outside Albert's cottage, much to the interest of the clients in The Two Pheasants, who gazed unashamedly as she waited on the doorstep next door.

The step, she noticed, was freshly whitened, and the windows gleamed. It boded well, thought Mrs Peters.

The door opened and Nelly stood before her looking a little puzzled. As soon as she saw her,

Mrs Peters realised that this was the fat lady who at one time had attended the Misses Lovelock as a char, and whom she had seen passing The Fuchsia Bush. She remembered now that she *cleaned,* but did she *cook?* She only had the two ladies' word for it.

'I'm from The Fuchsia Bush,' began its owner. 'I wondered if you could help me. Miss Bembridge mentioned you to me this morning.'

'Come in,' said Nelly.

The kitchen shone as cleanly as the doorstep, noticed Mrs Peters with pleasure. She took the chair offered her, and put her gloves and handbag on the checked tablecloth. A bunch of pinks, in an old-fashioned earthenware honey pot, scented the air. Mrs Peters had not seen such a honey pot since she was a child, and felt a warm glow of nostalgia for such a homely vessel.

Albert was out at his church duties with his young assistant, and Nelly had obviously been knitting a jumper so vast it could only have been for herself. A delicious smell of cooking mingled with the scent from the pinks.

'You said something about help,' said Nelly, tidying away the knitting.

Mrs Peters told the sad tale of Mrs Jefferson, and Nelly listened attentively. Her spirits rose with the unfolding of the story, but she tried to hide her excitement. It all sounded too good to be true.

'Well, I've never done cooking for *numbers,* if you follow me,' she said, 'and I always believe in having the very best ingredients. No substitutes or made-up stuff, I mean.'

'We only use the best at The Fuchsia Bush,' her prospective employer told her, with a touch of hauteur. 'I have my reputation to consider.'

'Oh, I only mentioned it,' replied Nelly hastily, 'because I occasionally cooked a meal for them Lovelocks, and the food wasn't what I've been used to at all.'

Mrs Peters unbent at once. The Misses Lovelocks' cuisine was a by-word in Lulling. Her heart warmed towards Nelly.

'I'm sure you would soon get the hang of coping with numbers,' she assured her, 'and of course I should be there to help you. It's mainly small cakes and biscuits, and at midday we offer a cold buffet or one hot dish, something simple like curried lamb and rice, or cottage pie. And there's always soup. We keep a very good stock pot.'

At the thought of a very good stock pot, Nelly was quite won over. It would be lovely to play in a really properly equipped kitchen, instead of this poky little place of Albert's. And she would be free of him for the best part of the day, and what's more earning some money of her own.

'What wages were you offering?' she asked.

Mrs Peters mentioned a sum which seemed extremely large and generous.

'Well, if you think I can do it,' said Nelly diffidently, 'I'm willing to try my hand with you.'

Something sizzled in the oven, and Nelly excused herself as she bent to open the oven door. A gust of delicious cooking odours blew into the room, reminding Mrs Peters how famished she was.

Nelly bore a magnificent pie to the end of the table where a wooden mat was waiting. The crust was golden brown and neatly indented round the edge. Four beautiful leaves splayed across the top, glossy with egg-yolk gilding. From the centre where the pie-funnel stood, came a little plume of fragrant steam. It was a vision of beauty. It was quite enough to convince that connoisseur of pies, Mrs Peters, that here was a mistress of her craft.

'Steak and kidney,' said Nelly. 'I like a bit of puff for that. Lighter than shortcrust, I always think, and my husband suffers with his stomach, so I have to be careful what I put in front of him. Personally, I enjoy making a nice raised pork pie, but it's too rich for him these days.'

'A raised pork pie,' echoed Mrs Peters, quite faint now with hunger. 'Perhaps you would like to make a really large one for the cold table when you come?'

'Nothing I'd enjoy more,' Nelly assured her. 'And when would you like me to start, ma'am?'

Now that she was engaged, Nelly started as she meant to go on, with due respect. Who knows? She might be taken on permanently if she proved satisfactory.

'You couldn't manage tomorrow, I suppose?' ventured Mrs Peters, her eyes still on the masterpiece before her.

'I'd just love to,' said Nelly sincerely, and stood up as her visitor rose.

'I'm so grateful,' said Mrs Peters. 'Tomorrow then at nine, or eight-thirty if you can manage it.'

'Eight-thirty, ma'am,' promised Nelly.

And with a last look of longing at Nelly's pie, Mrs Peters went to her car, her stomach rumbling protestingly at being denied its rights.

[AFFAIRS AT THRUSH GREEN]

Having this employment made all the difference to Nelly. She enjoyed the company at The Fuchsia Bush and the knowledge that her skills were appreciated. Also, she liked earning money of her own.

241

Matters at the Piggott household continued to run with unaccustomed harmony. Nelly, still happy in her job at The Fuchsia Bush, was made still happier when she discovered that she had lost almost a stone in weight and felt all the better for it.

It was not lack of food. She usually had a substantial lunch provided by The Fuchsia Bush, but there was no doubt that the semi-run downhill to Lulling, and the arduous plod back after work, were giving the lady much-needed exercise.

Better still, from Nelly's point of view, was the healthy state of her Post Office savings' account. It now stood at one hundred and seventy-five pounds, boosted most satisfactorily by the fifty-pound Bingo winnings.

All in all, Nelly found life at Thrush Green much pleasanter than she had expected on her nervous return from the perfidious Charlie. Of him, she had heard nothing. She assumed that his entanglement with his new love still engrossed him. They were both welcome, Nelly told herself. She had had quite enough of love. Good health, a nice job and money behind her really provided a much more satisfactory state of mind, and she said as much to her new friend, Mrs Jenner, as they puffed uphill one evening from a Bingo session.

'You're quite right, Nelly,' said Mrs Jenner. 'I know Albert's behaving himself very well at the moment, and looking forward to spending time with Miss Harmer's goat Dulcie, so he's in good spirits, but you watch your step, my dear! Put as much in your account as you can. There's nothing like a bit of money behind you. That way you can be independent, and I don't care what all the book-writers say about love and marriage. To my mind, you can't trust men.'

And with this sentiment Nelly heartily agreed.

[AFFAIRS AT THRUSH GREEN]

Nelly and Mrs Peters became good friends, and when the latter went down with influenza one bitter winter's day, Nelly was quite capable of running the restaurant. She was in for a surprise, however.

Just after twelve, Nelly hurried through from the kitchen. Only two tables were being used, she noticed, as she set a tray of freshly-filled rolls on the counter for the office workers and shop assistants who might be expected very soon.

The windows were steamy, but she noticed a figure studying the name above the shop. Soon the door bell gave its familiar tinkle, and a snow-plastered man appeared.

An icy blast accompanied him. He took off his snowy cap and shook it energetically.

'You get some cruel weather up here, Nelly,' he said.

To that lady's horror, she saw that it was her old paramour Charlie, once the visiting oilman at Thrush Green, who had turned her away from his bed and board when he had discovered a more attractive partner.

'And what,' said Nelly, in a tone as frigid as the world outside, 'do you think you're doing here?'

'You don't sound very welcoming,' replied Charlie, looking hurt.

'I don't feel it after the way you treated me,' responded Nelly. She became conscious of the interest of the two customers, and lowered her voice. A quick glance had shown her that this was not the spruce, confident Charlie that she remembered. Snow apart, there was a seedy look about his clothes, his shoes were cracked, he had no gloves, and the canvas hold-all was soaked. Despite herself, Nelly's heart was touched.

'Well, we can't talk here. Come through to the kitchen, and I'll put your wet things to dry.'

What a blessing, she thought agitatedly, that Mrs Peters was away! How to have explained this unwanted visitor would have been a real headache.

Charlie stood about looking awkward while Nelly hung up his outdoor clothes near the massive stoves. Gloria, Rosa and the two kitchen maids gazed at him open-mouthed.

'Just carry on,' said Nelly, 'I'll be with you in two shakes. Come through to the store room, Charlie.'

Here there was silence. Nelly pushed a pair of steps forward for Charlie's use, and sat herself in the only available chair.

'Well, Charlie, let's hear all about it. Where's Gladys?'

Gladys was her erstwhile friend who had usurped her place in Charlie's fickle attentions. It was Gladys who had caused Nelly's return to Albert a year or two ago. As can be imagined, there was not much love lost between the two ladies.

'She upped and left me. Went back to Norman, same as you went back to Albert. And how's that old misery?'

'You can keep a civil tongue in your head about my husband. He's no Romeo, but he's treated me right since I got back, and we've settled down pretty solidly. Don't think you've any chance of getting me back, Charlie, because I'm not coming. Times have changed, and I'm doing very well for myself here.'

'So I heard. That's partly why I came. Thought you might have a job for me.'

'A job?'

'The fact is things went from bad to worse for me. Gladys was always at me for more money. In the end I sold the business.'

'But what are you living on?'

'Social security mainly. I flogged the furniture, so that brought in a bit. Now I'm looking for a job.'

Nelly took another glance at the cracked shoes and the wet ends of his trouser legs. For a moment she weakened, for she was a kind-hearted woman. But reason held sway, and she spoke firmly.

'Look here, Charlie. There's nothing here for you in the way of work. Lulling's as badly hit as all the other towns, and no one's going to employ a chap your age with no real qualifications.'

Charlie looked down at his hands, twisting them this way and that in his embarrassment.

'Well, if that's the case, I'd better be off. I thought I'd make my way to Birmingham to see old Nobby.'

'Nobby?'

'Don't you remember Nobby Clark? Mary was his missus. They kept the ironmonger's on the corner. Nice pair.'

'Is he offering you a job?'

'Yes, in a way. When his dad died in Birmingham, he left Nobby his shop. A sweetshop,

246

it is, with newspapers and postcards, and all that lark. He said he could do with some help if I needed work.'

'Sounds the best thing you could do,' said Nelly decidedly. 'Does he know you're coming?'

'No. I thought I'd see you first.'

And worm your way into my affections again as well as finding a job, thought Nelly.

'Before you set off,' said Nelly, 'you're going to have a good hot meal, and you can ring Nobby from here to say you are on your way. Where are you staying?'

'With them, I take it.'

'In that case, she'll need a bit of notice to make up a bed. You can use the phone in the office, and then go straight through to the restaurant. I've got to be getting back to my work. We're short-handed with the boss away ill.'

Charlie nodded his agreement, and Nelly ushered him into the office while she bustled back to the kitchen.

'That's an old acquaintance of mine,' she said to the girls. 'Down on his luck, and off to Birmingham this afternoon. Don't charge him, mind. Give the bill to me.'

Within the hour, just as The Fuchsia Bush's regular customers were beginning to struggle in, shivering with cold, Charlie had finished his meal.

He went through to the kitchen to fetch his clothes and to say goodbye to Nelly.

He was looking all the better for his meal,

she noted approvingly. There was a hint of the old chirpy Charlie who had first stolen her heart, but she had no intention of succumbing to his charms again.

She was alone in the kitchen, and she took advantage of their privacy to enquire about the state of his immediate finances.

He held open his wallet. It contained two five-pound notes.

'I've got a bit of loose change,' he said, rattling a trouser pocket.

'That won't get you far,' said Nelly, opening her handbag. 'Here, take these two fivers. It'll go towards the fare. The bus to Oxford goes in ten minutes, and you'll have to get a train or bus on to Birmingham from there.'

He put them with the other two notes in his wallet, and muttered his thanks, so brokenly, that Nelly looked at him in surprise. To her amazement she saw tears in his eyes for the first time.

Much embarrassed, she hastened across the kitchen to the dresser where the remaining ham and tongue rolls lay in the wooden tray.

She thrust two into a paper bag and held out the package.

'Put those in your pocket, Charlie. It'll save you buying, and you can eat them on the journey.'

'You're one in a thousand, Nelly. I won't forget all you've done today.'

'That's all right. I'm glad to help, but take

note, Charlie! It's the last time. Don't come trying your luck again. I hope you get on all right with the Clarks. Don't write, nor telephone. It's the end between us now, Charlie, and best that way.'

He bent suddenly and kissed her cheek.

'That's my old love,' he said warmly. 'Don't worry. I won't embarrass you.'

'If you want to get that bus,' replied Nelly, more shaken than she cared to admit, 'you'd best get outside to the bus stop. Thank the Lord the snow's stopped.'

She watched him cross the restaurant, humping his hold-all, and saw the door close. Much as she would have liked to see him board the bus, and perhaps give him a final wave, she was too upset to leave the haven of the kitchen.

Gloria came in balancing a tray on one hip. 'Your friend nearly missed the bus,' she said brightly. 'Got out there just in time.'

'Good,' replied Nelly huskily. She blew her nose energetically.

'Don't you go getting the flu now,' said Gloria, 'or we'll have to shut up shop.'

She spoke with unaccustomed gentleness, but forbore to make any more enquiries.

Later, she said to Rosa: 'The poor old duck was crying when that chap went away. I bet she was sweet on him once, though what anyone could see in an old fellow like that, beats me.'

'One foot in the grave,' agreed Rosa. 'Must

be nearer fifty than forty, poor old thing, *and* going bald.'

'He ate pretty hearty though,' replied Gloria. 'Steak and kidney pie, mashed spud, broad beans, and then the Bakewell tart.'

'Well, she said he was down on his luck,' Rosa reminded her. 'Maybe he didn't have no breakfast. Look out, she's coming back.' The two girls began to stack plates busily by the sink.

Nelly, now in command of herself, bustled into the room. 'Now, Rosa, you can cut the iced slab into squares ready for the tea tables, and there's some fresh shortbread to put out, Gloria. Look lively now, there's plenty to do.'

The two girls exchanged glances. It was quite clear that things were back to normal.

[AT HOME IN THRUSH GREEN]

And that is the last we shall hear about Charlie. Nelly's infatuation with the oilman was over. She was determined to look ahead in her new circumstances.

Next door to the Piggotts' house stands Albert's second home, The Two Pheasants. In real life, a trim public house called The Three Pigeons stands on this spot on Wood Green, and the host and his wife are ever-welcoming, as I can testify.

Mr Jones in the Thrush Green books is equally zealous in his work, and discreet in his dealings with all and sundry.

Curried Lamb

The following recipe would serve 4-6 people. At The Fuchsia Bush, Mrs Peters and Nelly would make enough for about thirty helpings.

3 slices of cold lamb per person	1 dessertspoon curry powder
60 g (2 oz) butter	1 tablespoon chutney
1 large onion	60 ml (1 pint) stock
chopped parsley	1 tablespoon cornflour

Melt the butter, and slice onion into it with a sprinkling of parsley. Cook until light brown. Now add the curry powder, chutney and stock. Stir well and cook for a few minutes.

Thicken this mixture with cornflour, then add the sliced meat and cook for about 15 minutes over a gentle heat.

Serve with a border of rice or mashed potato, and sprinkle more parsley on the top.

Minced lamb or mutton can be used equally successfully, and a few sultanas can be added to the cooking, if liked.

Albert Piggott's first venture outside after his illness did not involve a long journey. He simply took a few paces northward from his own front door to the shelter of The Two Pheasants.

Mr Jones, a kindly man, greeted him cheerfully. 'Well, this is more like it, Albert! How are you then? And what can I get you?'

'I'm pickin' up,' growled Albert. 'Slowly, mind you. I bin real bad this time.'

'Well, we're none of us getting any younger. Takes us longer to get back on an even keel. Half a pint?'

'Make it a pint. I needs buildin' up, Doctor says.'

'Well, your Nelly'll do that for you,' said the landlord heartily, setting a foaming glass mug before his visitor. 'I hear she's doing wonders down at Lulling.'

'That ain't here though, is it?' responded Albert nastily. He wiped the froth from his mouth

The white building across Wood Green
is The Three Pigeons, which I made
The Two Pheasants, Albert Piggott's second home

with the back of his hand, and then transferred it to the side of his trousers.

'You going to get back to work?' enquired Mr Jones, changing the subject diplomatically.

'Not yet. Still under the doctor, see. Young Cooke can pull his weight for a bit. Won't hurt him.'

At that moment Percy Hodge entered and Mr Jones was glad to have another customer to lighten the gloom.

'Wotcher, Albie! You better then?' said Percy.

'No,' said Albert.

'Don't look too bad, do he?' said Percy appealing to the landlord.

'Ah!' said he non-committally. If he agreed, it would only give Albert a chance to refute such an outrageous suggestion, and maybe lead to the disclosure of various symptoms of his illness, some downright revolting, and all distasteful.

On the other hand, if he appeared sympathetic to Albert, claiming that he still looked peaky and should take great care during his convalescence, the results might still be the same, and Albert's descriptions of his ills were not the sort of thing one wished to hear about in a public place.

Mr Jones, used to this kind of situation, betook himself to the other end of the room, dusted a few high shelves and listened to his two clients.

Percy Hodge had a small farm along the road

to Nidden. His first wife Gertie had died some years earlier. For a time, he had attempted to court Jenny, Winnie Bailey's maid, but was repulsed. He then married again, but his second wife had left him. Since then, he had been paying attention to one of the Cooke family, sister to the young Cooke who looked after the church at Thrush Green and its churchyard.

'Still on your own?' asked Albert, dying to know how Percy's amorous affairs were progressing.

'That's right,' said Percy. 'And better off, I reckon. Women are kittle-cattle.'

From this, Albert surmised that the Cooke girl was not being co-operative.

'Here I am,' went on Percy morosely, 'sound in wind and limb. Got a nice house, and a good bit of land, and a tidy bit in Lulling Building Society. You'd think any girl'd jump at the chance.'

'Girls want more than that,' Albert told him.

'How d'you mean?'

'They want more fussing like. Take her some flowers.'

'I've took her some flowers.'

'Chocolates then.'

'I've took her chocolates.'

'Well, I don't know,' said Albert, sounding flummoxed. 'Something out of the garden, say.'

'I've took her onions, turnips, leeks and a ridge cucumber last summer. Didn't do a ha'p'orth of good.'

'Maybe you're not *loving* enough. Girls read about such stuff in books. Gives 'em silly ideas. Makes them want looking after. They wants attention. They wants —'

He broke off searching for the right word.

'*Wooing!*' shouted Mr Jones, who could bear it no longer.

'Ah! That's right! *Wooing*, Perce.'

Percy looked scandalised. 'I'm not acting *soppy* for any girl and that's flat. If they turns down flowers and chocolates and all the rest, then I don't reckon they're worth bothering about. If they don't like me, they can leave me!'

'That's just what they are doing,' pointed out Albert. 'I take it you're still hanging around that Cooke piece as is no better'n she should be.'

Percy's face turned from scarlet to puce.

'You mind your own business!' he bellowed, slamming down his mug and making for the door.

'There was no call for that,' said Mr Jones reproachfully, when the glasses had stopped quivering from the slammed door.

'I likes to stir things up a bit, now and again,' said Albert smugly. 'I'll have a half to top up.'

[THE SCHOOL AT THRUSH GREEN]

There is certainly a public house at Wood Green, but there is no village school. However, I remedied this defect when I started the Thrush Green novels, and inserted the school and school-house between

255

The Two Pheasants and Harold Shoosmith's abode.

The two school-mistresses, Miss Watson and little Miss Fogerty, continued to live in amity at the school-house for a number of years. A great many things happened here — not only were school activities discussed but of course the usual domestic problems. In due course, the two friends made plans to retire together to their favourite resort of Barton-on-Sea. Circumstances postponed the move once or twice, until one winter evening Dorothy suddenly decided that the time had come for action.

'Now who can that be!' exclaimed Dorothy when the telephone rang.

She heaved herself from the armchair and made her way to the hall. A freezing draught blew in as she opened the sitting-room door, and sparks flew up the chimney from a burning log.

Agnes closed the door quietly and hoped that the call would not be a lengthy one. She would have liked to spare dear Dorothy the bother of answering the call, but as headmistress and the true householder it was only right that she should take precedence.

Within a few minutes her friend returned, and held out her hands to the blaze.

'That hall is like an ice-well,' she shuddered. 'Of course, the wind is full on the front porch, and fairly whistling under the door. I fear that this house is getting too old for comfort.'

'Anything important?' queried Agnes. It was so like Dorothy to omit to tell one the main message.

'Only Jane Cartwright. Muriel Fuller has laryngitis and won't be able to come along tomorrow.'

'Poor Miss Fuller!' cried Agnes. 'It can be so painful! Has the doctor been?'

'So I gather. Anyway, it need not make much difference to the timetable. After all, Muriel's visits are very much a fringe benefit.' She picked up her knitting and began to count the stitches.

Agnes considered this last remark. It seemed rather callous, she thought. Her own soft heart was much perturbed at the thought of Miss Fuller's suffering, but Dorothy, of course, had to think of the school's affairs first, and it was only natural that she saw things from the practical point of view.

'Eighty-four!' pronounced Miss Watson, and gazed into the fire. 'You know, Agnes,' she said at length, 'I really think it is time we retired.'

'To bed, do you mean? It's surely much too early!'

'No, no, Agnes!' tutted Dorothy. 'I mean retired properly. We've been talking of it for years now, and the office knows full well that we have only stayed on to oblige the folk there.'

'But we've nowhere to go,' exclaimed Agnes. 'It was one of the reasons we gave for staying on.'

'Yes, yes, I know we couldn't get what we wanted at Barton-on-Sea, but I think we should redouble our efforts. I really don't think I could stand another winter at Thrush Green. Sitting in the hall just now brought it home to me.'

'So what should we do?'

'First of all, I shall write to those estate agents, Better and Better, at Barton, and chivvy them up. They know perfectly well that we want a two-bedroomed bungalow with a small garden, handy for the church and post office and shops. Why they keep sending particulars of top floor flats and converted lighthouses heaven alone knows, but they will have to pull their socks up.'

'Yes, I'm sure that's the first step,' agreed Agnes. 'I will write if it's any help.'

'You'd be much too kind,' said her headmistress. 'I think I could manage something sharper.'

'You may be right,' murmured Agnes. 'But when should we give in our notice?'

'The sooner the better,' said Dorothy firmly. 'We'll arrange to go at the end of the summer term. That gives everyone plenty of time to make new appointments.'

'We shall miss Thrush Green,' said Agnes.

'We shall miss it even more if we succumb to pneumonia in this house,' replied Dorothy tartly. 'We can always visit here from Barton.

We shall have all the time in the world, and there is an excellent coach service in the summer.'

She caught sight of her friend's woebegone face. 'Cheer up, Agnes! It will be something to look forward to while we endure this winter weather. What about a warming drink?'

'I'll go and heat some milk,' said Agnes. 'Or would you like coffee?'

'I think a glass of sherry apiece would do the trick,' replied Dorothy, 'and then we shan't have to leave the fire.'

She rose and went to fetch their comfort from a corner cupboard.

[THE SCHOOL AT THRUSH GREEN]

As anyone who has been house-hunting will know, the next few months were full of anxiety and frustration. An added complication was the arrival of a stray cat which Agnes fed regularly, becoming more and more attached to the animal. Dorothy, unaware of what was happening, reacted with vigour.

'There's that cat!' exclaimed Dorothy suddenly. 'Do you know, that's the second time I've seen him this week. I hope he's not coming regularly.'

Agnes made no answer. Dorothy turned round from the window.

'Agnes, are you *feeding* that cat?'

Little Miss Fogerty's hands trembled as she

put down the knitting into her lap. She took a deep breath.

'Well, yes, Dorothy dear, I am!'

It was Dorothy's turn to breathe in deeply, and her neck began to flush. This was a bad sign, as Agnes knew very well, but now that the matter had arisen she was determined to stick to her guns.

'Well, really, Agnes,' protested her friend, with commendable restraint, 'you know I think it is wrong to encourage the animal. We can't possibly take on a cat now when we are off to Barton in a few months. And what will happen to it when we have gone?'

'I can't see the poor little thing go hungry,' answered Agnes. 'I've only put down milk, and a few scraps.'

'When, may I ask?'

'First thing in the morning, and as it gets dusk. I don't leave the saucers down in case mice or rats come to investigate.'

'I should hope not. In any case, the mere fact of putting food out in the first place is enough to encourage vermin.'

'It's a very *clean* little cat,' said Agnes, becoming agitated.

'I daresay. Most cats are. But I think you have been very silly, and short-sighted too, to have started this nonsense. It's cruel to encourage the poor animal to expect food when we know we shall not be here to provide for it before long.'

'It would be far more cruel to let it starve to death,' retorted Agnes with spirit.

Dorothy rarely saw her friend in such a militant mood, and resolved to deal gently with her.

'Of course it would, Agnes dear. I'm simply pointing out that we must look to the future. If it becomes dependent upon us, it is going to be doubly hard on the animal when it finds we have gone.'

She noticed, with alarm, that Agnes was shaking.

'Perhaps we could find a home for it if it is really a stray,' she continued. 'So often cats go from one house to another for anything they can cadge, when they have a perfectly good home of their own.'

'This one hasn't,' snapped Agnes.

'And how do you know?'

Agnes explained about the Allens' departure, abandoning the cat, and its present plight. By now her face was pink, her eyes filled with tears, and her whole body was quivering.

'Then we must certainly try and find a home for it,' said Dorothy. 'Perhaps the RSPCA could help.'

'I don't see why we shouldn't take it on ourselves,' protested Agnes. 'It is getting tamer every day, and *whatever* you say, Dorothy, I

261

intend to go on feeding it. I am very fond of
the little thing, and I think — I'm sure — it
is fond of me.'

Dorothy gave one of her famous snorts. *'Cupboard love!'* she boomed.

At this the tears began to roll down little Miss
Fogerty's papery old cheeks, and splashed upon
her knitting.

Dorothy, curbing her impatience with heroic
efforts, tried to speak gently. 'Well, carry on
as you are, dear, if you think it right. You know
my own feelings on the subject.'

Agnes blew her nose, and mopped her eyes.
She was too overwrought to speak.

'I think,' said her headmistress, 'that we could
both do with an early bed tonight.'

[THE SCHOOL AT THRUSH GREEN]

Both ladies found the inevitable clearing up, the
farewell ceremonies and the general upheaval profoundly exhausting. A visit from Ray and Kathleen
during this time did nothing to help.

It had been one of those days when everything
had gone wrong. The milk was sour, the school
dinner particularly revolting, one child had hurt
his knee badly, another had spots which looked
suspiciously like chickenpox.

The ladies returned wearily to the school-house.

'I could well do without a visitation from Ray
and Kathleen,' commented Dorothy, as they
cleared away their teacups, 'but there it is. I

only hope they don't stay long. What a day it has been!'

The ladies went upstairs to change from their workaday clothes, and Agnes was just trying to decide whether the occasion warranted the addition of her seed pearls to the general ensemble, when the car arrived.

Dorothy admitted her brother, his wife and the boisterous labrador, Harrison, who luckily was on a lead.

'Is he going to stay indoors?' queried Dorothy, in a far from welcoming tone.

'He'll soon calm down,' Ray was assuring her as Agnes entered the sitting-room. 'He's very obedient these days.'

Harrison leapt upon Agnes and nearly felled her to the Axminster carpet. She sat down abruptly on the couch.

'Down sir!' shouted Ray in a voice which set the sherry glasses tinkling. 'D'you hear me? Down, I say!'

Dorothy put her hands over her ears, Kathleen bridled, and Agnes attempted a polite smile.

'It's just that he's excited,' bawled Ray, tugging at the lead. 'So pleased to see everyone. Awfully affectionate animal!'

The affectionate animal now attempted to clamber on to Agnes's lap. As it was twice her size and weight, she was immediately engulfed.

'Take him out!' screamed Kathleen. 'He's obviously upset. He's extremely highly-strung,'

263

she explained fortissimo, to the dishevelled Agnes.

Reluctantly, Ray tugged the dog outside and, to the relief of the two hostesses, Harrison was deposited in the car.

'Well!' exclaimed Dorothy. 'I should think you could do with a restorative after all that. Sherry, Kathleen?'

'Thank you, but no,' said Kathleen primly. 'I have to keep off all alcohol, my doctor says.'

'Tomato juice, orange juice?'

'Too acid, dear.'

'Perrier?'

'I simply can't digest it,' said Kathleen, with great satisfaction.

'A cup of tea? Or coffee?'

Dorothy was starting to sound desperate, and Agnes noticed that her neck was beginning to flush.

'If I might have a little milk,' said Kathleen, 'I should be grateful.'

'I will fetch it,' said Agnes, anxious to have a moment's peace in the kitchen.

It would be today, she thought, examining the dubious milk, that Kathleen wanted this commodity. For safety's sake, she took the precaution of pouring the liquid through the strainer into a glass, and hoped for the best.

Without Harrison, the sitting-room was comparatively tranquil. There was general conversation about the Dorset holiday, the state of their respective gardens, Ray's health, soon disposed of, and Kathleen's, which threatened to dominate the conversation for at least two hours if not checked.

Over the years, Dorothy had developed considerable expertise in cutting short the recital of her sister-in-law's complaints and their treatment. At times, Agnes had felt that she was perhaps a shade ruthless in her methods, but today, exhausted as she was with the vicissitudes it had brought, she was glad to have the conversation turned in the direction of their own future plans.

'It surprised me,' said Kathleen, 'to know that you haven't found a house yet.'

'It surprises us too,' replied Dorothy tartly. 'It's not for want of trying, I can assure you.'

'Time's getting on,' observed Ray. 'You ought to make up your mind. Prices seem to rise every week.'

Agnes trembled in case Dorothy responded with a typical outburst, but for once her friend remained silent.

'Once we have the car,' Agnes said timidly, 'Dorothy and I intend to have a thorough look at houses.'

'I imagine that you will be getting rid of a good deal of furniture,' remarked Kathleen. 'What do you propose to do about it?'

'Nothing, until we've seen what we need in the new place,' said Dorothy.

Kathleen drew in her breath. Agnes noticed that she cast a quick glance at her husband.

'I only ask,' Kathleen continued, 'because we wondered if we could help at all by taking it off your hands.'

'What had you in mind?' enquired Dorothy, with dangerous calm.

'Well, this nest of tables, for instance,' said Kathleen, putting down the glass of milk, 'and dear Mother's kitchen dresser, and any china which might be too much for the new home.'

'Anything else?' asked Dorothy, her neck now scarlet.

Ray, ill at ease, had now gone to the window, removing himself, man-fashion, from all source of trouble.

'There were one or two items that Ray was always so fond of,' said Kathleen, looking somewhat sharply at her husband's back. 'He often talks of that silver rose bowl his mother always cherished, and her silver dressing-table set.'

'I cherish those too,' said Dorothy.

'And I don't suppose that any of the carpets

266

or curtains will fit the new place,' continued Kathleen happily. 'So do bear us in mind if you are throwing anything away.'

At this point, a desperate howling from Harrison pierced the air, and Ray leapt at the excuse to hurry outside.

'He's probably seen a cat,' said Kathleen. 'Hateful creatures!'

Agnes, full of fears, betook herself to the window. There certainly was a cat in sight, but to her relief it was only Albert Piggott's, an animal which could well take care of itself, and was now sitting smugly on the garden wall, gloating over its imprisoned enemy.

'We must be on our way,' announced Kathleen, much to Agnes's relief. She drained her glass, and began to fidget with her gloves and handbag. 'Who would have thought it was half-past six?'

Ray returned, and seemed glad to see preparations for departure.

'Is he all right?' asked Kathleen anxiously. 'We don't want him unsettled with a journey before him.'

'Just a cat,' replied Ray, in what Agnes felt was an extremely callous manner. Just a cat, indeed!

'It was good of you to break your journey,' said Dorothy, her feelings now under control. 'We'll keep you in touch with our plans. I can't see us moving from here much before the late summer.'

'But won't the new head want it?' queried Ray.

Dorothy explained about the sale of the house, how it was on the open market, and quite separate from the school.

'But we are assured that we shall not be turned out,' added Dorothy.

'I wonder,' began Kathleen, making her way to the front door, 'if it would suit us, Ray?'

'We are quite happy where we are, dear,' Ray said firmly. 'Besides, it would be a terrible upheaval for Harrison. He's so used to his present daily walkies, and no one could be better with him than our local vet.'

'Of course,' said Dorothy, as she kissed them in farewell, 'it would save us taking up the carpets and curtains if you took over, and we might even come to some arrangement about the kitchen dresser. Mother's silver, of course, means too much to me to part with.'

Deafening barking put a stop to all further conversation, and the two drove off with much waving and hooting.

'Well,' said Dorothy, with infinite satisfaction, 'I think I had the last word there!'

[THE SCHOOL AT THRUSH GREEN]

But of course things were settled, and to echo E. M. Delafield's 'Provincial Lady's' favourite quotation: 'Time and the hour run through the roughest day', and the two friends set off at last to the house of their choice at Barton-on-Sea.

Promptly at eight-thirty, the removal van arrived and loading began.

In between supervising the bestowal of their household belongings, Dorothy prepared a substantial picnic lunch, and Agnes superintended the arrangements of Tim the cat's travelling basket.

The greatest worry, of course, was the strong possibility that he would stay well away from all the unaccustomed activity, and Agnes had opened a tin of sardines as a particular bribe.

Amazingly it worked, and Agnes secured the cat in the basket just as the removal men were about to set off.

The two ladies were to follow in the car, and to meet the van at Barton at two-thirty. The time now had come to say goodbye to Isobel and Harold who had been helping them.

But not only Isobel and Harold, it seemed, for although the children of Thrush Green school were supposed to be at school dinner, they were instead all at the railings of the playground, with the three staff standing behind them, smiling and waving.

'What a wonderful send-off!' said Agnes, as they drove off towards Lulling. 'What a nice idea of the headmaster's!'

'Yes, a kindly thought,' agreed Dorothy, negotiating the traffic in Lulling High Street. 'I think the school should do *quite well* under him.'

Greatly content, the two friends drove south-ward to their future.

[THE SCHOOL AT THRUSH GREEN]

Among her school equipment which Agnes left behind for the teachers' use were a set of short poems suitable for young children. These were printed in her own hand, and used to hang round the walls for the children to copy and learn.

One of her favourite poems was this by Humbert Wolfe.

The Lilac

Who thought of the lilac?
'I' Dew said.
'I made up the lilac
Out of my head.'

'She made up the lilac!
Pooh!' thrilled a linnet,
And each dew-note
Had a lilac in it.

Agnes was particularly sad to say goodbye to their neighbours, for Isobel Shoosmith was an old friend from college days, and the fact that she had come to live at Thrush Green was a delight to Agnes.

The two had always kept in touch, but rarely met after Isobel had married and settled in Sussex, and had had a family to rear. After the death of her husband, and when her children were out in the world, Isobel decided to return to the Cotswolds where she had been brought up.

She stayed with Ella for a time while she was house-hunting, and it was then that she met Harold Shoosmith. Over the months that followed, Harold assisted with the exhausting job of looking at houses.

'How I long to get back here!' said Isobel. 'Sussex is beautiful, but it's here I belong.'

'Then we'd better push on to see this house,' said Harold practically, letting in the clutch.

It was not easy to find. The little blue car nosed its way through narrow lanes, between steep banks starred with late primroses and early stitchwort. They passed signposts to Burford, to Asthall Leigh, to Swinbrook, to Witney, and were beginning to wonder if the house really existed when they saw the 'For Sale' sign.

The house was built on the side of a hill, and a steep path went from the lane to the front door. It was a substantial dwelling of honey-gold Cotswold stone, and a scarlet japonica covered the side wall.

'Would you like to come in?' asked Isobel.

'I won't, many thanks,' said Harold. 'It's easier for you to ask questions, and take in what the owners tell you, if you are on your own. I'll wait a little farther down the road, where it is wider.'

'Fine,' said Isobel, collecting her bag and papers. Obviously she was expected, for at that moment the front door opened, and a woman peered out.

Harold watched the two meet, and then drove to the arranged parking place. Here he got out, leant upon a conveniently sited five-barred gate, and surveyed the pleasant scene spread out below him.

He could well understand Isobel's longing to return. His own affection for the area grew with every year that passed. He had never regretted, for one instant, his decision to settle at Thrush Green. He had made many new friends, not an easy thing to accomplish when one was a middle-aged newcomer to a small community; and the countryside was a constant delight.

His own domestic arrangements were also satisfying, although of late he had begun to wonder if the years ahead would prove lonely. He had never regretted his bachelor state. After all, it was of his own choosing, and very contented he had been with it. But observing the happiness of the rector, Charles Henstock, had given Harold cause for thought.

Not that one should contemplate matrimony solely for the betterment of one's lot. Such selfishness would be a sure way to disaster. A true marriage, to Harold's mind, should be a joyous partnership, and if it were not to be so then it were better to remain single.

He had a healthy distrust of strong emotions, and viewed his own present disturbance with mingled amusement, pleasure and caution. But he recognised a deeper feeling towards Isobel which he felt that time would confirm. He hoped that she would soon be living nearby, and that time would prove him right as he grew to know her.

He walked down the lane between the hawthorn hedges shining with new leaf. The sun was warm, some lambs gambolled in the water meadow below, and a thrush sang as it bounced on a flowering spray of blackthorn above him.

When he returned, Isobel was waiting in the car.

'Any luck?' he asked as he climbed into the driver's seat.

Isobel shook her head. 'Too much needs to

be done. It would cost a fortune. And it's dark, and faces north-east. A pity, because the rooms were nice, and my stuff would have looked well there.'

Harold patted her hand.

'Never mind, there'll be others.'

'But I haven't much time. Only two more days. I think I must try and come again later on, when I've sorted things out at home.'

'Must you go this week?'

'I'm afraid so. There are various bits of business to attend to in the next two or three weeks, and I certainly hope to have a few offers for my house to consider.'

Harold nodded. At least it was some comfort to know that she planned to return in the near future.

'Will you stay with Ella again?'

'No, I think not. It's not really fair to her. There's The Fleece, though I'm not keen on staying at hotels. The evenings drag so. But don't let's bother about all that now. Who knows what the next two days may bring? And anyway, what about that cup of tea?'

'Burford may be crowded. What about having tea with me? I can offer you Earl Grey, or Lapsang Souchong, or plain Indian.'

'The last will suit me beautifully,' replied Isobel, with a smile which turned Harold's heart somersaulting.

'Thrush Green it is then,' he replied.

[RETURN TO THRUSH GREEN]

When Isobel returned to Sussex, Harold missed her sorely, weeks went by very slowly, and it was July before she returned to continue house-hunting.

This time, Isobel stayed at Tullivers, next door to Winnie Bailey, for the Hursts were in America and had offered her the house in their absence. It was here that Harold called on her again. He found her in a despondent mood.

'Anything wrong?' he asked, seating himself at the table where her writing things were littered.

Isobel put her hands flat on the table with a gesture of despair.

'A lot, I'm afraid. I was coming to tell you. I shall have to drive home again. There's a muddle about the sale of the house.'

'Can't the estate agent cope with that? Must you go today?'

'Either today, or tomorrow morning. The sale's fallen through again.'

She sighed, and looked so desperately unhappy that Harold could not bear it. He had never seen her cast down. In all their fruitless searchings for a house, she had always managed to maintain a certain buoyancy of spirit which was one of the reasons why he loved her.

He put a hand over one of hers, and spoke urgently. 'Isobel, let me help with this. I can't bear to see you so unhappy, and it's all so unnecessary.'

'Unnecessary?' queried Isobel.

'I've wanted to say something for weeks now, but it has never seemed the right moment. I don't know if this is — but hear me out, Isobel, I beg of you.'

He tightened his grip on her hand, and began his plea. Isobel sat very still, her eyes downcast upon their linked hands, and heard him out as he had asked.

'And will you?' he ended. 'Could you, Isobel?'

She smiled at him, and at last regained her hand.

'Thank you, Harold dear. You must let me think for a day or so. My mind is so confused with all that's happened, I shall need time. But I do thank you, from the bottom of my heart. It is the loveliest thing that has happened to me for a long, long time.'

'You dear girl!' exclaimed Harold. 'And please don't keep me waiting too long! I warn you, I've been in a state of near-dementia for the past months.'

Isobel laughed. 'I promise you an answer before the end of the week, but I must get back and sort out some of this muddle. Oh, the misery of selling and buying houses!'

'You know the way out now,' Harold pointed out.

'You would never know,' replied Isobel, 'if I'd married you or the house.'

'I'll take that risk,' Harold assured her.

[RETURN TO THRUSH GREEN]

276

Of course, the inhabitants of Thrush Green were well aware of the state of Harold Shoosmith's heart, and awaited the outcome with enormous interest. Betty Bell, who helped in the house, was particularly vigilant.

'I bet you miss Mrs Fletcher,' she remarked conversationally, over elevenses.

Harold ignored the remark.

'A real nice lady,' continued Betty, crunching a ginger biscuit. 'Miss Harmer was only saying yesterday as how it would be lovely to have her living here.'

'Here?' interjected Harold. Was it so obvious?

'In Thrush Green,' explained Betty. 'Or nearby. Everyone wants her back.'

Not as much as I do, thought Harold, pushing back his chair.

'Well, I must get on with my hedge-cutting,' he said, making his escape.

It was Betty Bell who answered the telephone half an hour later.

'Hang on,' she shouted cheerfully. 'I'll get him.'

She hung out of the kitchen window. 'Mrs Fletcher on the phone,' she yelled, and admired the speed with which her employer abandoned the shears and sprinted up the path.

She would dearly have loved to listen to the conversation on the bedroom extension, but decided to retreat to the landing where, with any luck, she would be out of sight, and might hear at least one side of the proceedings.

She had to wait some time, for there seemed to be a great deal said at the Sussex end, but at last her vigil was rewarded.

'Oh, Isobel!' cried Harold. 'You darling! Yes, I'll be with you at twelve tomorrow, with a bottle of champagne.'

There was another break, and then: 'I can't say all I want to, but I'll say it tomorrow. Yes. Betty's here, and listening too, I've no doubt. But who cares?'

When a minute later he put down the telephone, Betty sauntered down the stairs with as convincing an air of innocence as she could muster.

'Betty,' said Harold, his face radiant. 'I'm going to get married.'

'Really, sir?'

'To Mrs Fletcher,' said Harold.

'We all said you would,' said Betty, picking up her duster.

[RETURN TO THRUSH GREEN]

The marriage proved to be a happy one, and Harold Shoosmith and his wife were particularly popular in Thrush Green. They were on excellent terms with their next door neighbours, Dorothy and Agnes, and when Dorothy decided to take driving lessons in preparation for their retirement, Harold did his best to advise them.

As Agnes had guessed, Harold was proving most helpful on the subject of Dorothy's driving tuition and the buying of a small car.

The two ladies had been invited next door for a drink to discuss matters and Harold was waxing enthusiastic.

It was strange, thought Agnes, how animated most men became when discussing machinery. Her dear father, she recalled, could read a book without any sort of reaction to its contents. It was the same with a play or a concert. He was quite unmoved by these products of the arts, but his joy in his old tricycle, upon which he rode when delivering the shoes he repaired, was immense.

Later, he had taken to driving a three-wheeled Morgan and the same fanatical light had gleamed in his eyes. To Agnes, any form of locomotion was simply the means of getting from one place to another and she looked upon this male fever as just one more incomprehensible facet of man's nature.

'I've thought a good deal about driving lessons,' Harold was saying. 'I shouldn't get Reg

Bull if I were you. I'd offer myself, but I don't know that friends make the best instructors. Worse still are spouses, of course, but you are spared those.'

'I certainly shouldn't have allowed you to teach me,' said Isobel. 'As it is, you gasp whenever I let in the clutch.'

'Do I? I never realised that!'

'Well, you do. And very trying it is,' said his wife briskly. 'But go on. Tell Dorothy your bright idea.'

'It occurred to us both, that perhaps Ben Curdle would be willing to give you lessons. He's a marvellous driver, very steady and calm. I'm sure he'd be first-class. So long as he's willing, of course, to let you learn on his Ford. It's a good gearbox. You could do worse than buy a little Ford when the time comes.'

'Ben Curdle would be just the man,' agreed Miss Watson. 'But would he do it? He doesn't seem to have much spare time.'

'If you like, I will have a word with him and let you know the result. One thing I do know — he would be glad to earn some money in his spare time.'

'That would be very kind of you. I have the greatest respect for Ben, so like his dear grandmother. If he will take me on, I shall be delighted.'

'And, of course,' added Harold, 'I can take you out occasionally for a run in my car, just to get the hang of things.'

'How lovely! I should appreciate that. And I hope you will advise me when it comes to buying a car.'

Harold's eyes sparkled at the prospect. 'What was the car you drove earlier?' he enquired.

Dorothy frowned with concentration. 'Now, what was it? I know it was a red one, with rather pretty upholstery, but I can't think what make it was.'

Harold looked flabbergasted.

'I'm sure the name will come back to you when you are not thinking about it,' said Isobel soothingly. 'Like throwing out the newspaper and knowing immediately what ten down was in the crossword. Harold, Agnes's glass is empty.'

Recalled to his duties as host, Harold crossed to the side-table, but he still appeared numb with shock at the abysmal ignorance of the female mind.

[THE SCHOOL AT THRUSH GREEN]

The Shoosmiths, in common with the rest of the Thrush Green people, awaited the new headmaster of the school, and the arrival of new neighbours at the school-house. Whoever arrived would be thoroughly scrutinised, his history known, his family background explored, his character and his earnings discussed, in the time-honoured tradition of all country communities.

And so our gentle tour of Thrush Green ends, but there are two establishments which play important parts in our drama.

Dotty Harmer lived a few minutes' walk from Thrush Green. The narrow footpath beside Albert Piggott's cottage led across buttercup fields to Lulling Woods, and on the left-hand side was Dotty's cottage, sitting as snug and foursquare as a cat, in a slight dell.

As I remember that area in war-time, there was no such cottage to be seen if you walked down that footpath. But there were certainly fields, and buttercups grew there at the right and proper time.

The footpath ran parallel to one of the chief roads in Witney, called West End. One of the houses in that street had a particular claim to fame as it was the subject of the song:

The 'old-fashioned house' was about halfway along on the right-hand side of this photograph

In an old-fashioned house
In an old-fashioned street
In a quaint little old-fashioned town.

and Jill and I had the pleasure of having tea there one day. She was allowed to roll out the dough for the scones, the pastry board lodged on the kitchen chair for easier operation. Not many hostesses are willing to indulge a three-year-old with such understanding.

In the same street lodged two sisters, war-time evacuees as we were, and their three children were Jill's particular friends.

All the gardens on the northern side of West End led to the buttercup fields which I describe so often in the Thrush Green books, and some of them had gates between garden and field.

Now many houses have been built on the fields between the New Yatt Road and the Hailey road, and Lulling Woods and The Drover's Arms were, I must confess, only in my mind.

Dotty Harmer is one of my favourite dolls. She is, despite her idiosyncracies, brave, honest and a great lover of animals. She is also unpredictable and pig-headed, and when she was left a car in her brother's will, the inhabitants of Thrush Green were rightly alarmed. Surely, she would not attempt to drive it? It was years since she had possessed a vehicle, and even in those comparatively traffic-free days, Dotty's driving had been a public menace.

But drive it she did, and Harold Shoosmith, as

a newcomer to Thrush Green, clapped eyes for the first time on Dotty Harmer as a driver.

He became conscious of a cacophony of horn-blowing coming from the steep hill which led from Thrush Green to Lulling.

Harold strode over to the green, and stood by the statue of his hero, Nathaniel Patten, the better to see the cause of the fuss. The main road, leading northward to the Midlands, appeared to be free from traffic. Whatever the obstruction was which was causing such irritation to so many drivers, was out of sight.

Harold continued to wait. The children from the village school, just let out to play, crowded against the railings behind him like so many inquisitive monkeys.

Albert Piggott appeared on his doorstep. Joan Young, girt in her gardening apron, came across the chestnut avenue, trowel in hand, to join Harold, and at least a dozen twitching curtains told of more sightseers.

'Do you think there's been an accident?' asked Joan. 'Perhaps we should go over.'

Even as she spoke, a small car, jerking spasmodically, came into view. It was impossible to see, at that distance, who held the wheel, but Harold guessed, correctly, who it might be.

'Dotty!' cried Harold and Joan in unison, setting off across the grass at a brisk pace.

By the time they arrived, the car had come to another stop just outside Ella Bembridge's house. Behind it stretched a long queue, the end of it out of sight in the main street of Lulling. Immediately behind Dotty's small vehicle was a Land-Rover towing a horse-box.

'Get the bloody thing off the road!' shouted the driver. His face was scarlet with wrath as he leant out of the side window. 'Damn women drivers! No business to have a licence!'

Further protestations came from those behind, and the additional music of car horns rent the air.

Dotty, peering agitatedly at the car pedals, was pink herself and very cross indeed.

'Here,' said Harold, wrenching open the door, 'hop out, Miss Harmer, and I'll park her in the side road.'

'Why should I get out?' demanded Dotty. 'And what right have you to order me out of my own carriage, may I ask?'

'Pull the old besom out,' begged the Land-

Rover driver. He began to open his door, and Harold feared that battle would be joined.

'*Please,*' he pleaded. 'You see, there is such a long queue, and this road is far too narrow here to overtake safely. I'm afraid that the police will be along to see what's happening.'

'*You* may be afraid of the police,' said Dotty sharply, 'but I am *not*. Now kindly take your hand from the door.'

'But —' began Harold, but could not continue as, by some miracle of combustion, the engine had started again into spasmodic life and Dotty moved slowly, in a succession of convulsive jerks, into the side road leading to the church. There was a mild explosion, a puff of smoke, the car stopped, and Dotty put forth her deplorably-stockinged legs and got out.

'Stick to your bike, lady!' shouted the Land-Rover man rudely, as he quickened his pace along the main road. A few imprecations, some shaken fists and vulgar gestures were directed towards Dotty as other cars passed, but most of the drivers contented themselves with re-signed glances as they glimpsed the scarecrow figure of the one who was responsible for their delay.

The three of them waited until the last of the queue vanished northwards, before speaking.

'Would you allow me to have a look at the car?' asked Harold.

'Of course, of course,' said Dotty airily, as

if washing her hands of the whole affair.

At this moment, Ella appeared and crossed the road.

'What on earth have you been up to, Dotty? Never heard such a racket since just before D-day when we had all those tanks rumbling through.'

'I simply drove quietly from West Street up the hill here. Just because I do not care to *scorch* along, this queue formed behind me. I had some difficulty in changing gear at the bottom, I must admit, but there was no need for the vulgar demonstration of impatience which you have just witnessed. No manners anywhere these days! A pity some of these men weren't taught by my father. He wouldn't have spared the strap, I can tell you!'

Harold climbed out of the car and came towards them. 'It's quite a simple problem,' he said. 'The petrol's run out.'

'The *petrol?*' echoed Dotty. 'But we only filled it when we brought the car home, not ten days ago!'

'Nevertheless, it's empty now.'

'But how can you tell?' demanded Dotty. 'You didn't put in your dip stick.'

'There's a little gauge on the dashboard,' explained Harold patiently. 'Perhaps you would allow me to show you?'

'Don't trouble,' said Dotty, setting off towards the car. 'I'll just push her round, if you'll give me a hand, and coast down the hill to Reg

287

Bull's for some fuel.'

'But it's not allowed!' cried Joan.

'You'll stop halfway along the High Street, Dot.'

Dotty looked coldly at her old friend. 'I suppose there are still plenty of people capable of *pushing* me along to Reg Bull's,' she said witheringly. 'It's little enough to ask.'

Harold took command. Years of administration in far-flung corners of the world stood him in good stead.

'I have a spare gallon of petrol in my garage, and I shall put it into your tank, Miss Harmer. That should get you home safely, and then you can fill up next time you are out.'

'And while Harold's doing that,' said Ella, 'you can come and see my parsley. You know you said you wanted a root to take you through the winter.'

'Very well, very well,' muttered Dotty, allowing herself to be led away.

Joan Young accompanied Harold back across the green. Her expression was troubled.

'You know, she really shouldn't be allowed to drive that car.'

'I absolutely agree,' said Harold. 'But what's to be done?'

'I don't know, but I feel sure there's going to be some awful accident if Dotty is going to drive around these parts.'

'That might be a blessing in disguise,' said Harold, opening his gate. 'If she had to go to court, she might be taken off the road for a while.'

'Let's hope it doesn't come to that,' exclaimed Joan.

'There was a lot to be said,' remarked Harold reflectively, 'for a man with a red flag going ahead of a car in the early days of motoring.'

'Dotty could do with one,' laughed Joan, 'but I wouldn't volunteer for the job if I were you.'

'No fear!' said Harold, making for the garage.

[BATTLES AT THRUSH GREEN]

It was only to be expected that Dotty would drive into trouble, and this she did before many weeks had passed.

The overcast sky was beginning to darken as Dotty backed cautiously out of the car park and set the nose of the car towards Thrush Green.

The High Street was busier than usual. Housewives were rushing about doing their last-minute shopping. Mothers were meeting young children from school, and older children, yelling with delight at being let out of the classroom, tore up and down the pavements.

Some of them poured from the school gateway as Dotty chugged along. Several were on bicycles. They swerved in and out, turning perilously to shout ribaldries to their friends similarly mounted.

Dotty, still agitated at the thought of so much to do before nightfall, was only partly conscious of the dangers around her. She kept to her usual thirty miles an hour, and held her course steadily.

Unfortunately, one of the young cyclists did not. Heady with freedom, he tacked along on a bicycle too big for him, weaving an erratic course a few yards ahead of Dotty's car.

The inevitable happened. Dotty's nearside wing caught the boy's back wheel. He crashed to the ground, striking the back of his head on the edge of the kerb whilst Dotty drove inexorably over the bicycle.

She stopped more rapidly than she had ever done in her life, got out and hurried back to the scene. A small crowd had collected in those few seconds, expressing dismay and exchanging advice on the best way to deal with the injured child.

'You take 'is legs. I'll 'old 'is 'ead!' shouted one.

'You'll bust 'is spine,' warned another. 'Leave 'im be.'

'Anyone sent for the ambulance?'

'Where's the police?'

Amidst the hubbub stood the rock-like figure of a stout American boy, known vaguely to Dotty. His face was impassive. His jaws worked rhythmically upon his chewing gum.

He was the first to address Dotty as she arrived, breathless and appalled.

'He's dead, ma!' he said laconically, and then stood back to allow PC John Darwin 42469, stationed — unfortunately for him — at Lulling, to take charge.

[BATTLES AT THRUSH GREEN]

Within hours, of course, the news was all round Lulling and Thrush Green. There is nothing so potent as a disaster — to someone else, of course — to set tongues wagging.

'Bad luck about Miss Harmer, isn't it?' cried Betty Bell when she reported for her morning duties at Harold's. 'I called in to see her on my way up. She don't say much, but she looks a bit shook up.'

'She's bound to be upset,' said Harold diplomatically, watching Betty unwind the cord of the Hoover from the intricate figure of eight which she employed for its resting hours.

Harold had asked her, on many occasions, to wind it straightforwardly up and down, because of breaking the covering of the cord, but he might just as well have addressed the moon on the subject, and was now resigned to the habit.

'She's a funny old party,' announced Betty, dropping the plug with a crack on the kitchen tiles. Harold winced, but remained silent.

'I know she feels bad about that Cooke kid, but she won't say so. Says it was all the child's fault. He wasn't looking where he was going, and she was, and all that. Let's hope she's got some people as'll back her up.'

'There must have been plenty of witnesses

at that time of day.'

'Ah, *witnesses!*' agreed Betty knowingly. 'But who's going to *be* a witness? As soon as a policeman comes they all scarpers, don't they? Don't want to know. Might have to spend a day in court having questions fired at 'em. You can understand it really.'

'It's a duty, Betty, which every citizen must accept.'

'Well, you try telling that to some of them Lulling lot! The only person I've heard of so far is Mr Levy, the butcher. He saw it all evidently. Anyway, Mr Venables'll nobble him, I expect, to speak for old Dot — Miss Harmer, I mean.'

Harold was relieved to hear that the redoubtable Dotty had seen fit to call in help, even if it was in the ageing form of Justin Venables. However, he did not pursue that subject with Betty.

'Thought I'd make a start in the bathroom,' shouted his help, heaving the Hoover towards the stairs. 'You finished up there? Shaving, and that?'

'Yes, thank you,' said Harold. For a moment he felt as he had done at the age of six, when a particularly strict nurse had had charge of him, and demanded to know the most intimate details of his morning sojourn in the bathroom. It was only his advanced age, Harold felt, that kept Betty from just such an inquisition.

Halfway up the stairs she paused and put her

face over the banisters.

'Know what I told her? I said them Cookes needed more'n a crack on the head to knock them out. And what's more, it was no good worrying about going to court. If it comes, it comes, I told her. It's no good fretting about right or wrong, or what really happened. It's the chap who lies best wins the case.'

She resumed her ascent, leaving Harold to muse on the layman's view of the legal profession.

[BATTLES AT THRUSH GREEN]

In due course, Dotty was summoned to appear in the local magistrates' court. She was defended by her old friend Justin Venables, and many friends came to support her.

'I will call my client,' Justin said, when the prosecutor sat down.

Dotty entered the witness box and picked up the New Testament.

'Please remove your glove,' said the usher.

'As you wish,' said Dotty, tugging at the splendid suede pair.

She took the oath firmly.

'Now, Miss Harmer, will you direct your answers to the bench,' said Justin, 'although I am asking the questions?'

Dotty turned obediently, recognised Mrs Fothergill as an acquaintance, and wished her 'Good morning' affably.

Mrs Fothergill gave a sickly smile, but forbore to reply. Lady Winter and the chairman ignored Dotty's civility, and remained impassive.

'You are Dorothy Amelia Russell Harmer, residing at Woodside, Lulling?' said Justin, in dulcet tones.

'You know I am!' responded Dotty, astonished.

'A formality,' murmured Justin. Good heavens, was she going to be in one of her prickly moods?

He led her, with exquisite caution, through her narrative. It soon became clear, that despite her odd appearance and a certain impatience with some of the questions, Dotty was transparently honest about the whole affair. She was not in the least put out by some fairly searching questions by the prosecution, and even congratulated the police in having such a pleasant young fellow as Mr Darwin in the force, before Justin could quell her.

Mr Levy, enjoying every moment of his public appearance as witness, was equally hard to restrain.

'You saw the boy riding before the accident?' asked Justin.

'If you can call it riding,' said Mr Levy. 'He was on a bike far too big for him — sawing away he was, wobbling all whichways, and yelling to his mates. He swerved straight into Miss Harmer. She was well into the middle of the road. I'll take my oath on it —'

'You have,' put in Mr Pearson, the clerk to the court, drily.

'And I've known Miss Harmer since she was a little girl, and she's as straight as a die! She'd say if she'd been at fault. It was that ruddy boy — begging your worships' pardon — as crashed across her path.'

'Miss Harmer's integrity is not in question,' said Justin austerely. 'Just let us take your account of the boy's movements, point by point.'

With some difficulty he led his ebullient witness through his story. The prosecutor had no questions to ask. Nor had the bench.

Justin's last witness was one of the teaching staff who had been in the playground when the accident occurred. He was a nervous young man, but Justin soon put him at ease, and he agreed that the boys were rather noisy and excited when they left school, and did not take as much care as they should about traffic conditions. He agreed with Mr Levy that Cyril

Cooke's bicycle was in a poor state and much too big for him. He himself had told Mrs Cooke so, and suggested that the boy should walk to school. She had not been co-operative.

By now it was almost one o'clock, and Charles Henstock was beginning to get hungry. The rest of the spectators appeared unaffected and were obviously content to wait for the case to be completed.

Justin Venables gave a brief but well-expressed summing up on behalf of his client, pointing out that she had held a licence for almost half a century, and that she had no previous convictions. To his mind, the prosecution had failed to prove the charge and he suggested, with all due respect, that it should be dismissed.

'Bench will retire,' growled Mr Jardine, and Mrs Fothergill led out the three.

Charles remained standing so as to ease his aching back. Whoever had designed the public seats in Lulling Court deserved to be sentenced to sitting in them for twenty-four hours non-stop, he decided.

The Misses Lovelock, aflutter with scarves and gloves, came up to speak to him.

'Didn't Dotty do splendidly?' quavered Miss Violet.

'Surely she will not be found guilty?' said Miss Bertha.

'I always knew she was a cautious driver,' said Miss Ada. 'I hope that horrid boy gets sent to a penal institution.'

Charles did not feel equal to explaining that the boy was not being charged, only Dotty, and was spared further conversation by the return of the justices.

Dotty remained standing by Justin Venables. Suddenly pale, she looked incredibly old and tired. Charles felt shaken with anxiety for her. What an ordeal! He would be glad to get her into his car and back to the haven of the rectory and Dimity's ministrations.

Mr Jardine cleared his throat with peremptory honkings.

'We find you not guilty of the offence with which you have been charged.'

Dotty looked with bewilderment towards Justin Venables, who was smiling and bowing.

'The case,' explained Mr Jardine, looking directly at Dotty, 'is dismissed.'

Dotty inclined her head graciously, and murmured thanks.

'The court will adjourn until two o'clock,' said Mr Jardine.

Everyone stood, as the bench retired. The door to the magistrates' room had scarcely closed when Dotty's clear voice was heard.

'Could you, by any chance, lend me a handkerchief, Mr Venables?'

Head up, back like a ramrod, Dotty faced her solicitor. Tears were coursing down her papery old cheeks and splashing unchecked upon the fur coat.

But, through the tears, Dotty's expression was one of utter triumph.

[BATTLES AT THRUSH GREEN]

Odd Dotty might be, but she was respected by all, and not least by Albert Piggott. The two had a strange affinity.

Albert Piggott's first real outing was down the footpath at the side of his cottage to visit Dotty Harmer.

He had, of course, visited The Two Pheasants daily, and during the brief spell of warm weather, had shared a seat on the green with Tom Hardy and Polly one bright morning.

But this was his first proper walk, and he sniffed the air appreciatively as he made his way towards Dotty's cottage some quarter of a mile away.

It was good to be out and about again after his enforced sojourn indoors. Some young dandelion leaves caught his eye, and he pulled a few as a present for Dotty's rabbits.

Bending down caught his breath, and he had to stand still for a while in case a fit of coughing followed, but all was well.

He watched a coral-breasted chaffinch hopping about the hawthorn hedge where it had its home. A rook floated down across the field on its black satin wings, and in the distance he could hear the metallic croak of a pheasant, now safe from man's guns.

Albert felt almost happy. He liked being alone. He liked all the country sounds and smells. They reminded him of his boyhood in these parts when he had run across this same meadow at buttercup time, and gilded his broken boots with their pollen.

He looked forward to seeing Dotty after so long. The two strange people had much in common. Neither cared a button about appearances or other people's opinions of them. Both loved the earth and all that could be grown in it. Both had a way with animals, preferring them to their own kind, and each respected the other.

Dotty was well wrapped up in a man's old duffel coat girded at the waist with orange binder twine. She wore a balaclava helmet, knitted in airforce-blue wool, which was obviously a relic from the days of war.

Wellington boots, much muddied, hid her skinny legs, but her hands were bare and as muddy as her boots.

Her face lit up as Albert approached.

'My dear Albert! This is a lovely surprise. Come and sit on the garden seat, and tell me how you are.'

'Not too bad, considering,' replied Albert, secretly much touched by the warmth of her welcome. 'You better now?'

'Never had anything wrong,' asserted Dotty roundly. 'But you know what families are.'

'I do that,' agreed Albert. 'Everlastin' worryin'.'

Dotty waved towards a small, freshly constructed pond, around which half a dozen Muscovy ducks were sliding happily.

'You haven't seen that, have you, Albert? Kit dug it out and lined it. So clever. The only thing is, I want your advice about shady plants.'

Albert considered the problem. He did not like to criticise the work done by her niece's husband, but it would never do. The ducks were slithering about on the muddy edge of Kit Armitage's creation, and it was obvious that nothing much would grow there while the birds disturbed the surroundings.

'If I was you,' he said, 'I'd put some sort of stone edging round it.'

'But it would look *horrible!*' cried Dotty. 'Like those paddling pools you see in municipal parks!'

Albert could not recall ever seeing a paddling pool nor, for that matter, a municipal park though he supposed she meant something like the playground at Lulling.

'I never meant concrete,' he explained. 'Some nice flat bits of Cotswold stone. Percy Hodge has got no end of odd slabs lying about where his old pigsties was. Settle in nicely round that pond they would.'

'But the plants? I thought of shrubs. Some sort of willow perhaps.'

'You'd be best off standing a few tubs around with some nice bushy fuchsias or lilies. That way you could shift 'em about where you wanted 'em, and them ducks couldn't flatten the plants. Keep the edges dry too. Ducks slop enough water about to drown growing stuff.'

Dotty was silent, envisaging the picture sketched by her companion. It could be the answer. It was practical too.

'Albert,' she said, putting her skinny claw upon his sleeve, 'you are quite right! What a comfort you are!'

Albert smirked. He was seldom praised, and had certainly never been told that he was a comfort to anyone.

He cleared his throat awkwardly. He was as pink with pleasure and embarrassment as a young suitor.

'Well, I don't know —' he began deprecatingly.

'Well, I do!' replied Dotty. 'Now when can we get hold of Percy to discuss buying the stone?'

Albert straightened his shoulders. He looked as determined as a military commander.

'You leave it to me, miss! You leave it to me!'
[THE SCHOOL AT THRUSH GREEN]

It was lucky that her sensible niece Connie and her husband Kit Armitage lived with the old lady. The incomparable Betty Bell, who looked after the Shoosmiths and Thrush Green school, also included Dotty among her employers.

She called in one day to find Dotty trying to fill in a form. The day was hot, and several flies buzzed about the kitchen table.

'You've got some real nasty flies in here,' said Betty.

'Poor things,' said Miss Harmer, putting down her pen. 'So persecuted. I often wonder if they are as dangerous to health as modern pundits suggest. My grandmother used to sing a charming little song to my baby brother when flies were *quite accepted*.'

She began to sing in a small cracked voice, while Betty watched her with mingled exasperation and amusement.

Baby bye, there's a fly,
Let us watch it, you and I.
There it crawls, up the walls,
Yet it never falls.

I believe with those six legs
You and I could walk on eggs.
There he goes, on his toes,
Tickling baby's nose.

'Well!' said Betty, 'fancy letting it! Downright insanitary!'

Dotty tapped the neglected form with her pen. 'Now, how did it go on?'

Round and round, on the ground,
On the ceiling he is found.
Catch him? No, let him go,
Do not hurt him so.

Now you see his wings of silk
Dabbling in the baby's milk.
Fie, oh fie, you foolish fly!
How will you get dry?

'Did you ever?' exclaimed Betty. 'I mean, flies in the *milk!*'

'Well, it only goes to show how kind-hearted the Victorians were. And really so much more sensible about disease. My brother grew into a splendid specimen of manhood, despite flies.'

Betty looked at the clock. 'Tell you what, Miss Harmer, I'll come back for that form this afternoon. It'll give you time to work it out, and anyway Willie don't collect till five o'clock.'

Besides that, she thought privately, there was her shopping to do, and heaven alone knew when that would get done if she stayed listening to old Dotty.

'Perhaps that would be best,' agreed Dotty,

turning again to her task, while Betty made her escape.

[GOSSIP FROM THRUSH GREEN]

I have never seen that particular ditty written down, but my mother, who would have been over a hundred had she lived, used to sing it when we were small. I must say that I like the concern shown for the wet fly in the last two lines. Bad luck on the baby though!

Among my dolls, the three Misses Lovelock are some of my favourites. I think that most of us have our own particular streak of parsimony, hoarding lengths of string, storing the wrappings from butter ready to grease baking tins, cherishing chipped dishes which 'might come in useful', but never do.

We also know, I suspect, people who carry these economies into every part of their lives. They will walk the length of the High Street to buy sultanas at a halfpenny a pound cheaper than elsewhere. The fact that they are dog-tired and have probably worn out three penn'orth of shoe-leather on this excursion, does not dim the triumph they feel in obtaining the sultanas. And why not, if it gives them pleasure? Quite often such people are well-to-do, and have no need to seek out bargains. But that is beside the point. It is the feeling of success which gives them such satisfaction, and the Misses Lovelock are prime examples.

It has always been recognised in Thrush Green

that an invitation to a meal at the Misses Lovelock necessitated a substantial snack before setting off for the occasion.

Dotty Harmer, who usually made a meal of an apple or any handy crust of bread whilst gardening, or concocting some of her deplorable wine, pickles or preserves, did not bother to take the usual precautions.

Food meant little to her, which was just as well when she went one day to have lunch with Bertha, Ada and Violet.

The luncheon party was a great success. The meal was served on a fine drum table. The four chairs drawn up to it were of Sheraton design with shield backs. The silver gleamed, the linen and lace cloth was like some gigantic snowflake. Nothing could be faulted, except the food. What little there was, was passable. The sad fact was that the parsimonious ladies never supplied enough.

Four wafer-thin slices of ham were flanked by four small sausage rolls. The sprig of parsley decorating this dish was delightfully fresh. The salad, which accompanied the meat dish, consisted of a few wisps of mustard and cress, one tomato cut into four, and half a hard-boiled egg chopped small.

For the gluttonous, there was provided another small dish, of exquisite Meissen, which bore four slices of cold beetroot and four pickled onions.

The paucity of the food did not dismay Dotty in the least. Used as she was to standing in her kitchen with an apple in her hand at lunchtime, the present spread seemed positively lavish.

Ada helped her guest to one slice of ham, one sausage roll and the sprig of parsley, and invited her to help herself from the remaining bounty. Bertha proffered the salad, and Dotty, chatting brightly, helped herself liberally to mustard and cress and two pieces of tomato. Meaning glances flashed between the three sisters, but Dotty was blissfully unaware of any contretemps.

'No, no beetroot or onion, thank you,' she said, waving away the Meissen dish. There was an audible sigh of relief from Bertha.

The ladies, who only boasted five molars between them, ate daintily with their front teeth like four well-bred rabbits, and exchanged snippets of news, mainly of a scurrilous nature.

'I saw the dear vicar and Mr Shoosmith pass along the street this morning. And where were they bound, I wonder? And what was dear Dimity doing?'

'The washing, I should think,' said Dotty, eminently practical. 'And I can't tell you what the men were up to. Parish work, no doubt.'

'Let's hope so,' said Violet, in a tone which belied her words. 'But I *thought* I saw a picnic basket on the back seat, with a *bottle* in it.'

'Of course, it's racing today at Cheltenham,' said Ada pensively.

The second course consisted of what Bertha

termed 'a cold shape', made with cornflour, watered milk and not enough sugar. As it had no vestige of colour or flavour, 'a cold shape' seemed a fairly accurate description. Some cold bottled gooseberries, inadequately topped and tailed, accompanied this inspiring dish, of which Dotty ate heartily.

'Never bother with a pudding myself,' she prattled happily, wiping her mouth on a snowy scrap of ancient linen. 'Enjoy it all the more when I'm given it,' she added.

The Misses Lovelock murmured their gratification, and they moved to the drawing-room where the Cona coffee apparatus was beginning to bubble.

What with one thing and another, it was almost a quarter to four before Dotty became conscious of the time. She leapt to her feet like a startled hare, and grabbed her handbag, spectacle case, scarf and gloves which she had strewn about her en route from one room to another.

'I must get home before dark. The chickens, you know, and Ella will be calling for her milk, and Dulcie gets entangled so easily in her chain.'

The ladies made soothing noises as she babbled on, and inserted her skinny arms into the deplorable jacket which Lulling had known for so many years. Hasty kisses were planted on papery old cheeks, thanks cascaded from Dotty as she struggled with the front door, and descended the three steps outside.

The three frail figures, waving and smiling,

clustered in their doorway watching the figure of their old friend hurrying towards the car park.

'What sweet old things!' commented a woman passing in her car. 'Like something out of *Cranford*.'

Needless to say, she was a stranger to Lulling.

[BATTLES AT THRUSH GREEN]

The amount of silver in the Lovelocks' household was prodigious, and a great deal was on display in the drawing-room. It did not surprise anyone to learn that an opportunist thief had swiped the major part of the silver so readily on view, and the general feeling was that 'those Lovelock sisters had asked for it'.

But not long afterwards the word went round that the police had recovered a substantial amount of silver, and that Bertha, Ada and Violet had been summoned to the police station to see if they could identify any of their property.

Full of hope, the three sisters tottered along one bright morning, stopping only by the Corn Exchange to read some extraordinary messages, written in chalk, on the walls of that building. The words were not familiar to the three ladies, but the content of the slogans was. The writer presumably did not approve of the Prime Minister nor of the country's police force.

'But, Violet,' said Ada in bewilderment, 'does one spell that word like that?'

'Ada dear,' said Violet with some hauteur, 'it is not a word that I find myself needing to spell.'

Bertha, as usual, took charge.

'We must draw the attention of the officer on duty to this defacement, when we call in. I'm sure he will deal quite competently with the matter, correct spelling or not. It is not the sort of matter for ladies to concern themselves with.'

'Should you end your sentence with a preposition, Bertha?' asked Violet innocently.

But she was ignored, and the three mounted the steps of the police station.

Sadly, there was only one of the Lovelocks' lost objects among the display set out on the trestle table in a back room with Police Constable Darwin on guard.

'Father's rose bowl!' cried Ada.

'What a miracle!' cried Violet.

'Given to him on his retirement!' cried Bertha. 'How wonderful of you to recover it.'

They walked slowly round and round the table, gloating over the beautiful objects before them.

'And where did you find all these lovely things, officer? So clever of you.'

'Well, miss,' said Police Constable Darwin, 'I'm not at liberty to say, but it wasn't us chaps at Lulling as came across this lot. But several people, besides you ladies, have lost stuff around here, so it's our turn to show it.'

'And have the other people found theirs here?'

'You was the first to be asked,' the constable told them.

'Well, that is most gratifying. Most kind. We feel quite honoured, I assure you. Now, are we allowed to take home Father's rose bowl?'

'I'm afraid not, miss. It'll have to be exhibited in court, see, when we've picked up the thieves. There's still a lot missing. If you notice, miss, all this is the big stuff, salvers and bowls and that.'

With commendable delicacy he ignored a seventeenth-century toilet set, with a pair of silver chamber pots to match, and directed the Misses Lovelocks' attention to trays, teapots and other tableware, including the rose bowl, which stood at the farther end of the table.

'We reckon this is only about a quarter of

what's missing. The smaller stuff's probably been passed on. Melted down already, I don't doubt.'

There were horrified gasps from the ladies, and Police Constable Darwin hastily tried to make amends for his gaffe.

'But let's hope not. After all, this lot's turned up. Keep your fingers crossed, ladies. Anyway, I'll mark this rose bowl down in the book as belonging to you. Want another look round to make sure?'

'No, thank you, officer. You have been most helpful. There was just one other little matter,' added Bertha, the natural spokesman of all three.

'Yes, miss?'

'Have you been on outside duty this morning? On your beat, I believe is the correct expression?'

'Well, no, miss. I was detailed by Sergeant Brown to stand by this lot this morning. Very valuable stuff here. But I'll pass on any message.'

Bertha wondered if this fresh-faced young man would really be experienced enough to deal with the unpleasant matter of the Corn Exchange's graffiti, but she decided swiftly that he had probably been adequately trained and was quite used to seeing — and perhaps even hearing — the phrases written on the wall.

'We just wanted to direct your attention, officer, to some quite dreadful messages written with some prominence on a public building nearby.'

'Oh, them scribbles on the Corn Exchange,' replied the constable, with relief. He had begun to wonder just what else these old tabbies were going to disclose. 'Don't you worry about them. One of the Cooke boys, no doubt. Anyway, a chap's been told to clean it up, so everything's under control.'

'I'm delighted to hear it,' said Bertha graciously.

'In very bad taste to deface a building with such words,' added Ada in support.

'And not even correctly spelt,' said Violet, adding her mite.

'I think,' said Bertha ominously, 'it is time we returned home.'

[GOSSIP FROM THRUSH GREEN]

Getting help in the Lovelocks' house was, as we have seen already, something of a problem. Nelly Piggott had had her spell there, but was quick to hand in her resignation from the post.

Later, Doreen Lilly, a young single woman with a little boy to bring up, applied for the job. Her mother Gladys had mentioned it to Nelly Piggott at bingo one evening. Naturally, Nelly was hesitant.

'I know some old ladies who want some help,' said Nelly hesitantly. 'But I'm not sure whether the job would suit her.'

'She can but try,' responded Mrs Lilly. 'She knows she'll have to knuckle down to a bit of hard work to keep herself and the boy. But she's certainly not living with me! For one thing I've no room, and after two days we'd be fighting like Kilkenny cats.'

'I'll do what I can,' promised Nelly, feeling some sympathy for the daughter and her problems.

The Misses Lovelock were duly informed at their next Wednesday lunch at The Fuchsia Bush, and word was sent to Gladys Lilly that they would be pleased to interview Doreen as soon as possible.

'Not that I am altogether happy about the idea of employing an unmarried mother,' observed Ada, when they were back in their cluttered drawing-room.

'Oh, really, Ada,' exclaimed Violet, 'what difference will it make to her housework?' She was struggling with that day's crossword puzzle, and finding an anagram of 'grenadine' particularly elusive.

'It's not her *housework* that is in question, but her *morals*,' pointed out Bertha.

'Well, we can't do much about that,' said Violet flatly. 'It sounds to me as though she has had a hard time. Nelly said the father has vanished completely, and left this poor girl in the lurch.'

'It is very unwise,' pronounced Ada, 'to try and pre-judge the girl, and to let our hearts rule our heads. All we can do is to sum up her abilities when she comes for interview, and to show her what will be required of her. I gather from Nelly that the girl has first to find lodgings, as Mrs Lilly has no room for the daughter and child.'

'What about the top floor?' said Violet. 'There's our old nursery and the maid's bedroom.'

'Out of the question,' said Ada, rolling up her knitting. 'This house is *quite* unsuitable for a young child.'

Violet was about to say that all three of them had been born and reared in this same house, but Ada had on the look which brooked no arguing, and in any case Violet had just realised that 'endearing' fitted her clue, and so busied herself in filling it in.

[THE SCHOOL AT THRUSH GREEN]

And so Doreen Lilly made her way along Lulling High Street to her appointment. She had been warned by her mother, and by Nelly Piggott, that the job might be a hard one, and that the three sisters would be demanding. Even so, she was taken aback by the size of the house and by the old-fashioned formality of the ladies.

The Misses Lovelock interviewed Miss Lilly in their dining-room. They sat in a row at one side of the immense mahogany table, and Doreen on the other, facing them.

She was a wispy little thing with fluffy fair hair, and a permanently open mouth, indicative of adenoids. But she was clean and polite.

Miss Violet's kind heart warmed to her. She looked so young to be the mother of a three-year-old.

The girl confessed that she had no written references from her previous post, but said that she knew her employer's name and address and the number of her telephone.

'I was there nearly two years,' she said. 'She'll speak for me, I know. It was after that row with my boyfriend I decided I'd be better off nearer my mum.'

'A row?' queried Bertha.

'That's when he lit off,' explained Doreen.

'Lit off?' said Ada.

'Cleared out,' said Doreen.

'Cleared out?' echoed Bertha.

'Slung his hook,' agreed Doreen.

'Slung —' began Violet. 'You mean he left you?'

'S'right,' acknowledged the girl.

'And you do not expect to see him again?' asked Ada.

'Hope not. About as much use as a sick headache he is.'

'Well, in that case,' said Ada, 'you had better come and see the kitchen first.'

The three old ladies shepherded the girl all over the house. She made no comment as she was led from the kitchen's archaic grandeur, to the drawing-room, study, and then up the lofty staircase to the over-furnished bedrooms above.

After twenty minutes all four returned to their seats in the dining-room. Violet thought that the girl looked somewhat over-awed at the prospect before her.

Miss Ada produced a paper and pencil. 'Perhaps you would write down the name, address and telephone number of your last employer. That is, of course, if you feel that you want the post.'

'What wages would you be offering, miss?'

Ada told her.

'But I was getting twice that before,' she protested, 'and only half the work as you've got here.'

'My sisters and I will consider an increase, and let you know,' said Ada.

She pushed the paper and pencil towards the girl, and with some hesitation the prospective maid began to write.

'I'm not putting my name to it,' she said, looking bewildered.

'There's no need,' Ada assured her. 'I simply want to speak to this Mrs Miller — or is it Mitter?' She squinted at the paper, holding it at arm's length.

'Mrs Miller.'

'If all is satisfactory, could you start next Monday?'

'Well, I could, I suppose. Nine till twelve, my mum said.'

'That is correct. Three mornings a week. Definitely Mondays, and we can arrange the other mornings to suit you. I think a week's notice either way would be best. If you call again on Friday morning I can let you know what we have decided would be a fair remuneration, and you can give us your decision then.'

The three ladies rose, and ushered Doreen to the door.

When she had vanished round the bend of Lulling High Street, the three sisters discussed the affair.

'I do think,' said Violet, suddenly emboldened, 'that you were rather high-handed, Ada.

317

Why couldn't we have had a word together and raised her wages then and there?'

'One doesn't want to rush into these things,' replied Ada. 'I still have to discover from Mrs Miller what sort of person she is.'

'She didn't look very *strong*,' observed Bertha.

'And one must check her *truthfulness*,' continued Ada. 'How do we know that she was getting twice the amount we offered? We'll be in a better position to discuss terms when I have telephoned Mrs Miller this evening. Do the cheap rates start at six or six-thirty? I can never remember.'

[THE SCHOOL AT THRUSH GREEN]

It was hardly surprising that Doreen Lilly vanished from her post only a few weeks after this. It was only to be expected, the good folk of Lulling and Thrush Green told each other. Even the Lovelocks' most loyal friends agreed that the three sisters were becoming more difficult as the years passed.

Luckily, the Misses Lovelocks were the exceptions in an otherwise happy community, and none knew this better than the children as the Fifth of November approached.

The celebration of Guy Fawkes's attempt to blow up the Houses of Parliament in 1605 was always a communal affair at Thrush Green.

The schoolchildren helped to build the bonfire

and to supply the guy. Fireworks were given by various people who still enjoyed such things, and Harold Shoosmith and his friend Frank Hurst were among the most generous donors.

Percy Hodge always gave a sack of large potatoes which the Boy Scouts baked in the ashes of the bonfire for everybody, and Mr Jones of The Two Pheasants brought out glasses of beer and mugs of cocoa for the assembled throng.

A light breeze sprang up round about five o'clock on Guy Fawkes's day, and the children rejoiced. Now the bonfire should blaze merrily, and the guy catch fire without recourse to unseemly proddings with paraffin-soaked rags and such demeaning aids to combustion.

It sat upon its funeral pyre looking splendidly remote. Harold Shoosmith's topee had tilted a little on its way to the summit, and gave the guy a slightly rakish appearance, but all agreed that it was one of the best efforts of Thrush Green school.

At six-thirty sharp the scoutmaster thrust a flaming torch into the base of the pyre and within minutes yellow and orange flames leapt skyward. Cheers went up from the spectators, and the boxes of fireworks began to be sorted out by those in charge, ready for display.

A few minutes later, the first rocket of the evening whooshed upwards, and sent down a cascade of pink and violet stars.

'Ah!' sighed the crowd in great contentment.

'Where's the next?' shouted one wag.

And, as if in answer, the second streaked away towards a black velvet sky.

[AT HOME IN THRUSH GREEN]

Across the green, Winnie Bailey and her maid Jenny had been watching the fireworks from the house. At last the final rocket had sped upwards and the final Catherine wheel had whirled itself to darkness. When the last of the sparklers had been used, the children were sent, protesting a little, to their beds.

It was very peaceful after the din. Winnie leant from her window to survey the scene. There was a moon showing between silver-edged clouds. It was almost full, and lit Thrush Green with a gentle light.

Nathaniel Patten's statue gleamed opposite, and wet branches glistened as the moonbeams caught them. An owl hooted from Lulling Woods and, high above, the landing lights of an aeroplane winked rhythmically.

Little drifts of smoke wavered across on the air, bringing that most poignant of autumn scents from the bonfire's remains.

Tomorrow morning, a ring of white ash and a few cinders would be all that would remain of the past hours' splendour. The children would scuffle among the debris, hoping for a stray burnt potato, or the gnarled metal of a firework component to treasure. Miss Watson and Miss Fogerty would deplore the state of pupils' shoes and the yawns which would be the outcome of an evening's heady bliss.

They won't mind, thought Winnie fondly. They've had their fun, and nothing can take away those thrilling memories.

[AT HOME IN THRUSH GREEN]

Once the excitement of Guy Fawkes's day was over, the children began to look forward to Christmas. By the beginning of December, everyone in the school was involved with preparations in some way.

End of term was now in sight, and Agnes and Dorothy were in the throes of rehearsing the children for a concert, in rooms bedizened with paper chains, bells, friezes showing Santa Claus, reindeer, and lots of artificial snow made from pellets of cotton wool which fell from windows, as well as the mural frieze, and was squashed everywhere underfoot.

Miss Watson's children were attempting two carols played by the few who had recorders. The noise produced was excruciating, and Dorothy sometimes had difficulty in distinguishing 'Hark, The Herald Angels Sing' from 'O Come All Ye Faithful'. At times, she despaired. On the other hand, it was only right that the young musicians should be encouraged, and the parents would be gratified to see the expensive recorders being used.

The lower juniors, in charge of a young probationer on the other side of the partition, were being rehearsed endlessly, it seemed to Miss Watson, in some hearty mid-European dances which involved a lot of stamping and clapping. As the stamping and clapping never seemed completely co-ordinated, the resultant racket was hard to bear, but the young teacher, to give her her due, was persistent, and it was to be hoped that all would be well before the great day.

Little Miss Fogerty, with years of experience behind her, opted for two simple songs with actions which she had first tried out with success at several Christmas concerts in the past, blessing the ancient copy of *Child Education* held together with Scotch tape, which supplied the subject matter.

As always, the children were over-excited and belligerent. Agnes sometimes wondered if the expression 'the season of goodwill' was wholly correct. There was some acrimony between infants fighting over the brightest colours when making paper chains, harsh and wounding criticisms were made about desk-fellows' portrayal of Christmas trees, Christmas fairies, carol-singers and other seasonal matters. Two ferocious little girls, having a tug of war with a strip of tinsel, had to have their wounds dressed before being sent home, and poor Miss Fogerty's head ached with the unusual clamour in her classroom.

The two teachers were thankful to get back

to the peace of the school-house at the end of the day.

[AT HOME IN THRUSH GREEN]

In the week before Christmas, Lulling was chock-a-block with cars, with vans delivering extra goods, and with frantic shoppers who were more often than not accompanied by over-excited children. A local brass band played carols at irregular intervals and with less than perfect notation.

By the time Christmas arrived, most of the inhabitants of Lulling and Thrush Green were quite exhausted with all the many preparations, and were looking forward to having a rest as soon as possible.

The weather had turned mild and tranquil, as is so often the case at this time, making a mockery of the Christmas card scenes of stage coaches in deep snow, children constructing

323

snowmen and winter landscapes complete with skaters.

In Lulling gardens a few tattered roses still clung to unpruned bushes, and one or two early crocuses and snowdrops were thrusting through the damp soil. The more morose inhabitants, such as Albert Piggott, reminded each other saying that a green Christmas meant a full churchyard.

But on the whole, people rejoiced in the mild spell, and among them Charles Henstock. He had been able to go about his visiting, and to attend the plethora of pre-Christmas festivities, unencumbered by slippery roads and snow drifts.

On the morning of the great day, he awoke early as usual. Dimity was still deep in sleep, and the rector thought of the duties before him with real pleasure. It would be a busy day. The churches would be full and he would have the joy of seeing almost all his flock.

He looked forward keenly to his Christmas Day. It was still dark, but by the illuminated dial of the bedside clock he saw that he must rise if he wished to be in good time. He edged gently out of bed, hoping not to disturb his wife, but she stirred as he moved.

'Happy Christmas!' she murmured, her eyes still closed.

'It will be,' said the rector with conviction.

[AFFAIRS AT THRUSH GREEN]

Afterword

The years I spent in Witney, although overshadowed by the war, were among my happiest. Friendships were made which still endure, and affection for the Cotswolds has grown deeper over the years. Perhaps that is why I really prefer to write about Thrush Green rather than the village of Fairacre.

Writing, however, is not the unmitigated pleasure that so many people imagine. It seems that most writers feel a sense of relief and loss on finishing a book and I am among them.

The relief comes first. It is like casting away a heavy burden from one's back, and the feeling of freedom is most exhilarating. At this stage, I take a vow never to write another book, never again to face the onerous task of filling up ten or twelve exercise books in longhand.

Sometimes people ask me if it is hard work. It certainly is, and one writer on being asked this question made the following answer:

'Take any book from your shelves and set about copying it out. Then add the superbly difficult job of actually thinking about the contents first. That should give you some idea.'

I think it makes the point neatly.

But after a month or two, there seems to be

something lacking in one's life. An idea surfaces. Some particularly useful descriptions come to mind. One reaches for a notebook and starts to make a few reminders. Who knows? One day they may be handy.

And then the publisher says: 'What about another book?' and after the first spasm of horror at the very suggestion, one starts to ponder on the possibility. It will be the *last* book, of course. The work is too burdensome to undertake more than this last volume and, in any case, I have already written thirty-five or thirty-six — more than enough. Somehow, the next book is always the last — until the next one.

Perhaps it is time to play with my dolls again . . .